VENERA DREAMS

A WEIRD ENTERTAINMENT

MIROLAND IMPRINT 12

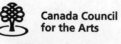

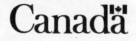

Guernica Editions Inc. acknowledges the support of the Canada Council for the Arts and the Ontario Arts Council. The Ontario Arts Council is an agency of the Government of Ontario.

We acknowledge the financial support of the Government of Canada.

VENERA DREAMS

A WEIRD ENTERTAINMENT

Claude Lalumière

MiroLand
publishers

MIROLAND (GUERNICA)
TORONTO • BUFFALO • LANCASTER (U.K.)
2017

Connie McParland, series editor
Michael Mirolla, editor
David Moratto, cover and interior book design
Guernica Editions Inc.
1569 Heritage Way, Oakville, ON L6M 2Z7
2250 Military Road, Tonawanda, N.Y. 14150-6000 U.S.A.
www.guernicaeditions.com

Distributors:
University of Toronto Press Distribution,
5201 Dufferin Street, Toronto (ON), Canada M3H 5T8
Gazelle Book Services, White Cross Mills
High Town, Lancaster LA1 4XS U.K.

First edition.
Printed in Canada.

Legal Deposit—Third Quarter
Library of Congress Catalog Card Number: 2017932213
Library and Archives Canada Cataloguing in Publication
Lalumière, Claude, author
Venera dreams : a weird entertainment / Claude Lalumière. -- 1st edition.

(MiroLand imprint ; 12)
Issued in print and electronic formats.
ISBN 978-1-77183-216-8 (softcover).--ISBN 978-1-77183-217-5 (EPUB).
--ISBN 978-1-77183-218-2 (Kindle)

I. Title. II. Series: MiroLand imprint ; 12

PS8623.A465V46 2017   C813'.6   C2017-900608-8   C2017-900609-6

in memory of
Baird Searles & Martin Last

CONTENTS

CONTENTS

OVERTURE

BEDTIME STORIES

THE ODOURS OF SEX envelop the two of them. Already Isabelle is asleep, Pierre spooning her. Sweat makes their bodies stick together. He sniffs her skin, and its feminine fragrance catches in his throat. He has come only moments ago, yet his cock stirs, poking the soft cushiness of her rump. A rush of excitement jolts him out of his post-orgasmic daze.

He raises his head to look at Isabelle. In sleep, her round face relaxes into an even more beautiful countenance, framed by her long black hair.

Pierre is restless, feels confined by the smallness of the apartment, his senses hungry for more stimulation. He considers rousing Isabelle, for them to go out and explore the night together. But he is again struck by how lovely she is asleep, and he can't bear the thought of waking her. He peels himself away, the film of sweat eliciting a soft kissing sound as their bodies separate.

Isabelle moans Pierre's name, but she doesn't emerge from her dreams.

Pierre dresses, careful to do so quietly. He steps out of the bedroom, out of their apartment, down the stairs, and onto the sidewalk. Into the hot summer night air.

⬧ The odours of sex envelop him. The taste of Isabelle's juices on his lips, the smell of her ass on his fingertips. The pungent blend of sweat and semen and girl adhering to his skin. As Pierre wanders the Main, brushing past the nocturnal denizens stepping in and out of clubs, bars, restaurants, cafés, and late-night alternative art galleries, he imagines a cloud of sex wafting from his body, insulating him from direct contact with the nightlife.

⬧ The poster on the bookshop window intrigues Pierre. THE BED-TIME STORIES READING SERIES AT LOST PAGES PRESENTS *The Darkbright Book of Scheherazade*. The description is followed by a list of names Pierre has never heard of. Not surprising; although the evidence is all around him, he rarely notices the Anglo demimonde of the metropolis. Over a lifetime spent on the island, he has come to think of it as two cities occupying the same physical space: Montreal, Anglophone and multicultural; Montréal, Francophone and international. The Montrealers and the Montréalais each ambulating through their respective city, only peripherally aware of the twin metropolis coexisting subtly out of phase with their own.

Tonight, in a lingering post-orgasmic altered state, Pierre feels out of phase with mundane reality altogether, participating in neither iteration of his city. Instead he feels like a phantasm — remote, yet unusually receptive, his senses drinking in every detail.

On a whim, he opens the door to Lost Pages and walks in.

The interior is dim, but bright lights draw Pierre's gaze to an area near the far window that has been cleared for the performance. A balding man in his fifties, wearing fashionable jeans and a jacket that's a size too large, is reading at a podium, without a microphone. Pierre stands near the door unsure whether to stay or go. He tries to concentrate on the words emanating from the makeshift stage, but his command of English is not up to the task of fully comprehending the convoluted narrative. Suddenly people start clapping. The reader has finished. Another writer walks to the podium. A curvy redhead whose trendy glasses and retro clothing give her an air that is at once hipster and scholarly. Pierre turns to leave, wondering why he bothered to come in at all, but he unexpectedly locks eyes with a stunning beauty: jet-black skin, long dark hair; dark eyes with long lashes; petite to the point of improbability yet exuding uncommon strength and confidence.

Two other women sit on either side of her. One is tall and Slavic, with long blond hair and a perverse mouth; the other is of average height, with a Mediterranean complexion and a posture of casual elegance, yet radiating an edginess that hints at a punk past. These two aren't listening to the performance, but rather are intensely trying to engage with the woman sandwiched between them; she appears to be mostly ignoring them. The Slavic woman notices the exchange of glances with Pierre, and cold fury seizes her features. She speaks to the short dark woman with obvious anger; Pierre is too far from them to catch the words. He feels like a voyeur for staring at the women while they're fighting, but he's drawn to their drama, feels connected to them, especially to the dark woman, the other people in the venue reduced to the status of anonymous extras.

Abruptly, the Slavic woman leaps to her feet. She's very tall — over six feet — taller than Pierre. She knocks down her chair. A few eyes turn toward her, but the storyteller keeps going. The blonde stands frozen, embarrassment and rage reddening her cheeks. Without bothering to replace her chair among the haphazardly arranged seating, she rushes toward the exit, elbowing Pierre in the ribs on the way out — hard enough to let him know it was no accident. The former punk replaces the chair, then she too gets up and leaves, shaking her head in confused disappointment. The dark woman, now alone, nods from Pierre to the empty chair on her left, inviting him to join her.

Pierre barely hesitates.

"I apologize for Petra and Renata," she whispers as he sits, but her tone suggests the opposite. Even at a murmur, her voice is deep and sultry, like a song. She leans in closer toward him. He catches a whiff of her aroma — a subtle spiciness redolent of salt and cinnamon and burnt butter.

She halts in the act of leaning back, as if something has caught her attention, and pushes her face closer to his neck. She sniffs him, which he finds electrifyingly intimate and erotic. "I thought so."

He mouths more than utters: "What?"

"You've just had sex. You reek of it. Of love. Of your fluids and hers. Whoever she is."

It strikes Pierre that the woman is speaking neither French nor English — the only languages he knows — and yet he understands her every word.

Before Pierre can formulate a response, the crowd erupts in applause. The reading is over. Some people immediately move to leave the store, but several others line up to buy books and get their copy signed by the assembled authors. While all this activity is going on, the mysterious woman grabs Pierre's hand and leads him deeper into the shop. She is even shorter than he thought, no taller than a tween girl, but there is nothing childlike in her penetrating gaze, her arrogant body language, her sensuous grip, her musky scent. They sit down on the floor, isolated from the bustle by bookshelves.

She takes a clear glass flask from her bag and offers it to him. The colour of the beverage is burnt orange with hints of red. He twists open the cap. The bouquet reminds him of the woman's own aroma, as if the two originated from the same source. Pierre takes a sip; the liquid is powerfully intoxicating. From the taste and texture, it is clearly wine of some sort, mulled with a peculiar blend of spices, but it spreads through his body like the best whiskey — a comforting warmth that softens the edges of the world.

He replaces the cap and hands back the flask.

She says: "Kiss me?" There's only the merest hint of question in her voice. She assumes he's going to do it. She touches his chin with her finger. No polish on the nails. He likes that. The sound of her voice pronouncing those two words — *kiss me* — echoes in his mind, like a unshakeable refrain, drowning out all other sounds, all other thoughts, taking on the imperative of a command.

He leans in toward her mouth — the closer he gets, the more heady and delicious her aroma; all that remains in his mind is the compulsion to kiss her, to lose himself in her. He moves his hand to cup the stranger's cheek, and as his fingers pass near his face he catches a trace of Isabelle's lingering odours, which breaks the stranger's spell. He pulls back before their lips make contact.

Pierre runs his fingers over his stubbly chin, releasing more of Isabelle's scent. Rubbing his fingers on his nose, he breathes deeply, lets himself be imbued with Isabelle and with his memories of her. His flesh still tingles from fucking Isabelle, the musk of their passion clinging to him.

The stranger says, laughing, not unkindly: "You love her."

Pierre feels himself blushing.

The dark woman once more leans in toward him, as if to whisper something, but instead her hand falls into his lap, where it lands on an erection.

Pierre abruptly rises, without affording her another word or another glance. All he wants now is to get away from this confusing woman, to go back home, to get back to Isabelle, and to forget this ill-advised excursion. He flees outside. Into the hot summer night air.

❧ The hot summer night air envelops him. Pierre walks quickly, on automatic, without thinking or looking at his surroundings. The city seems darker than usual, as if there were a power outage, and unusually, even for the middle of the night, there's no traffic noise. He stops and closes his eyes. Although he is eager to return to Isabelle, before slipping next to her in bed, Pierre wants to shake off his lingering agitation from the encounter at the bookshop. He thinks about how much he enjoys walking through Montreal; his favourite route consists of drinking in the always-bustling atmosphere of the Main, then veering off to skirt Jeanne-Mance Park and stroll on Avenue de L'Esplanade, continuing north to Mile End and zigzagging back south to the Plateau. He is forever enchanted by Montreal's unique style of residential architecture, with the outdoor winding stairs, the porches and balconies, the colourful and varied gables, the closeness and tightness of everything.

Finally, Pierre opens his eyes to get his bearings, to plot a course that will take him through the neighbourhood and eventually back home to Isabelle.

But he has no idea where he is.

Pierre's environment is unfamiliar and strange. The air is thick with the smell of the mulled wine the strange woman offered him, mixed with the pungency of seawater brine.

As his eyes adjust to the darkness of the night, he notices the ornate architecture, the shapes and configurations so unusual that he can't entirely grasp what he sees. Vegetation and masonry merge into one another in confounding patterns. The sidewalk follows not a city street but a canal. Across the canal, he spots a handful of pedestrians; their body language is disquieting, as if their bodies, echoing the architecture, are assembled in somewhat inhuman configurations.

Did the woman slip him a hallucinogen?

Or perhaps he's still in bed with Isabelle, and this whole evening has been a weird dream?

Pierre steadies himself on the railing at the edge of the waterway, and a hand covers his own with a subtle squeeze. Looking up, Pierre says: "It's you."

⁂ The Slavic woman's name is Petra. Petra Maxim. "But that's not my real name. I'm originally from Smolensk. I fled to Romania and lived with my punk friends in a deserted warehouse." Her accent is subtle, softening the edges of the otherwise Parisian lilt of her French. He hadn't spotted she'd been a punk, too, but now he sees the signs — in her posture, in her subtly but artfully mismatched clothes, in the tilt of her chin. She walks like a caged animal — there's something fierce and unforgiving about her, like an Amazon warrior who you know will take no prisoners.

And yet, despite her earlier fury, there's almost tenderness — or is it pity? — in how she addresses Pierre. As they talk, the two of them hang onto the guardrail, looking out onto the quiet canal.

"Then *she* found me," Petra pauses and gives Pierre a long silent stare, "nursed me back from an overdose of vermilion dragon, and gave me a new life. Do yourself a favour: don't mix heroin and vermilion. I live in London, now. With this new name, this new identity. I am hers. Her creation. I'm a photographer. I travel around the world. But I often come back here. This is the most magical city in the world. Also, because I love *her*."

Pierre hesitates — there is so much he does not understand that he doesn't know which question to ask first.

"You're so confused. Poor little man. Let me ask you a question: in which city were you before you entered the bookshop?"

"I'm from Montreal."

"I visited Montreal once. I do not like North America, but I enjoyed Montreal. A real city. A city with many layers of myth and history. Few places in North America possess even a hint of that potent brew, unlike in Europe. I did a photo essay for *Metropolis Now* on the vestiges of Man and His World, the 1967 World's Fair. The photographs of the original event make me yearn to have been there."

Finally Pierre settles on the most important question: "How can I get back home?" He refuses to be ensnared by the overt obliqueness of these women. They can keep their mysteries. All he wants is for all this to end.

"I can't help you. *She* has plans you. It's not for me to interfere."

Behind Pierre, another woman says, in English: "Why don't you let me speak to him, Petra?"

Pierre turns. It's the third woman from earlier, at the bookshop. The one with the Mediterranean look who, Pierre suspects, also has a punk past. He can recognize it. He was a punk, too, briefly, when he was an exchange student in Bordeaux. Pierre wonders if this confluence of punk backgrounds is a coincidence, or if it points to yet another mystery.

Petra answers the other woman, also in English: "He's all yours, Renata. I'm tired anyway."

By the time, Pierre turns back to say goodnight, Petra is gone.

⤸ They walk arm in arm. As they wander through this bizarre maze of alien architecture, briny canals, and dense vegetation, Pierre keeps expecting the illusion to fade and Montreal to reappear. Certainly the linguistic composition of their conversation is familiarly Montreal: he addresses her in French, she addresses him in English; and they both understand each other.

"Why are all three of you so coy, so indirect? Can you not simply answer any of my questions?" Pierre laughs nervously; his attitude flip-flops between being convinced that this is all an elaborate dream or hallucination and believing that he truly is stranded in a foreign city he can't identify.

"You really have no idea where you are? Surely you must recognize this city? Everyone has heard of this place. The home of vermilion spice. The notorious city of unrequited dreams."

"No, I tell you, this entire place looks impossible. And what is this 'vermilion' that you and your friend Petra keep mentioning?"

"I have never met anyone who did not know these things ... and I have travelled all over the world ... unless you're from another ..." A worried glance appears on Renata's face.

"I don't really care where I am or about the answer to any of these riddles. I simply want to go home. To my girlfriend. To Isabelle. If all this is real, if I truly am in a city far from my own, then, regardless of how I got here, surely I can fly back home. How can I get to the airport?"

"I don't think it'll be quite that simple to get you home. Let me ask you something: the bookstore where you met us — Lost Pages — had you ever seen it before?"

"No, but then I do not pay much attention to the Anglo side of Montreal. So there's nothing unusual about that."

"Perhaps, but there's something unusual about Lost Pages. You were in Montreal before you stepped inside, but I was not. I was here. In Venera. But we both walked into the same bookshop."

"Is that what this place is called — Venera? I've never heard of it."

"And you've never heard of vermilion? Know this, then: even if I did get you back to Montreal, I don't think it would be the Montreal you call home."

"None of what you say makes sense. All this is too absurd to be real. Eventually I'll wake up from this frustrating dream."

"I wish that were true. I'm sorry. For you and for your Isabelle. I wonder what Scheherazade wants with you."

"Scheherazade? Is that your other friend's name? Like the story-teller from *The Arabian Nights*? What an unusual name. Beautiful, though." Slipping into English, Pierre adds: "Wait — the reading. It was for an anthology called *The Darkbright Book of Scheherazade* ..."

"She'll find you again. Let her tell you everything. You wouldn't believe me. But you'll believe her. She knows how to tell a story ..."

Renata's evasiveness exacerbates Pierre's impatience with this delusion.

The darkness lightens; dawn faintly hints its inevitable re-emergence.

Renata says to him: "Let's watch the sunrise. A sunrise in Venera is a magical experience."

They disentangle and lean against the guardrail.

The lighter the sky becomes the more the mist enshrouds the city. Within minutes the fog is so thick that he can see nothing but the shimmering whiteness of it. *Now*, he thinks, *when the mist lifts, so will the hallucination. I'll be back in Montreal. I'll be home.*

⌒ The emerging sunlight burns through the mist, and the city teasingly sheds it veils.

Renata has left — unnoticed; without word or acknowledgement. Pierre waits alone, witnessing the revelations of dawn. Figures — not all of whom seem entirely human — ambulate through the white haze. In time, the morning mist entirely dissipates, revealing an architecture that blends lush nature and dense cityscape, with flourishes that hint at Arabic, Italian, Iberian, Scandinavian, and Chinese influences, and elements too alien for his mind to distinguish.

At the edge of his consciousness, Pierre perceives a song. He recognizes the singer's voice as that of the third woman, the one Renata called Scheherazade. The language is unknown to him, yet he understands Scheherazade's words. The song tells a story. The story of Venera.

He fears that he will never again see his Montreal, his Isabelle. He wonders how differently the night might have unfurled if he'd woken her.

Scheherazade stands beside him now. She takes his hand — so softly, as if the moist air itself were enfolding him — and whispers the song of Venera in that eerie language of hers. Breathing in the damp and potent atmosphere of this new day, Pierre ponders the sights and sounds and aromas of the surreal city. It would be easy, so easy, to be seduced by the strange and extravagant beauty of this unlikely woman and of this even more unlikely metropolis. To surrender to Scheherazade's song. Surprising himself, he finds that a part of him yearns to be so seduced. Yet ... the emotion that suffuses him most powerfully is an unravelable tangle of grief and foreboding.

⮑ Via pedestrian streets and ornate bridges and lush canals and bustling plazas and opulent parks and dense woods and iridescent tunnels and damp caverns, Scheherazade pulls Pierre along, his hand firmly nestled in hers. Pierre is so exhausted that he sometimes sleeps as he walks. The flickering phantasmagorical images of the city merging indistinguishably with snippets of his dreams.

Eventually, Pierre wakes up in bed. Alone. Naked.

There are no windows, but there is a door.

The bed is large and too soft. On the wall opposite the bed, there's a large table, on which rests a burning candle providing just enough illumination for him to know that the room is unfamiliar and from which wafts the now-familiar smell of cinnamon, burnt butter, and brine. The scent of that woman — Scheherazade — and of her city.

He gets up — the marble floor is smooth on his bare feet — and tries the door. He is unsurprised to find it locked.

Next to the door is a chair, on which his clothes are folded. He doesn't bother putting them on.

Pierre finds other candles in a basket on the floor. He lights three more with the flame of the first one.

The brighter light reveals that the walls are decorated with line drawings depicting creatures only vaguely humanoid involved in scenes of disquieting violence and eroticism.

Besides the bed, there's an empty chamber pot, much too ornate considering its purpose. And in the corner a love seat also designed in an extravagantly gaudy style.

Also on the table there's a carafe of wine — the bouquet tells him it's the same beverage he shared with Scheherazade at Lost Pages — and two wooden mugs. And a book — no; a notebook. Its pages are blank, a fountain pen hooked on the cover.

Pierre knocks on the door, calling out Scheherazade's name — but there's no answer. Time goes by with nothing to mark it. He eventually goes back to bed and succumbs to sleep.

When he wakes up, Scheherazade is sitting in bed next to him. Also naked.

Pierre says: "Let me go home." He doesn't care what this bizarre woman wants from him. All he desires is for this strange odyssey to end so he can return to Isabelle.

Scheherazade ignores him. Instead, she takes his hand and begins to tell him a story. A story of Venera. A fast-paced story of swashbuckling adventure and unrequited love and bloody rituals.

Only a few scenes in and Pierre falls asleep again. In his dreams, Scheherazade's story becomes increasingly unlikely and fantastical. When it reaches its tragic conclusion, Pierre is jolted awake. Scheherazade is still in bed with him.

Pierre explains that he never heard her full story, that he dreamed his own continuation. Despite himself, he's curious. Her songlike narration is addictive. He craves more, and he hates himself a little for being so easily beguiled.

Scheherazade says: "Venera is built of stories. They are all lies; and they are all true."

She climbs out of bed. Pierre can't help but notice the alluring sway of her hips and derriere, but his arousal does not lead him to desire his captor; it only reminds him of Isabelle, to whom he yearns to return.

Scheherazade grabs the pen and notebook and comes back to Pierre. "Tell the story. Your version of the story." She gives him the writing implements.

"Why?"

She answers only: "Write."

So he starts recording what he remembers of Scheherazade's tale and his own dream that followed it.

When he's finished, he discovers that Scheherazade has left the room.

He goes to relieve himself and notices that the chamber pot has been cleaned since he used it last.

His stomach growls. There's nothing to eat or drink aside from the aromatic wine, and so he pours himself a cup. It satisfies both his thirst and hunger. And it also relaxes him, sending him off to sleep, and to dreams of Venera.

≈ And so the cycle goes: Scheherazade slips unnoticed in and out of his prison; she sings him stories that lull him to sleep and to dream his own endings; he wakes and writes stories of Venera; he drinks more wine, and dreams more of Venera. The carafe of wine is never empty. The pen never dries.

Occasionally, his body urges him to reach out so as to taste and savour Scheherazade herself. She would not deny him. Her gaze and her touch make that amply clear. But the bereavement he feels over his isolation from Isabelle never dissipates, and so he leaves his lust unquenched.

Dozens of nights and days pass. Hundreds. Perhaps a thousand. Perhaps more.

Until ...

One day, Pierre has filled every page of the notebook.

He waits a long time, but Scheherazade never returns.

Finally, he again takes to knocking on the door and calling out to Scheherazade. He tries to open the door ... to find it unlocked.

Quickly, he dresses. Grabbing his storybook, he leaves.

⟶ The hot summer night air envelops him. Pierre runs, without thinking or taking careful notice of his surroundings. Electric lights punctuate the darkness. The sounds of automobiles fill the air. Dripping with sweat, Pierre slows to a more customary stride. And he notices that he's walking along the Main in Montreal. He accelerates again. He veers off to skirt Jeanne-Mance Park and sprints up Avenue de L'Esplanade, continuing north to Mile End and zigzagging back south to the Plateau.

He's eager to return to Isabelle, to slip next to her in bed. But he's been gone so long — how long exactly he has no idea — how can she possibly still be waiting for him? She must think him dead. So he prevaricates and wanders, afraid of what might be awaiting him.

Finally, Pierre gets his bearings and plots a course that will take him through the neighbourhood and eventually back home to Isabelle. If home and Isabelle are still there waiting for him.

His key still fits the lock. He walks up the stairs as quietly as he can.

In the bedroom, Isabelle is asleep.

He should wake her. Talk to her. Do whatever he can to lessen the alarm he will cause her. But all he can bear to do is to take off his clothes and slip into bed next to her. As he spoons her, Isabelle mumbles Pierre's name without emerging from her dreams.

⟶ The next morning Isabelle wakes him. "Where were you all day yesterday? I was worried."

"All day? I was gone so much longer ..."

"What are you talking about?"

Did he hallucinate the entire experience? That wine at the bookstore must have been drugged. He fell in a stupor somewhere and dreamt the whole thing up. There's no such place as Venera; that woman wasn't the legendary Scheherazade — his subconscious picked up the name because of the title of the anthology that was being launched.

But his eyes fall on the notebook, lying on the floor next to his clothes.

He grabs it. "Can I read you a story?"

"You're weird today. What happened to you?"

"Humour me."

"Okay. Of course. Always. Read me a story."

She rests her head in his lap and closes her eyes. He's overwhelmed by her trust, her love.

Pierre opens the notebook, eager to share with Isabelle ... whatever it was that he experienced. Every page is filled with handwriting, but ... the words are nonsense, incomprehensible. Hundreds of pages of gibberish, uncontestably in his script. He digs through his memory, but he can't recall any precise details from Scheherazade's songs or from his Venera dreams beyond blurry images of adventure, sex, romance, blood, danger, fantasy, and myth.

Isabelle says: "I'm waiting."

PART 1

STRANGE ROMANCES

THE CITY OF
UNREQUITED DREAMS

⤴

On my seventeenth birthday, I finally heard from Vittorio. He sent me a box of chocolates, accompanied by a picture of himself on a rooftop, with a spectacular view of a colourful city easily recognizable as the fabled island-state Venera and, beyond, the Mediterranean. In the four years since I'd last seen him, my best friend had hardly changed. Or at least he looked the way I still imagined him. On the back of the picture, he'd scrawled "Buon compleanno!" — nothing else.

Had Vittorio been in Venera all this time? Was he there now? Alas, the return address on the package was too smudged to decipher.

The list of ingredients had been peeled off. It was easy to guess why. In the privacy of my bedroom, I opened the box and bit into one of the sweet and spicy delicacies. That first taste of vermilion — the Veneran export was barely available in Canada, and then only at tremendous cost — was so intense that I experienced a tactile hallucination of Vittorio kissing me, of his hands fondling my erection. Not the first time I'd had such a fantasy, but it had never so consumed all my senses, surprising me with a sudden ejaculation. I was still dressed, but my cock had wormed out of my underwear. My jeans were sticky and uncomfortable. The orgasm had been bittersweet — as was the memory it had awakened: my first kiss, that time Vittorio's mouth had tasted mine, so briefly, in the school library, two days before his abrupt departure.

One morning, a mere three months after Vittorio and his parents had immigrated to Canada, Mrs. Dorchester, our sixth-grade teacher, announced that Vittorio would no longer be in our class, as his family had moved away. How could that be true? Vittorio would never leave — never leave me — without at least saying goodbye.

I went to his house. There was a For Rent sign on the front lawn. I rang, but there was no answer. I broke the basement window and went in, hoping to find some clue, some reason why my friend had abandoned me, some way to contact him. But the place was empty, as if no-one had ever lived there; so bare and lifeless that I could no longer visualize the hours we'd spent sequestered in Vittorio's room, conspiring against the monotonous conformity that constantly threatened to extinguish the fire that we, and no-one else, saw in each other's eyes.

≈ I graduated high school, although I forgot each day as it was over. Several of my university applications were successful, but I never bothered replying to any of them. My father threatened to throw me out unless I either went to school or paid rent. My mother stopped talking to me entirely.

I didn't care about any of that. All I wanted was to reach Venera and find my friend. After receiving that package from Vittorio, I read countless books and articles on the mysterious city-state. The best that I could conclude from this miasma of contradictory information was that almost none of these writers had any direct experience of the decadent metropolis. And then I hit on Petra Maxim's *1001 Days and Nights in Venera* — a gorgeous coffee-table book filled with breathtaking and surreal pictures of the glamorous city. One photo depicted a party at the Velvet Bronzemine ballroom — so extreme in its gaudiness and tastelessness that it achieved an unexpected beauty. Among the party-goers, there he was: Vittorio — dancing, arms enlaced, in a trio with the massive Tito Bronze himself and a petite but voluptuous nude girl with jet-black skin and long, braided hair.

My father was careless with his PIN numbers, keeping a list of them in his sock drawer. The day after my eighteenth birthday, I stole one of his bank cards while he slept. I took out all the cash I could — two thousand dollars — and booked the cheapest flight to Europe.

⤻ Located on Rue de Seine, just north of Boulevard Saint-Germain, Venera's Parisian embassy betrayed nothing of the city-state's celebrated decadence, at least from the outside. Its facade was a dull greyish white, like most Parisian facades, and lacked any distinctive details. A metal plaque next to the door announced, in both French and Italian, what was housed in this drab building.

A short dark-haired man with a comically large nose welcomed me in French with disconcerting warmth. After only a few days in Paris, I had already grown accustomed to the French capital's oppressive sterility. He led me to a small office — unadorned, save for a modern ergonomic desk, a computer, and a filing cabinet. At the desk sat a taller, German-looking man who immediately picked up on my accent and switched to English.

The embassy's austerity shocked me. Where were all the erotic paintings? The gaudy colours? The outré architectural embellishments? Most of all I was surprised that everyone I had seen so far was male — ordinary men in dull business suits. Venera was, after all, a city ruled by women, its population reputed to be more than 75 percent female.

I had an appointment with a Mr. Sangralia, who handled all visa and immigration requests. The receptionist asked to see my passport. He inspected it with much greater care than the customs official at Aéroport Charles de Gaulle had when I first landed in Europe. After a few minutes of scrutiny, the receptionist was satisfied and returned it. He nodded; his gaze focused past me. I turned my head, noting the dark-skinned giant behind me; more suave than his colleagues, he wore his black business suit as comfortably as a second skin. The receptionist shook my hand. "Vincent will take you to see Mr. Sangralia."

Vincent led me up two flights of stairs and down a long hall. Now, this floor reflected more closely my idea of Venera. The doors and doorframes were sensual, ornate wooden sculptures opulently gilded and adorned with precious gems. On the walls hung portraits of famous Veneran women from throughout history against surrealist back-drops — the work of the notorious Errata Maximilia, whose torrid affair with the even more notorious Tito Bronze had been conducted with exhibitionist glee across all of Europe, providing juicy fodder for the rapacious paparazzi.

We stopped at the very end of the hall; Vincent opened the door, and immediately I was hit by a cloud of smoke. The tangy fragrance was unmistakable: vermilion. Vincent gave my shoulder a gentle nudge, and I entered Mr. Sangralia's office — although *office* was a misleading word.

Sangralia, sprawled among cushions on the floor, greeted me in English, but forming each syllable as if it were in Italian. He motioned that I join him, then handed me a smoking tube. I hesitated a moment, afraid of how the spice might affect me and thus my chance for permission to enter Venera. But I also feared that refusing would guarantee my failure.

I breathed in the aromatic smoke — and the strength of the blend, much more intense than the small dose in Vittorio's chocolates, hit me like an orgasm. Then everything got blurry. I floated on smoke and swam in voices — Sangralia's and my own. But I could make sense of neither his words nor mine.

... I awoke in a plushy armchair in a nook adjacent to the embassy's lobby, my head pounding. Vincent towered over me. His musical voice, tinged with unexpected softness, surprised me. "I am sorry to inform you that your application has been rejected." Not so softly, he took me by the arm, raised me up, and escorted me outside.

Under the glare of the harsh early afternoon sun, I felt exposed, shamed, ridiculed.

⟿ In London, atop the Serpentine Bridge in Hyde Park, under the damp cover of a light, misty rain, I pretended to stare at the water below. The woman I had been shadowing for the past three weeks stood only a few feet to my left. She appeared deeply lost in thought. I should have talked to her last month, when I first spotted her coming out of the *Metropolis Now* offices, but the merciless cut of her severe Slavic features and the determined, military stride of her long legs had shattered whatever courage I could muster.

I turned to look at her now. The rain had flattened her hair, accentuating the aristocratic beauty of her cheekbones. She turned her head and locked her eyes with mine. Her stare paralysed me as she walked up to me. She leaned in, brushed her lips against my ear, and said in an icy, commanding voice: "It's time you told me why you've been following me."

Without planning to, I grabbed hold of her and kissed her — hard, pushing my tongue deep into her mouth. She tasted like vermilion. Her fingernails dug into my cheeks, tethering her, as her knees buckled. She kissed me back, drawing blood as she bit my lips. Eventually, we gasped for air and laughed. She whispered obscenities in my ear, then took my hand and led me to her apartment, a luxurious flat only a few minutes' walk from the park.

I never answered her question, and she never asked again. Without even discussing it, I moved in with this woman: Petra Maxim, author of *1001 Days and Nights in Venera*; a Russian expat who had abandoned her real name along with her past. She was currently a photojournalist for *Metropolis Now* magazine, but, to be able to afford to live in such luxury in this city, she clearly had other sources of income — I never inquired into her affairs, and she never volunteered anything. Petra was not one for conversation, and we were never close emotionally. Often, I felt like nothing more than a sex toy, a prop in her vermilion-enhanced debauched fantasies. Nevertheless, she was kind to me in many ways: besides making available all the vermilion I could crave; besides her casual, animalistic eroticism; besides allowing me free entry into the elite world of London chic; more practically, she also helped me get a gig at the magazine, copyediting and occasionally interviewing emerging artists for a series of sidebar profiles. It was an easy life, too easy. Too comfortable to shatter with the truth. Instead, I avoided dealing with my cowardice by wallowing in self-loathing, absenting myself with increased frequency from Petra's bed, losing myself in vermilion binges and anonymous sex with the all-male clientele of The Adonis Baths.

The next spring, Petra was granted a two-month visa for a return trip to Venera, in order to complete an architectural photo-essay for *Metropolis Now*. She refused to even try to see if she could bring me along. I finally told her about Vittorio, showed her the picture in her book, and asked if she knew him. She looked straight into my eyes for a few seconds, weighing or judging ... something, but I wasn't sure what.

Then, abruptly, she laughed at me and told me that she would not be sleeping at home that night. I had until morning to clear out and get out of her life. "And you will be quitting your job at the magazine to-morrow. Or should I have them fire you?" She turned away from me and left before I could respond.

Everywhere in that apartment her cold stare mocked me. I didn't wait till morning. I packed my bag and took the next Eurostar train to the continent.

~ Tito Bronze's Roman extravaganza, the *Festival dei Sensi*, provided a glimpse of Venera for the pleasure of the outside world. The festival snaked its way into and infested all of Rome, tapping into the simmering paganism that growled beneath the city's twin veneers of tourism and Catholicism.

Desperate for any clue to Vittorio, I took in as much of the festival as I could: films, gallery hangings of paintings and photographs, theatre, performance art — all the works of Bronze and his Velvet Bronzemine entourage. But neither Vittorio nor his image were anywhere to be found.

If only I could go backstage, speak to someone, perhaps even to the imposing Bronze himself — he had, after all, at least one time danced with my Vittorio. But then I realized that it might be possible: I still held my press ID from *Metropolis Now*. I hurried to the festival's publicity office. After examining my card and passport carefully, the festival's press coordinator asked me to wait a moment and excused herself. She came back within a few minutes, and to my surprise informed me that I would be allowed a fifteen-minute breakfast interview with Bronze, at his hotel room at 6 a.m. Coffee and croissants would be served.

A feeling of accomplishment surged within me. It was an unusual sensation. I savoured it, treasured it. I could almost feel Vittorio's skin on my fingertips, hear his laughter tickle my ears. Vittorio. Venera. Bronze was the key. I knew it for certain. Under no circumstance would I allow that key to slip from my grasp.

~ I showed Tito Bronze the photograph in Petra's book. The snap-shot of him dancing with Vittorio.

"Yes, I remember that boy. Tragic."

Tragic. The word hit me like a punch in the solar plexus.

"You're not really here to interview me for *Metropolis Now*, are you, young man?"

I stammered: "N-n-no."

His face betrayed not the slightest hint of disapproval. Instead, he spoke to me slowly, empathically: "You knew this boy, this Vittorio?"

Knew. Nononono. Bronze could not be telling me this.

"I think I shall spare you the details. I, certainly, am in no mood to dredge up the past. Perhaps we should end this conversation now. I'm sorry." He snapped his fingers, and a naked girl — that lithe gymnast's body told me she was, at the very most, twenty years old — slithered into the room with inhuman grace. "But it may be that our acquaintance is only beginning. Sherry — would you ...?"

She circled behind me and blew into my ear. Far from aroused, I was frozen with fear and dread. Something sharp stung the side of my neck.

I awoke on a park bench, under the glare of a bright, hot mid-afternoon sun. A half-dozen large dogs — obviously strays, or even feral, judging from their gauntness and the state of their fur — lazed about not far from me. Some children were playing a little farther off, totally unconcerned by the presence of the animals.

I took stock of myself. I was wearing clothes I did not recognize, but they fit me well enough; in my pocket was a wad of bills (several hundred euros!), a new passport with a new identity but my own photo (I was now an Austrian citizen), and a small plastic bag of vermilion snuff. My skin felt raw, and when I ran my hand under my shirt I discovered fresh scars, welts, and bruises. My arms had been shaved and were covered with bright, erotic tattoos.

What had happened to me? Where was I? How much time had elapsed since my meeting with Tito Bronze? I was not so concerned with the abuse I had no doubt suffered under the notorious Bronze's direction. I was much more intrigued, and even moved, by Bronze's gesture — that he had granted me the opportunity to start my life anew. I was reborn, and, if I wanted, I could be free of my past desires. I laughed at the naivety of such a romantic notion, so at odds with Bronze's reputed elitist egotism and chic hedonistic nihilism.

Disoriented and wobbly, I wandered out of the park and noticed that all the street names were spelled in both Roman and Cyrillic characters. I was in Greece. Athens. Farther from Venera than Rome had been, but what did it matter? There was no longer any reason for me to seek access to the debauched city-state.

∽ Using up almost all the money Bronze had left me with, I booked passage on a boat that was to circle around the south of Greece and then eventually travel across the sea all the way to Barcelona. But I had no intention of reaching Spain.

A little more than two full days after we left Greece, as the sun set among the clouds gathering from the west, I finally caught sight of Venera, far in the distance. Save for the lights from the city-state, once the sun was completely swallowed up, darkness enveloped us like a cloak. The first hints of rain brought with them a chill that cut me to the bone.

Rain was good. It hid tears so well.

From my jacket's inside pocket, I drew the last of my vermilion snuff. Up my nose it went. The euphoria was instantaneous. So why was I crying even harder?

The rain had driven the other passengers inside. I was alone on the deck. I climbed over the rail and without hesitation jumped into the Mediterranean. I was so deeply under the spell of vermilion that I didn't even notice the impact; but, completely submerged, I choked on the cold briny seawater. I had never been a good swimmer. This would be over quickly.

Nevertheless, I was buoyed back to the surface. In the distance, I glimpsed the lights from Venera — the lights of unrequited dreams. I let myself sink. Deeper and deeper. The underbelly of the great Venera revealed itself: glowing with colours I could never have imagined, shimmering, pulsating, undulating — as if it were alive and in constant metamorphosis. A glorious, farewell hallucination, courtesy of the vermilion tingling through me? Or was I being allowed to perceive an aspect of the true, perhaps unfathomable, nature of this strange metropolis?

My lungs clamoured for air. I almost opened my mouth and swallowed; almost let water fill my lungs. Ignoring the pull of both life and death, I closed my eyes — and the afterimage of Venera lingered, its intensity growing instead of fading.

Again I surfaced, gasping and shivering. Once my breathing settled back to normal, my gaze locked on the distant Venera.

I possessed neither the strength nor the skill to undertake such a long swim, but the city-state's tendrils had by now snaked deeply within me and I could not ignore the eerie beckoning.

XANDRA'S BRINE

❦

The smell of brine wafted inland from the Mediterranean; Camille
breathed it in, its pungent saltiness making her feel as if her
bones had lost their solidity, adopting a malleability that held
the promise of profound transformation. She welcomed the spongy sensation and the potential of change. Ten years spent in the north, in
Rouen, and nothing to show for it. No friends worthy of the name; a
string of humiliating service-industry jobs that had led nowhere; and,
worst of all, Armand. She didn't despise him, nor did she blame him
for leeching off her while he pretended to work on his music; she
wouldn't even have resented it if he'd been fucking other girls — not if
he'd also paid attention to her. But he had done neither. Inhaling the
burnt-orange smoke of vermilion from his hookah, he masturbated off
internet porn while she was at work, and recently even when she was at
home, barely registering her presence. He never looked at her with lust
anymore, let alone touched her, and had long ago stopped writing the
songs that had made her fall in love with him.

She'd left Armand behind in Rouen, hoping to shed her own
apathy, but with no idea of what she wanted anymore. All she knew was
that the south beckoned: the view of the horizon from the Riviera, the
brine of the Mediterranean, the comfort of the heat.

Showers had hit Nice throughout the afternoon, and now, even
though dusk was descending, in the summerlike heat of the Riviera
spring the evaporated rainwater lingered heavily in the air.

That morning, she'd tried to enjoy the beach, but she'd forgotten
how painful it could be to walk barefoot on the pebbles. All around

her, others had seemed untroubled by the discomfort. Now, from the rampart above the beach, Camille saw only one person down there: a naked woman with a long, elegant back and meaty, round hips that swayed alluringly with every step toward the sea. Her ethereally pale skin almost glowed in the near dark.

Obeying an impulse she felt no need to question, Camille hooked the straps of her heeled sandals through the fingers of her right hand and made her way down to the beach, toward the woman. The hard, smooth pebbles still hurt her feet but not as much as they had earlier. For a few steps she even thought she'd gotten the hang of it — felt as though the pebbles were massaging the soles of her feet rather than digging into them — but then a misstep caused her to yelp at the sharp pain, and the other woman turned to look at her.

The nude woman had uncommonly large eyes, their irises as black as the pupils. Camille gasped as she felt herself fall into the dark, moist, comforting embrace of the stranger's gaze. Camille hurried to breach the distance between them, overcome with the desire to talk to this woman.

The stranger turned back toward the sea. Her hair was oddly braided, like seaweed, in strands of blue, purple, pink, brown, and green. The tide nipped their ankles. Camille introduced herself. The woman shifted subtly to catch Camille's eye but remained silent, waiting for Camille to continue. Camille surprised herself by starting to talk about her childhood on the Riviera, in Menton.

Camille was shocked into silence when the stranger reached out and clasped her hand. The stranger's grip had a spongy quality that was oddly reassuring. Together, they stood there as the sun set and darkness settled in. At one point, perhaps hours later, the stranger disentangled herself and left Camille alone on the beach.

When the sun rose, revealing the stark blue of the Mediterranean sky, Camille brought her hands to her face to rub the tiredness from her eyes. She sniffed the hand that the stranger had held and was astonished at how strongly it smelled of brine.

Camille slept through the day at the hostel, occasionally and dimly aware of the noise and bustle around her. When she woke, she felt different, as if the previous night truly had had a transformative effect. She was skeptical, however, as she could not articulate what might have changed in her, and simply dismissed the sensation as elation at the previous night's odd encounter and as disorientation at rising at dusk rather than dawn.

She bought coffee and a croissant from the boulangerie across the street and once again made her way down to the seashore.

This cloud-free evening, unlike the day before, the crowds gathered on the beach to enjoy the glorious sunset. Still, she spotted the strange woman easily. Camille hadn't been aware that she'd been scanning for her until her gaze settled on her. The stranger wore a dark orange, almost burgundy summer dress, the hem kissing the curve of her buttocks, the back in a deep V that highlighted her graceful shape.

Camille spied at the woman for a few minutes, with the growing realization that she was moved by the stranger's unusual beauty. Camille walked toward her and, when she reached her, brushed her fingers against hers. The woman glanced shyly at Camille but reached out to her and clutched her hand tightly. Once again, they stood together as they watched the sun set.

⤬ The stranger's name was Xandra, and she knew no French. Camille's nearly nonexistent Italian was only good enough to recognize that Xandra spoke nothing but that peculiar dialect in use only in Venera, that archipelagic city-state known primarily as the world's only supplier of vermilion. It was notoriously difficult to obtain a visa to Venera, but every European dreamed of exploring its decadent vias and waterways. For Continental Europeans, Venera was in such tantalizing proximity, but the city-state remained as aloof from their attentions as it did from anyone else's.

In her late teens and early twenties, Camille, like almost every girl she knew, had covered her body with tattoos made from vermilion henna. It was said to heighten the sensitivity of the skin and, thus, make sex more intense. But, as Armand's interest in her body had faded, she had gradually stopped adorning herself with the tincture. Had it ever really made a difference? She could scarcely remember what sex felt like, with or without the vermilion enhancement.

Xandra shared Camille's bed at the hostel. Although she allowed Camille to kiss and lick her slippery body, she never gave Camille her mouth, nor did she open her legs for her. Camille was intoxicated by her companion's pungent briny aroma; she constantly craved the taste of her skin on her tongue.

Together, the two women walked through Nice hand in hand, rarely exchanging a word but somehow sharing an unarticulated complicity that filled a gulf in Camille's life. Occasionally, Camille would get a glimpse of Xandra's teeth; the sight was always a bit unnerving. They were sharp and pointy, as if they'd been filed to look like the teeth of a shark.

Xandra's skin exuded a briny moistness that always left a damp area in the bed. Every day, just before the break of dawn, when Xandra disappeared for a few hours, Camille rolled in that damp spot, luxuriating in her lover's fragrance.

After a few days, Camille realized that she had never seen Xandra eat. She accepted that as easily as her unexplained absences, lest this delicious spell be broken.

As hot spring turned into blistering summer, Camille had to face reality: she was running out of money, with no plan as to what she would do once her funds were entirely spent. One afternoon, she tried to describe her situation to her Veneran companion, but Camille broke into tears mid-explanation, convinced that the impassive Xandra hadn't understood a word.

That night, Camille, anxious and uncertain, did not kiss Xandra's body. The two women lay next to each other, their hands awkwardly clasped. Xandra let go of Camille's hand and propped herself on an elbow to stare at Camille's face. She ran her fingers through Camille's hair and bent down to give a light peck on her cheek. Camille breathed in the brine of Xandra's breath and instantly fell asleep.

Just before the break of dawn, like every morning since they'd been sharing a bed, Camille felt Xandra slip out. By noon, Xandra had still not returned, and Camille, finally deciding to force herself to get out of bed, was certain that the other woman had left her for good.

Camille was completely at a loss. She felt not at all transformed by the surreal intimacy of the past several weeks but rather utterly emptied, a hollow vessel with no life of her own. She sat on a bench for the remainder of the day, staring out at the sea, ignoring thirst and hunger, defeated.

As dusk began to temper the blue of the sky, someone sat close enough to Camille that their hips touched. She immediately recognized Xandra's briny aroma, and she sighed in desperate relief.

Xandra handed Camille an envelope: two train tickets to Villa Santa Mariagiovanna, a small port city in the south of Italy. They were taking the 13:45 train the next day. Camille had no idea why they were heading there, but she was thrilled at the idea of a mysterious adventure in the company of her equally mysterious lover. Besides, there was nothing and no-one else waiting for her.

Camille was surprised by the seeming revelation that Xandra had money, or at least access to it somehow. She had booked them on a sleeper car for the overnight leg from Milan to their destination, which, despite the crampedness, felt luxurious after weeks at the hostel. Meals were included with the fare, and, since Xandra still exhibited no desire to ingest anything, Camille indulged in double portions, even if overeating usually made her a little sick to her stomach.

In their compartment, Camille went to bed feeling ill and bloated. Xandra tucked her in with solicitous tenderness and rubbed a viscous tincture on the Frenchwoman's belly and face. Camille almost vomited at the concoction's reek: a too pungent blend of brine and vermilion overpowered by rot and decay. The stink of rot, Camille realized, could be caused by her own nausea and not by the tincture itself, but she was beginning to have trouble distinguishing sensations. Soon, she started sweating, erupting in fever, and it became difficult to think or to make sense of things.

When she woke in the morning, her fever broken, Camille struggled with odd memories of the past night.

Xandra was already up and dressed, staring out at the sea from their window, her bag packed.

Camille had had strange dreams — or perhaps waking delusions.

Most vividly she'd imagined Xandra naked, her body covered in glowing fishlike sigils, vermilion in colour. She was chanting in a language Camille could not recognize. One word was repeated more than any other: *nayadaga*. Xandra paused to sip from a burgundy-coloured bottle. She swished the liquid around in her mouth and spat it out into her hand. She brought her wet hand down between her legs, rubbing and fingering herself to orgasm. A dark orange mist seeped out from Xandra's cunt; the mist took a shape and solidified into a floating creature, undeniably female, that seemed a cross between a fish, a human, and something else Camille could not begin to identify. Again, Xandra repeated *nayadaga*, this time with reverential awe; Camille softly echoed the syllables, understanding as she intoned the word that this was the creature's name. At the sound of Camille's voice, both Nayadaga and Xandra looked at Camille with fury. From Nayadaga's gills spewed a burnt-orange substance that Camille, in her dream-logic, understood to be the essence of the goddess Nayadaga herself. Camille then lost consciousness, her mind adrift in delusions too bizarre to accurately recollect or describe to herself.

But looking at Xandra now in the light of day, all traces of the fever dissipated, the nighttime episode seemed so absurd. Yes, Xandra was odd and more than a little mysterious, but Camille was also aware of vermilion's reputed hallucinogenic properties; she easily dismissed her memories as the result of the fever and the vermilion ointment.

Camille rose and cuddled next to Xandra. Xandra stretched out her arm so that Camille could rest her head on her shoulder. They squeezed each other. Camille breathed in her lover's aroma and let herself be infected by Xandra's serenity.

The train pulled into the Villa Santa Mariagiovanna station at 8 a.m. They spent the morning walking by the port, until Camille got hungry. Camille used her last few euros to buy some lunch: macaroni with slices of spicy sausage, chunks of ricotta cheese, diced bright-red tomatoes, and hot green peppers — everything dripping with garlic-flavoured olive oil. It was the most delicious meal Camille had enjoyed in years. As usual, Xandra simply watched her eat.

Camille was now completely broke. She tried to explain this to Xandra, but the other woman curtly shushed her, as if it were of no import. Camille reminded herself that this was an adventure, reminded herself to roll with whatever would happen.

⌒ Villa Santa Mariagiovanna lacked the romance so characteristic of Italy. A small grey, business-like port where the shore and the town itself were entirely given over to commerce, to big ships loading and unloading their wares, to trucks carrying cargo to and from the boats. Beyond, the vibrant blue of the sea and the lush greenery of Sicily beckoned. Camille had never before come this far south in Italy. The mere idea of Sicily thrilled her. She broke the customary silence and tried to ask Xandra if that's where they were heading. Xandra seemed to make no effort to try to understand or respond to Camille's half-French, half-mangled-Italian query.

After lunch, Xandra dragged Camille through the grey streets of Villa Santa Mariagiovanna, until they reached an alley of some sort, with overflowing dumpsters that reeked of rotting fish. Xandra knocked on a nondescript wooden door; an old man answered, and he looked upon the Veneran woman with unashamed adoration. The two spoke in the Veneran dialect, but Camille thought she detected a few words that sounded utterly alien, much like the words Xandra had intoned during Camille's dream or delusion that night on the train. The old man stepped aside to let the two young women in. As Xandra crossed the threshold, with the Frenchwoman right behind her, Camille noticed, above the doorway, a small dark-orange statuette nailed to the wall. Camille squint-ed to get a better look and gasped with unexpected fear: she was certain she had recognized Nayadaga. How much of Camille's nighttime vision had in fact been hallucination? What had really happened on the train?

Xandra reacted to Camille's disquiet. At first, Camille thought she read anger in Xandra's features, but perhaps she had been mistaken. Xandra took her hand between the two of hers and squeezed it reassur-ingly. When she smiled at Camille, there was only concern and tenderness on her face. Still, Camille trembled a bit, unable to shake a chill of dread.

The old man led them to a small room with a cot no bigger than a child's bed. The door shut, Xandra removed her own clothes and enfolded the worried Camille into her arms. The proximity of Xandra and her briny odour finally soothed Camille's anxiety. Xandra's permanent dampness soaked into Camille's clothes. The two women exchanged a grin at this recurring incident. Camille made to slip out of her clothes, but Xandra grabbed her wrists to stop her. Instead, the naked Xandra slowly removed Camille's clothes herself.

Sex between the two women was never genital, and barely reciprocal. Xandra would passively lie there, with her legs and mouth firmly closed, letting Camille caress, lick, kiss, and otherwise have her way with her body. Occasionally, Xandra would utter strange, almost inhuman moans in what Camille assumed to be pleasure. The unique taste and scent of Xandra's flesh were intoxicating to Camille, providing a high more blissful than any orgasm she'd ever experienced before, with boys or by herself.

Camille swooned when now, for the first time, Xandra began to nibble on Camille's breasts with her sharp teeth, when she slid her rough tongue on her flesh, when she reached between Camille's legs with her moist hand to slip two wet, spongy, slippery fingers into Camille's own wetness.

Camille came immediately, screaming her orgasm, and promptly fell asleep on the tiny, cramped cot.

Camille woke shortly after sunset to find tiny, blood-red bite marks all over her body. Xandra avoided her gaze but firmly took hold of Camille's hand when the old man led the two women to a small pier, concealed beneath a bigger pier. From that secret location, they boarded a vehicle stranger than anything Camille had ever seen. Camille surmised that it was a sort of submarine, but, instead of metal, it was made out of a transparent, spongy substance. Its overall shape — that of a giant fish — was firm, but the hull was warm and soft and subtly yielding to the touch, as if it were organic, fleshly; the more she probed at it, the more it reminded her of Xandra's flesh.

Xandra took off her shoes before boarding and indicated that Camille should do the same. They got aboard through the vessel's open, gaping mouth, as if they were willingly sacrificing themselves by walking into the belly of an enormous marine creature. At that moment, Camille grew convinced that the ship was indeed alive.

The submarine was crewed entirely by women, all of whom bore an unmistakable family resemblance to Xandra. The interior of the vessel, and all the women aboard, smelled of the same distinctive briny aroma as Xandra herself.

They lost no time and quickly set off and submerged into the darkness of the Mediterranean at night.

In total darkness, Camille lost track of time and direction. But before long something glowed in the distance — a vermilion glow sparkling with other colours too otherworldly to name. The fishlike vessel approached the source of light: it seemed alive, but gigantic — bigger than a large city. It pulsed, shimmered, undulated, and erupted in multicoloured tendrils, like the underbelly of a leviathan squid or jellyfish.

As they drew even nearer, Camille grew increasingly confused by the nature of what she was seeing. At times, it appeared to be nothing more than rock — the underside of a large island, perhaps — but always there remained at least an afterimage of the pulsating, colourful tendrils.

As one, many of the women on board uttered the same word: "Venera."

The submarine navigated into the underbelly of the great city-state, following a stony labyrinth, until it emerged into a lush, underground cavern, lit with the glow of leaves and moss of iridescent vermilion.

The cavern was so big that Camille could not see its limits. Dozens, perhaps even hundreds of women were gathered here. Each of them naked; each of them resembling Xandra to an alarming degree; their bodies decorated with the same sort of glowing vermilion fish tattoos as Xandra's had been on the train during what Camille had believed to be a dream or delusion. The intensity of their collective briny aroma almost caused Camille to faint, but she pushed herself to stay conscious, refusing to abandon herself to that scent, which she associated perhaps too closely with pleasure and comfort.

The ground beneath her bare feet was covered in thick, iridescent spongy moss. It was a strangely soothing sensation.

By reflex, Camille reached out to take Xandra's hand, but she clasped only emptiness. The women were all crowded close to each other, but they had left a wide berth around Camille. She scanned the gathering but could not locate Xandra anywhere.

An older woman separated herself from the throng and approached Camille. To her surprise and relief, the woman addressed her in French. She was direct: "Do you love and trust Xandra with all your heart?"

Camille had not known what to expect, but she hadn't expected this. It took her a moment to collect herself, but she didn't pause to think: "Yes. Yes, I do. More than I ever believed I could love or trust anyone."

The woman lowered her eyes with a thin and somewhat ominous smile.

Camille heard a splash behind her. She turned to see Xandra climbing out of the water, also naked, also covered in the same fish sigils as the others.

Xandra came to stand next to Camille, grabbing her hand fiercely, her large, moist eyes radiant despite their darkness.

The woman spoke again. "Xandra loves you, Camille. She is willing to submit to anything the goddess demands to be with you. Will you, too, surrender yourself to Nayadaga in honour of your love?"

This was a wedding. Xandra had brought her here to get married. Camille had never idealized marriage, had never thought much about it, really, but suddenly she felt herself melt at the strange, compelling romanticism of this moment and of all the other moments with Xandra that had led her here, to this place, this time, this life-changing event. "I would do anything to make Xandra happy. To love Xandra."

The woman replied: "I will ask you again; but know that the goddess will exact a price from each of you to bless this love. Once you have formally agreed, there is no turning back, no possibility of refusing the goddess her due. Will you, Camille, surrender to Nayadaga in honour of your love for Xandra?"

"Yes, I will. Yes. Yes!"

Camille felt Xandra's hand squeeze hers tighter.

The woman addressed Xandra in the Veneran dialect. In response, Xandra turned to her bride, fixing her large, inhuman eyes on Camille's until the Frenchwoman felt utterly submissive and compliant to the will of her lover. Xandra then removed Camille's clothes. The officiator gestured, and another woman appeared, carrying a burnt-orange ewer, which she gave to Xandra, who dipped her fingers into it. When she brought them out, the tips of her fingers glowed with vermilion ichor, which Xandra used to cover Camille's body with the same fishlike sigils all these women bore.

The congregation began chanting. The chant grew louder and louder, until it rumbled like thunder. They were intoning a single name: Nayadaga.

Vermilion smoke seeped out from between the legs of every woman save the wedding couple. The fish goddess materialized from the smoke and took solid shape, a hundredfold larger than she had appeared on the train.

The two brides stood facing each other, their hands clasped. Camille breathed deeply; she felt the damp, smoky essence of the goddess Nayadaga seep into her. Camille's bones seemed to lose their solidity, adopting a malleability that held the promise of profound transformation.

AT THE
WORLD TREE HOTEL

⌇⌇

For the past five days, as the cruise ship *Venusian* languorously travelled the Mediterranean from Barcelona to Venera, the weather had been perfect: bright blue skies tempered by the occasional white cloud with not a hint of rain; never dipping below fifteen degrees centigrade at night, never going above 25 in the daytime; a steady breeze that carried the mesmerizing aroma of the sea. Jana had worked on her tan, sipping vermilion-tinged cocktails, which gave her deliciously vivid erotic daydreams, while Dean snapped away at the aquatic horizon with the camera she'd recently given him for his birthday.

But this morning, now that the boat is docking at the port of Venera, the rain pours down in dense sheets, rendering the legendary city-state all but invisible. The precipitation is accompanied by an unseasonal damp chill that lodges itself in Jana's bones. She shivers, even under the double protection of sweater and raincoat. She's not sure their luggage is rainproof enough to withstand such intense weather. She clutches Dean's arm, rubs her cheek on his shoulder. The smell of him chases away some of her agitation — having imbibed vermilion nonstop for five days her sense of smell is now animalistic — but she's still disappointed: she had looked forward to witnessing firsthand the celebrated sea view of the Venera cityscape. How often will she get to sail into what is reputed to be the most strangely beautiful metropolis on Earth? The weather is bound to clear up, though, and then maybe they can book a boat tour around the archipelago and get a good eyeful of the cityscape as seen from the sea.

At the exit of the boat, someone is waiting for them. A sturdy man with a crew cut dressed in a formal uniform that sits uncomfortably on his rough frame holds a sign with Dean's name. Next to the man is an enclosed two-wheel cart; after vigorously shaking Dean's hand and kissing Jana's, the latter in a manner that manages to be both brash and polite, he introduces himself — Carlo — and tucks away their luggage safely in his impermeable conveyance.

He motions for them to follow him, and they venture into the rain-darkened metropolis. Jana can barely see more than two arms' length anywhere around her. She holds on tightly to Dean as they zigzag into the unknown. To Jana's surprise, Dean is sure-footed, easily keeping pace with Carlo, who, even laden with the cart, navigates the narrow claustrophobic streets with a dancer's grace, belying her first impression of the bulky hotel employee. Then Dean surprises her even further when he starts to shout to Carlo through the percussive din of the rain, and the two men engage in a boisterous exchange punctuated with roars and laughter.

Besides her native English, Jana can barely squeak by in Spanish and French; to her Toronto ears Dean and Carlo are speaking something close to Italian, but tinged with Arabic, French, and Spanish. It must be Veneran, a language few people learn outside the archipelago itself. Jana and Dean have been together for nearly two years now — their second anniversary will occur here in Venera, and Jana suspects that the entire trip, paid for by Dean, is an elaborate setup for a marriage proposal — but she still doesn't really know much about his past, and now that he's displaying familiarity with mysterious, glamorous Venera she's more curious than ever — and more drawn to him.

Without Jana having noticed that they ever passed through a doorway or any kind of threshold, the three of them are now standing at the desk of the World Tree Hotel, its green and rust-red logo — depicting Yggdrasil, the World Tree of Norse myth — embossed on the front panel so realistically that it is as if the tree's roots reach into the soil underneath the hotel's marble floor.

Jana is drenched to the bone, shivering in spite of the heat. The heavy, confining layers of raincoat and sweater suffocate her. She removes them, hungry for air. Even her shirt and bra are uncomfortably damp, but she feels a moment of relief. Suddenly it's all too much: the incomprehensible Veneran language, the confusing organic architecture, the oppressive clamminess of the air, the pungent odours, the lobby filled only with men. Their palpable masculinity assails her senses, as if some primordial phero-mone receptor had just been kickstarted — perhaps another side-effect of vermilion? Dean had warned her not to overdo it with the cocktails. She had never tasted the notorious Veneran psychotropic spice before. Without realizing she's doing it aloud, she moans, and all those male eyes turn toward her, intensifying her sense of being trapped, surrounded, surveilled. She shivers violently, a penetrating cold icing through her veins.

Dean cries, "Jana ..." He steps toward her, but as he moves he is transformed into a grotesque caricature of himself, half-tree, half-wolf-man. The entire lobby and all in it are also transmogrified into some-thing otherworldly, so otherworldly that she cannot distinguish what is alive from what is not.

She closes her eyes. Hands grab at her. At first, they feel like rough bark scraping against the skin of her arms. But she hears Dean's voice, repeating her name gently. Then she recognizes the grip. Dean's hands. Not soft like a woman's, but softer than bark. Firm masculine hands. She opens her eyes, and there he is, holding her. The lobby is back as it was. But she is still cold and shivering. And weakened.

Dean supports her as Carlo leads them to their room. Jana keeps her eyes closed the whole way, surrendering herself to her man.

⤚ That night, Jana gets no rest. Feverish, she keeps getting jostled awake by the ceaseless clatter of the heavy downpour. The rain is so thick that she cannot even identify morning when, at 7:30, Dean rises from his deep, snore-filled slumber. He pulls open the drapes, but it's still so dark outside. Will she ever get to lay eyes on Venera?

⤚ Dean emerges naked from the bathroom, his skin still glistening from the shower. She thinks of inviting him back to bed for a morning romp, and the thought of sex makes her aware of feeling queasy. She rushes out of bed, but she doesn't quite make it to the toilet in time and she vomits all over the bathroom floor.

Dean finds her trembling on all fours. He dampens a clean towel, cleans her up, and brings her back to bed. He slips under the covers and presses her against his chest; she lets herself breathe him in. She shivers a few times, but she eventually starts to feel warm and drowsy …

… The sound of Dean's voice brings Jana back to consciousness. He's on the phone, talking in Veneran. She still hasn't asked him about that.

He hangs up, and she asks, yawning: "Who was that?"

"I called the front desk. They're sending a maid over to clean the bathroom."

That jars her out of her torpor. "What? No! Don't embarrass me like that. Call back. I'll clean it." But she's thinking: *You should clean it, Dean. And I shouldn't have to ask.*

"You'll do no such thing, amora. I'm taking care of it. There's nothing embarrassing. We're paying for service, and we're getting it. You need fresh air, though, but you also need to keep warm. Did you bring any sweaters?"

She nods; Dean rifles through her luggage, pulling out her clothes carelessly. Defeated, Janna feels weak again. She's hungry, but the thought of food turns her stomach.

He comes to bed and dresses her. She lets him, neither cooperating nor hindering. He wraps her in extra blankets pulled from the bottom drawer of the dresser. He leads her outside; it's still raining: a cascading wall of grey obscuring everything. But there's no wind, and the balcony is well protected and dry. So he sits her on a chaise longue, and she closes her eyes, exhausted.

Despite the rain, the air is hot; the balcony is almost as sweltering as a sauna. Yesterday's unseasonable cold spell has entirely dissipated. Nevertheless, there's still a hint of chill in her bones. Jana breathes in the moistness of Venera. It smells intoxicating: flowery fragrances mixed with salty brine; sex in a woman's bedroom.

Under the blankets, under her clothes, she places a hand between her legs. She's wet, hungry to be touched. She slips two fingers inside herself, wishing it were Dean's fingers. She lets herself glide on that fantasy …

... Until she hears a woman yelling, from within their room.

Jana gets up and walks inside. Dean is gripping the maid's wrists together. While she struggles, the maid continues to yell at him in Veneran. There are fresh, red scratches across Dean's cheek. There's barely controlled anger in his face: he wants to hit this dark-haired woman, hurt her, whoever she is. Never in the past two years has Jana seen Dean violently angry.

The scene leaves Jana confused; already sexually alert, she can't help but respond to Dean's show of strength. But it scares her, too, as does her own arousal.

The pair notice Jana. The distraction is enough for the maid to escape Dean's hold. She hisses at the couple, but the effect is more caricatural than menacing.

Dean and Jana catch each other's eye; as if on cue, they both start to guffaw. Scowling at Dean, the maid, gesturing like a madwoman, screams something Jana can't decipher, then flings the door open and flees.

As abruptly as the laughter began, it ends. The weight of secrecy, strangeness, alienation, and tension that has been mounting since their arrival in Venera — momentarily dampened by that unexpected burst of complicity — bears down on Jana. Now, it is Dean himself who appears secretive, strange, alien, and the source of Jana's disquiet.

Almost as quickly, the mood shifts again; Dean's customary male brashness dissolves under Jana's gaze. He closes the door, then stands awkwardly, his face flickering concern, culpability, love, vulnerability. He extends a hand toward her, and she takes it. They sit on the bed. A few times in short succession, he opens his mouth as if to speak but seems unable to find the words.

Now, Jana thinks. Now is the time to clear up all the mysteries aggregating around Dean and his relationship to Venera. All he needs is a persuasive nudge ... Jana brushes his ear with her mouth and whispers: "Talk to me, love."

And he does. But Jana is immediately angered by the sounds he utters. He's speaking Veneran.

She interrupts him, shouting: "I can't believe you're making fun of me like this!"

Instead of laughing or escalating the heat of the argument, Dean looks bewildered, frightened.

He speaks again but trails off after only a few words of Veneran. Again he tries; but, still spouting Veneran, he stops abruptly. He hurries to the desk. Picking up a pen, he writes on the hotel notepad, but tears off sheet after sheet. He yells a foreign word that has the unmistakable blunt venom of an oath. He slams his fist on the desk. Turning to Jana, he repeats pleadingly: "Amora, amora, amora ..." — his favourite endearment, which she now gleans is not his own romantic coinage but the Veneran word for *love* — followed by a string of syllables she cannot understand, punctuated by a final, defeated "Amora ..."

Then, he grunts angrily and, shaking his fist, spits out a sentence in Veneran. With one final, tender "Amora" for Jana's benefit, he rushes out the door.

Jana thinks of following him, but the adrenaline rush that followed her discovery of the altercation between Dean and the maid has dissipated, and now she feels weak, her skin burning. Remembering her hallucination in the lobby, she doubts everything that she has just witnessed. Sleep. Sleep will restore her and restore reason to the world. She buries herself in the bed, but her feverish slumber is anything but peaceful. She slips in and out of consciousness, haunted by nightmares and nightmarish hallucinations, by half-human monsters and distorted memories of past humiliations and betrayals, by visions of Dean and the maid conspiring against her.

When Jana wakes, despite the tumult of her time in bed, she feels like herself again. Whatever fever or ailment or virus or poison had assailed her has run its course. If she's still weak at all, it is because of hunger. It feels good, though, to want food again. She has no idea how long she slept. There's no sign of Dean. A quick hot shower, and she'll go down to the hotel restaurant. And then she'll deal with Dean's absence on a full stomach. For now, she's ready to dismiss everything that's happened since their arrival here as a fever dream.

But Jana had forgotten about the state of the bathroom. It still has not been cleaned. Best to deal with it on an empty stomach, she reasons.

Being careful to set aside one clean towel for herself, she gets the job done. Part of her wants to indulge in a long shower, but she's too hungry; she makes do with a quick in and out.

The layout of the hotel is labyrinthine, echoing her first impression of the city as she and Dean were led to the hotel upon disembarking. The halls are cavernous — badly lit and undistinguishable one from another. Which floor is she on? Has she passed by her own room repeatedly? Jana's hunger makes her disorientation more acute. Finally, she is rescued by a solicitous young porter who finds her wandering in the halls and leads her to her destination, the restaurant. The same porter once again comes to her rescue afterward, once she has spent nearly an hour trying to find her room. Both times, in fractured English, he refuses her offer of a gratuity.

The next day, the rain still shows no sign of abating. Daytime or nighttime, there's scarcely any variation in the light; a relentless dark grey aura shrouds Venera.

Dean has yet to come back. Suspecting that the maid is her best lead to find her wayward lover Jana goes to the front desk, which, to her surprise, she finds with no difficulty.

It's her first time in the lobby since they arrived and she suffered that disquieting hallucination. The sight of the embossed Yggdrasil on the front desk unnerves her. She can't shake the impression that it's somehow organic, alive. That some kind of preternatural life force pulses through it, emanating outward in concentric circles of corrupting energy, decaying the fabric that coheres reality.

Jana swallows her apprehension and strides toward the desk with what she hopes is confidence. She's not certain, but she thinks she recognizes the clerk from when they arrived. A tall, bony man whose extreme thinness makes it difficult to estimate his age. The hue of his pitch-black hair, gelled in place tightly against his skull, probably comes from a bottle. "Excuse me — do you speak English?"

"Of course, miadama."

Jana gives him their room number. "Two days ago, we called to have the bathroom cleaned. I'd like to speak to the maid, please."

"One moment, miadama." He opens a cumbersome ledger and murmurs, "Si, Natasha," then he *tsks*.

Jana asks, "Is something wrong?"

"The maid in question has not reported for work since being sent to your room."

"What's her full name? Is there a way I can get in touch with her?"

"Miadama, that is confidential information. We have been unable to contact her ourselves. Why did you want to talk to her? Is there any information you could give us as to her whereabouts or what happened to her?"

The clerk's tone is now accusatory. She hesitates, not knowing how to respond. The prospect of revealing that Dean has fled with no explanation, leaving her alone, is too humiliating. Under the clerk's probing gaze, she can feel guilt spell itself on her face, although she is guilty of nothing. Another man emerges from the back offices. He is portly, dishevelled, exuding stern paternalistic authority. The two Venerans confer in hushed tones — not that Jana could understand what they say, anyway. But she does catch the name "Natasha" a few times. Interrupting the men, she mumbles incoherently: "No ... I mean ... How could I ... I don't — " They turn to look at her, staring at her, judging her silently. Finally, she blurts: "If you hear from this Natasha, please let me know. I need to speak to her. It's a private matter," and turns on her heels before either man can say anything else to her.

But the geometry of the hotel once again confounds her. Instead of locating the stairs that would lead her back to her room, Jana finds herself at the threshold of the exit, the relentless rain, falling a few centimetres in front of her, splatters from the ground to her bare calves. As Jana ponders whether to go forth in the heavy downpour and explore Venera with no raincoat or umbrella — she can't spend the entirety of her time here, in the world's most exotic city, holed up in a room waiting for her boyfriend — a familiar voice addresses her. "Miadama?" It is Carlo, the porter who greeted them at the boat, now brandishing an umbrella. "Miadama, the weather has not been kind since your arrival."

Although she barely knows this man at all, Jana experiences a flood of comfort at his proximity. For an instant, she feels safe; yet, she knows her face betrays her distress. She quickly recovers, but in the silence Carlo has been studying her. She softens and nestles into the male possessiveness of his gaze, finding refuge in its brash, unspoken promise of protection.

He asks: "Have you yet seen anything of Venera?"

She shakes her head.

"I think, miadama, that you need to get out, to explore. Let me guide you in this terrible weather. Let me show you what I know of Venera, for she is the most beautiful and mysterious of cities." Carlo opens the umbrella, his left hand extended in invitation.

Jana ducks under the umbrella and grabs his arm, unashamedly kneading his strong biceps. She smiles at him, as chastely as she can manage under the circumstances. "Thank you. Let's go!"

∽ Although Carlo is from Venera, and not Italy, to Jana's ear his accent has that same musicality that she associates with Italian. His English is near-perfect, peppered with the occasional local expression or mistranslated colloquialism. As they walk arm-in-arm, he speaks non-stop, acting the eager tourist guide. Amid the dense downpour, Jana cannot see anything, cannot attach his words to any concrete reality. She soon stops paying attention to the words themselves, letting his voice and his male musk lullaby her into forgetting her anxieties and the strangeness of everything that's befallen her since arriving on the island.

∽ Finally, Carlo and Jana take refuge in a small restaurant. "It is unusual for the island to be hit by such heavy rain, miadama," he tells her after exchanging a few words in Veneran with the hostess.

"Please, call me Jana."

He bows his head. "Si, Jana."

They are led to a small booth, near a roaring fireplace. The fire is delicious. Jana closes her eyes and lets the heat caress her face.

Once she opens her eyes, she says: "Order food and wine for us, please. Surprise me. Delight me. It's all on me, of course. You've been so kind."

He starts to protest but catches himself. "It is you who is so kind." He gets up, finding the waitress at the bar.

Jana takes in her surroundings. The mood is warm, earthy, intimate. Eschewing electric light, the entire place is lit by fire: candles, lanterns, and, of, course, the fireplace. The walls are of vermilion-red brick and the structure and furniture is some dark brown — in this light, almost black — wood. The decor is minimalist: no artwork, no photographs — although some of the wood panels have carved details; she can't quite make out the shapes in the near dark, but the flickering light seems to reveal monstrous, nightmarish, even menacing faces. She assumes the horrific character of what she perceives in the carvings is the result of her own somewhat grotesque frame of mind, which Carlo's charming — almost too charming — company has only superficially suppressed.

Carlo returns. She asks him about this place. "The Kibbudea is an old establishment," he explains, pointing to the placemats, on which the name is spelled in Romanesque script under an ornate logo; although Janna cannot grasp what it depicts she is repulsed by its ferocious aura of obscenity, "predating even the Roman conquest, when the goddess Hecate sent her shapeshifting soldiers to take over the vermilion trade for the empire. Neither Hecate nor the Romans ever did find the gardens. Venera waited them out, and eventually the Romans retreated as their empire collapsed. So, too, the Northern hordes who built their temple to Yggdrasil where now stands the World Tree Hotel hoped to discover the holy secret of the sacred spice and profit from it. Over the centuries, some of the Vikings left, others died out or were assimilated."

Jana finds none of these digressions interesting. All this superstition about gods and worship ... she tries not to let her irritation show — Carlo is being so nice to her — but she sees in his reaction, now that he pauses for breath and takes a good look at her, that he has become aware of her impatience with the directions the conversation has taken.

Clearing his throat, Carlo answers her question more directly: "The priestesses of the goddess — the true goddess, Venera herself; not this counterfeit New Age Earth Goddess the current government espouses — once prepared food for the deity in these kitchens. But there has been no sign of Venera herself for generations. At least since the Nazi occupation. Maybe even before. In her absence, the Kibbudea — in Classical Veneran that means 'food for the goddess' — has passed into laic hands."

Jana fidgets uncomfortably, barely acknowledging Carlo. The near dark, already somewhat disquieting, takes on a suffocating quality; the carvings now appear even more monstrous, inspiring a gnawing, creeping terror. She admonishes herself for being so easily susceptible. "Surely, you don't believe all this. Shapeshifters? Goddesses?" She regrets her disdainful tone even before the words are out of her.

Carlo's face betrays a flash of hurt and anger, which settles into disappointment. He forces a smile. "Venera is like nowhere else on Earth. The gods may be dead everywhere else, but here many of them still thrive, miadama." Carlo puts an unmistakable cold emphasis on that formal word of address, announcing to Jana that he's shutting down the complicity that had been building between them.

The wine arrives, interrupting the palpable awkwardness. To Jana's surprise, it's a mulled wine, served in a glass decanter mounted on a trivet, below which oil burns in a boat-shaped terracotta dish. The wine is so dark, its charred redness is almost black. It smells delicious, its aroma already sumptuously intoxicating.

Carlo inhales the bouquet of the warm alcohol and instantly — Jana can see in his face — snaps back into his persona of the subtle charmer, as if it were an inevitable reflex. Good — she wants things to thaw again between them. She needs a friend, here in this faraway island and now in these bizarre circumstances. He pours her a drink in a wooden mug into which are carved demonic — or perhaps angelic? — figures engaged in an orgy of oral sex. Venera is notorious for this kind of grotesquely erotic artwork. She clutches the warm offering to her chest and, despite her skepticism, is overcome with a sense of ritual, maybe even transcendence. Jana closes her eyes, taking in the rich odours of the wine. In a near-whisper, she tells Carlo: "You're right ... Venera is like nowhere else." As she sips the dark liquid, she notices his gaze soften with a hint of genuine warmth.

They sip the wine in companionable silence, for which Jana is grateful. She doesn't want to say the wrong thing again, and with every sip she feels her inhibitions slip away. In this lightheaded state, she fears it would be too easy for her to let loose some ill-considered words that might again break this comforting illusion of intimacy.

Meanwhile, the wine continues to weave its spell, making her feel giddy, despite the nagging mysterious unpleasantness with Dean, despite the grotesque surroundings. She recognizes by now that the beverage is laced with vermilion. A small part of her is concerned about once again imbibing the powerful euphoric spice that left her so ill recently, but she suppresses her worries and lets herself relax.

The antipasti are brought to the table. Carlo describes it all with the enthusiasm of a sensualist gourmand, but Jana makes no effort to understand. She lets his sensuous words flow like music as she bites into the exotic concoctions, not caring what they are or what they contain. Every bite is a tiny orgasm. Everything is delicious. And everything, she suspects, is laced with yet more vermilion.

Yet more food is served. Every bite is more meltingly succulent than the previous. She hears herself talking, but by now she pays as little attention to her own words as she does to Carlo's. She cares not at all what they are discussing, or if even anything they say makes any sense. She abandons herself to the euphoria induced by the vermilion ... until she hears Carlo say that name: "... Natasha ..."

Jana forces herself to focus, although it's very difficult. The more she tries to fight the euphoria, the more she tries to concentrate, the more nightmarish hallucinations of sight, sound, and smell gnaw at the edge of her perception. She tries to ignore the subtle terror creeping inside her and asks Carlo: "Can you say that again? What about Natasha?"

"She and your man, Dean, were teenage sweethearts. She told me that he left Venera without telling her, without ever writing, without letting her know that it was over between them."

This was not entirely a surprise to Jana. "How did she find him?"

"Fate, Jana. *Masara.* Or perhaps you would prefer to think of it as coincidence. She has worked at the World Tree Hotel for many years. Longer than I have. She's a very passionate woman. Perhaps too passionate, I would say."

"How do you know all this about her and Dean?" She's unable to suppress the accusation in her tone.

"Natasha likes to talk. Especially when she is angry. And she was very angry when she left your room the other day."

"Have you seen them together? Or him? Have you seen Dean?"

"No, Jana. I do not know where your man is."

"Take me to her. Take me to Natasha. She knows. And you know where to find her."

"No, Jana. I cannot do that. Whether or not I know where to find Natasha, it is not my business to intrude on her privacy. Or to involve myself in this drama of yours. You are a stranger here. Your man, Dean, is not. He is Veneran. Perhaps he is where he belongs, now. Perhaps you should return to your home. Forget Venera. I do not mean to be unkind, but I do not think you are well suited to this place."

The monstrous carvings on the walls and ceiling disengage from their perches. They move in the shadows, never allowing her a clear glimpse of their shapes and sizes.

"You drugged me on purpose. You're in on it with her!"

"No, Jana. No. There is no plot against you. I am trying to be your friend. But you do not understand life here."

Fearing for her safety, Jana rises from her seat. She rushes outside without even glancing back. The rain is still torrential. She has no idea how to find the World Tree Hotel. She doesn't want to go back to her room, though. Maybe there's a Canadian embassy or consulate where she could seek refuge. Then take the first boat out to the mainland and fly back home. Save herself.

She wanders aimlessly in the rain, shivering down to the bone. How will she ever find her way? She could be anywhere. The whole world is nothing but rain, dense and impenetrable. Rain is all she sees, all she smells, all she feels. It's as if her own body were dissolving, merging with the downpour.

Strong arms enfold her. It is Carlo.

"Miadama. Jana. You will catch your death. Let me bring you back to the hotel."

Jana feels week, defeated. She leans into Carlo's muscular frame and lets him take over, not knowing whether she is saved or doomed. Barely caring which.

As soon as she is back at the World Tree and sheltered from the weather, the paranoia once again focuses her mind. She claws at Carlo's face, drawing blood, and escapes his grip.

She runs deeper into the World Tree Hotel, not really knowing what she is running from or where she is running to.

⮑ Jane recognizes the architecture and decor of the hotel — its aquamarine and earth-brown colour scheme; its hopelessly labyrinthine corridors; its disorienting ceilings of varying heights; its cavern-like lighting — but she finds no comfort in that recognition. She has no clue for how long she has been wandering this neverending, oppressive, deserted sameness. In desperation, she finally decides to knock on a random door. There's no answer. She tries the handle but finds it locked. She repeats her attempt on dozens of doors, but it's always futile: all the doors are locked, and there is never anyone who answers. Occasionally, she believes she hears the murmur of voices inside. Those times, she knocks more insistently, shouts her desperation at the anonymous patrons. Always, she is ignored.

At some point, probably before she and Carlo reached the World Tree Hotel, Jana lost her handbag. Along with her room key, her money, and her passport.

Jana needs to think her way out of this. She's aware that the vermilion is still influencing her perceptions but unsure to what extent reality is being distorted by the drug. Still, there must be a way out of this nightmare. The pressure on her bladder makes it impossible for her to concentrate. Seeing no other option, as all the doors are locked to her, she squats against a wall and relieves herself.

The deserted hallway now reeks with the musk of her piss. But Jana has regained some clarity of mind. She must locate the lobby. And from there get a word to Canadian authorities and find her way off this island. Carlo was right. She has to forget Dean and return home. There's nothing for her here.

In time, desperation once again clouds her mind. No matter how far she walks, Jana cannot escape the stench of urine — and worse. She peers at the floor in the near dark. With increasing frequency, she finds suspicious wet spots, piles of feces, rotting carcasses of small mammals and lizards. Gradually, the halls no longer look merely cavernous; gradually, the signs of civilization are stripped from her surroundings. No matter which direction she takes, Jana steps farther into a maze of narrowing caverns. Iridescent vermilion veins crisscross the surface of the rock walls, providing faint illumination. She had believed vermilion to originate from a plant, but here it appears to be a mineral.

Aware that she is straying deeper and deeper into the bowels of Venera and farther away from any possible exit, Jana tries to climb back up to the surface, but the labyrinth defeats her. Regardless of the direction she attempts to take, Jana continues her unwilling descent.

She has moved beyond the zone of decay and animal waste. The air is getting damper, almost palpable. It is not dank, however, but numinously clean — like breathing psychotropically potent mineral water: at once reinvigorating and heady, refreshing and dizzying, bringing about both clarity and confusion.

Her surroundings are now in perpetual transformation, taking on configurations she can neither recognize nor fully comprehend. Sometimes, her situation no longer seems claustrophobic. Vast alien subterranean vistas open up before her, exotic formations — which she cannot distinguish as fauna, flora, mineral, or artificial — spread outward for unfathomable distances. And then, with a step, her world shrinks again to a confining tunnel. The only constant is the faint burnt-orange glow of the strains of vermilion illuminating every surface.

Jana now stands at a threshold. At her feet are gigantic roots emanating from the chamber before her. The roots break through the stony ground, burrowing deeper still into the earth.

There's the flickering light of a fire coming from inside. Its warmth beckons her. Its aroma is intoxicatingly familiar: vermilion.

She steps inside. At first, her senses are drawn to the flames of the vermilion fire. On the ground rests a large terracotta pot onto which is carved the weird, obscene logo of the Kibbudea; the reddish flames that sprout from the vessel make the air inside the chamber shimmer, as if the reality revealed by the firelight were not any more substantial than a projected image.

And here, having abandoned any desire to locate him, she finds Dean. His naked body is chained to the trunk of a giant tree. Blood leaks from multiple small wounds in his flesh, running down the bark into the soil. The roots near where the blood pools pulse like veins.

Kneeling before the tree is a naked woman with long, dark hair. She turns her neck to greet Jana with a solemn nod. Jana recognizes the maid, Natasha, Dean's former lover.

In Natasha's hand is a dagger made of wood. She plunges the dagger into the ceremonial fire. The flames roll over the dagger and the bare skin of her hand, but do not burn either. She pulls out the dagger, which is now incandescent with vermilion, as is her hand. She reaches toward Dean and with the dagger cuts two small slivers of flesh from his calf.

Dean moans slightly, as if he were dreaming.

Natasha stares at Jana, but the meaning of the Veneran's stoic gaze is impenetrable.

Although her head is spinning from inhaling the vermilion fumes, Jana makes a decision. It feels as if she has no other option: she disrobes and joins the other woman.

Natasha hands a slice of Dean's flesh to Jana, keeping the other for herself. At the same time, they consume the meat of their common lover.

Natasha presents the wooden dagger to Jana. Splinters dig into the palm of her hand as she grips it firmly. With the intrusion of the slivers of wood into her flesh comes communion with Yggdrasil, from whose bark, it is thus revealed to her, the dagger was formed.

The flesh Jana carves with this dagger is hers to ingest; but not the blood that flows from the wounds. The blood seeps into the soil, sustaining the World Tree.

THE VENERA
FANTASY CONVENTION

⌇

I have now attended thirteen consecutive Venera Fantasy Conventions, and almost each occasion has been an epic event, host to intense emotions, unlikely encounters, professional breakthroughs, and welcome depravities. My publishers, Sanderson Grecko and Bettina Easton of Darkbright Books, the illustrious Guests of Honour at this year's VFC, have asked their staff and authors to share their favourite memories of VFC 50, but, as part of ongoing tensions between us, I was singled out and specifically instructed to "keep it clean" — and so I shall not be able to regale you, dear readers, who were not present to enjoy the unfettered festivities, with the full account of the debauched decadence that unfurled during the last weekend of March in wondrous Venera.

No ... I must refrain from telling all. I will not divulge the unspeakable obscenities committed on each other's bodies, in a profound moment of shared existential gloom, by two of my Darkbright Books colleagues, authors Brad Blue (*Vermilionarama*; *Melancholia Girls*) and Chas Roberts (*Whores and Other Horrors*; *The Ascension of Sex*), during the overnight ferry from the Italian mainland to Venera — which, at the World Tree Hotel bar, farcically intoxicated from their first-ever exposure to the Veneran psychotropic spice, vermilion, they drunkenly admitted to me, their ersatz confessor, in order to expunge their lingering shame. No, neither shall I mention the throng (or is that thong?) of scantily clad sorority girls who — after my latest book, *The Back Door to Lost Girls*, had been passed frantically among them — lined up outside my room at the break of dawn and who one by one bared their bottoms, hungry to be administered a spanking the likes of which their unformed, inane, and self-important frat-boy companions were too immature to provide with an adequately confident and wry hand. No, on such subjects, and others like them, I shall remain absolutely mute.

Nor shall I detail my epic struggles to reach the Mediterranean oasis of Venera, facing extreme weather, mechanical failures, and all sorts of unlikely obstacles, including nearly being left stranded in foreign territories such as Montreal, Chicago, London, Budapest, Belgrade, and Rome. Fate seemed determined to keep me from Venera, but that only strengthened my resolve. That tumultuous odyssey, although mythic in scope, was too unsettling to rank among my favourite moments. Were it not for the intervention and friendship of literary critic Roger Lobo, I might not have survived the Chicago flash flood, which was responsible for thousands of deaths; probably not counted among the official numbers were the scores and scores of homeless, all too invisible, alas, due both to their socioeconomic status and the darker colour of their skin, a reminder of an even darker history that has yet to be fully resolved.

Instead, I shall fondly remember joining up with my Darkbright Books brother-in-arms Daniel Dimes as soon as I stepped off the boat in Venera on the Wednesday, to then together spend a quiet evening (first over a Chinese buffet and then over vermilion cocktails in the hotel bar) ruminating on the greatest wonders of the world; that is, women and girls — and, more precisely, what makes some girls and others women, and the differences that make them each so fascinating and desirable. Daniel and I were supposed to have been discussing our contracted collaboration for Darkbright Books, *The Phantasmagorical Odyssey of Scheherazade*, a mosaic of nested fantasies tinged with dark eroticism, set in the Venera of antiquity, but perhaps that is a book best written without too much planning. Alas, in the aftermath of violent altercations during VFC 50 between myself and various staff members of Darkbright Books — all, I believed at the time, meant in good if somewhat extreme fun — my erstwhile publisher has since cancelled the contract, which has killed Daniel's interest in pursuing the project.

It was with great joy that, the second day, for the first time in a decade, since VFC 40, I re-encountered avant-garde writer Sandy Irish, who composes fiction out of hand-crafted jewellery instead of words;

Sandy introduced me to her friend Renata Austin, a singularly alluring and enchanting woman whose first action upon meeting me was to hug me in a most lascivious way, whispering in my ear: "I loved your novel *Echoes of the Ice Age* with a violent passion." Renata was a jetsetting Veneran expat with no permanent address, author of two books, the novel *The Pull of Heaven* and the obliquely titled poetry collection *And*, both winners of the prestigious Venera Fantasy Award. I have read neither but am now compelled to seek them out and perhaps ask their seductive author to collaborate with me on my now-orphaned project, *The Phantasmagorical Odyssey of Scheherazade* — but I'm getting ahead of myself.

After this rather electrifying introduction to this sultry former Veneran, she then proceeded to ignore me and flirt with every man in the room and no small number of the women. In fact, I am nearly certain that, at one point, I espied her reaching into a man's lap to pull out his cock and stroke it, right there in bar, among the gathered literati — a bold and shocking move, even in libertine Venera. However, the crowd was so thick that I cannot be certain of what I saw. Was it even her hand? Did I extrapolate from fragmentary glimpses an erotic vision, fuelled both by my already inebriated state of mind — it was still only mid-afternoon — and by the lust this woman had instantly provoked in me?

To my astonishment and, I will admit, my pleasure, as dinnertime neared, Renata took my arm, her other arm already entwined with Sandy Irish's, and then led us to this most bizarre restaurant, whose speciality was a fusion of Spanish and Japanese cuisines. The three of us shared a companionable evening, drinking too many sake margaritas tinged with vermilion, and eating exotic concoctions whose name and taste I entirely forget. Yes, partly due to the alcohol and the Veneran spice, which was present in every menu item, but also due to the fact that, under the table, Renata had coiled her bare leg around my own leg— alas I was wearing trousers and thus could not fully enjoy the proximity of her flesh, but it nevertheless kept me oh so very distracted. Despite that, with a great effort of concentration, I kept up my share of the conversation with these two lovely women and remember, even, amusing them to laughter, although my witticisms are also lost to intoxication and memory. It does not escape me, with the clarity of sober hindsight, that they were most likely laughing at me rather than with me.

Later that evening I was delighted to once again encounter cult writer Sandrine Columbia — many believe that she, like her notorious creation, Patricia Edge, is a centuries-old vampire; I know the truth, but I am sworn never to reveal it. This I can say: Sandrine's true nature is not easily categorized. She is a veteran of shared, sacred bacchanalias at the previous year's VFC, the 49th edition. But propriety, editorial edict, and legal caution forbid me to be more candid on such salacious topics as to what pranks and indiscretions we engaged in either this or the previous year.

Saturday afternoon, I took great pleasure in performing my scheduled reading (those who are familiar with me know how much I enjoy performing public readings) — a chapter-long excerpt from my work-in-progress, *Venera Dreams*, followed by several short Cryptolegends. I was later pleased to discover that, at the award banquet that closed off the convention, my performance had earned me the annual award for Best Reading Performance at VFC. (Please forgive this moment of boastful pride.)

Soon after my reading, on that same afternoon, I joined my fellow Canadians Chas Roberts, Brad Blue, and anthologist of the macabre Kevin Angel in the inner yard of the hotel; we held court, amusing ourselves with the Perverse Golems of Istanbul and other exotic and taboo delights my companions would rather I keep hidden from their spouses. Already, rumours abound regarding that gathering, which has now passed into legend.

The Sunday — a usually quiet day at these events, by which time the intense conversations, flirtations, and rivalries have relaxed into something akin to survivalist camaraderie — was disrupted by a notorious trio of party crashers: the filmmaker and surrealist pornographer Tito Bronze, accompanied by two writers — the pompous, self-aggrandizing Bram Jameson and the mad genius Magus Amore. These unavoidable icons yet pariahs of the Veneran arts scene have in recent years been made unwelcome at the Venera Fantasy Convention. The three men were awarded a lifetime ban three years ago, each for different reasons:

Tito Bronze for a partly hushed-up sex scandal involving the tween-age triplets of VFC 47's Guests of Honour, fantasy opera composer Neal S. Palmer and his paramour and star performer Mandy Gay; Bram Jameson for heckling every panel, reading, talk, and performance by those same Guests of Honour; and Magus Amore, simply for being insane beyond redemption — the former bestselling author has long ago lost all sense of propriety, parading his scrawny naked body everywhere, pissing and defecating like a wild animal, relentlessly spewing incomprehensible gibberish at the top of his lungs. Still, all three of them are famous, exuding an aura of larger-than-life grandeur — thus, none dared block them or invoke the ban. These three old tricksters had each of them, on numerous occasions over the past decades, faked their deaths, and a significant number of gullible VFC 50 attendees were thus awed when these celebrities showed up alive at the gathering. Eager sycophants swarmed to them, gaggling like overexcited geese, disrupting that day's schedule and entirely spoiling what had been shaping up to be a pleasantly congenial day.

Finally, on the Monday afternoon, mere hours before I had to catch my ferry back to the mainland, Fullbright Byrne (editor of the sumptuously designed journal of outré horror, *The Illuminated Doom*) and I were guided through the mysterious inner-city streets of Venera, where the expat trendsetter Renata Austin unveiled for us the sordid secret history of the mysterious metropolis. Throughout the Dantean odyssey — the Zoological Museum housed creatures whose existence I doubted even as I could see, hear, and smell them; the Gallery of Sexual History celebrated eldritch perversities of which I would rather have remained ignorant; the Vegan Fashion Cooperative engaged in atavistic rites much more disturbing than their genteel, politically correct appellation would suggest; I am not at all convinced that all the politicians I saw seated in the High Parliament of Venera were in fact human; the wares of the Society of Culinary Transcendence (and their enthusiastic use of the psychotropic vermilion spice) affected my consciousness in such a way that much of that afternoon remains a vague blur of disquieting imagery (now when I sleep alone I wake screaming as, in my dreams, those images unfurl one by one into dreadful memories) — Renata used Byrne's presence to avoid my lustful gaze, my eager hands, or any attempt to rekindle our secret intimacies. My days are still haunted by the coy eroticism exuded by her every gesture.

The above is only a brief, sadly perfunctory glimpse of the revelries that took place during this latest Venera Fantasy Convention ... What of the time Daniel Dimes and I explored the gorgeously decadent and haunted Devilscock Hotel in downtown Venera? What conspiratorial secrets lurked behind the laughter bestselling thriller author Rex Montagnard and I shared in plain view of his publishers and mine? What unspeakable truths did antiquarian Dennis Spider reveal to me? Was the Lost Pages booth in the dealers' room really a portal to other worlds, or was the whole setup simply an elaborate marketing prank? Do Daniel Dimes and Martin Less, our Darkbright Books publicist, really want me to relate the curious incident of the giant turtle of living marble and all it entails? What of the various colours of Veneran foods shared with, for example, comics scripter Rod Mann and eager groupie Sylvia Stephens — what truly transpired during those "friendly" Mediterranean meals? Did Rod Mann and I really come to blows over the merits of cartoonist Jake Kurtz's oeuvre, as claimed by an obviously doctored photograph posted online? What Canadian perversities did a subset of the Darkbright Books contingent — myself, Daniel Dimes, Brad Blue, Chas Roberts, Martin Less, Elaine Sherman, Jessica Red, Sanderson Grecko, and Bettina Easton — engage in as we drank bottle after bottle of anything we could get our hands on while intimately and cosily holed up in the guest-of-honour suite? And I must refrain from stating exactly what I did to induce the mistress of gothic zombie pornography Gabriella Jaymes to squee, no matter how insistent your prying might be.

And yet ... Already, I must question my recollections. Memory is an unreliable, untrustworthy mistress who lies, distorts, manipulates, and cheats with wanton abandon, often for no reason other than being able to. Did any of these things actually happen? Venera is such an alien, phantasmagorical environment that anything occurring within the archipelagic city-state becomes improbable at best the instant one has left the lush metropolis and its surreal architecture. I am, with each passing day, increasingly convinced that my entire escapade was nothing more than a fever dream that washed over me as I lay stranded in Chicago, lost among its homeless population while I sought shelter from the flood rains.

The only physical evidence I possess of my passage in Venera and of its unbridled excesses is a neatly folded tissue left on my hotel bed, gilded with a kiss of vermilion lipstick — a memento I carry with me still.

But perhaps I'm lying about that, too.

INTERLUDE

VERMILION DREAMS: THE COMPLETE WORKS OF BRAM JAMESON

PIRATES TO NOWHERE (1961)

IN *PIRATES TO NOWHERE*, a group of seven plunderers invade
Venera, seeking its lucrative stores of vermilion, the euphoria-inducing
spice manufactured from a plant that reputedly grows nowhere but in
the soil of Vermilion Gardens, an inner borough of the archipelagic
city-state. The vermilion plant has never been successfully smuggled out
of Venera.

No outsider knows, exactly, how to locate Vermilion Gardens, never
mind how to recognize the plant or even find the building (or buildings)
where the precious stores are kept. One of the pirates, a Canadian
named Bram Jameson, who may or may not be the same person as the
book's author, boasts of having been in Venera as a child. The captain
is counting on Jameson's memory to guide them all to riches.

To the pirates' surprise, no-one opposes them; in fact, at first, Venera appears deserted. The would-be thieves almost immediately lose
their way in the unfamiliar streets of Venera, their poorly laid plans in
shambles. The five men who comprise the rest of the crew blame both
the captain and Jameson for this failure. The ensuing mutiny causes
Jameson to be separated from his fellow criminals. He tries in vain to
retrace his steps, to find the harbour where their ship set anchor. But,
as he navigates the streets of Venera, his sense of direction fails him. He
loses himself in this alien cityscape, so unlike any other metropolis on
Earth and so unlike his memories of it. He loses sight of the sea and
cannot locate any of the aquatic vias that so famously serve as Venera's
main thoroughfares. Instead, he is caught in a maze of claustrophobic,
cobblestone streets that zigzag through the geometrically confusing
architecture of Venera. Often, he can barely see the sky through the
overhanging maze of passageways, balconies, arches, bridges, and vegetation. For days on end, the vegetation grows so dense that he comes to
forget that he is in a city at all, believing himself lost in a labyrinthine

primeval forest. Eventually, albeit temporarily, the jungle becomes more recognizably urban, although the bizarre geometry confuses his sense of logic and, even, of self. Throughout his journey, Jameson encounters visionaries, prophets, lunatics, sadomasochists, holy whores, defective automata, and deformed doppelgangers of his former crewmates.

Time ceases to have any meaning for Jameson. Eventually, he wends his way into a garden. Cubist paintings hang from trees. The paintings are all different, but each of them is a stylized, distorted closeup of someone's face, perhaps his own. Each in turn, the cubist heads spring to life, asking Jameson a series of surrealist riddles too arcane for Jameson to answer.

He ventures deeper into the garden. A path leads him to the edge of a whirlpool made of light. The book ends mid-sentence as the hero descends into the luminous whirlpool.

THE GREAT DISASTERS (1964)

Starting in 1965, the US paperback house Full Deck Books planned to release Bram Jameson's gargantuan opus *The Great Disasters* as a series of four slim mass-market paperbacks. They published the first three as *A World of Ice*, *A World of Fire*, and *The Great Flood* — and had advertised the fourth, *The New World*. However, assaulted by lawsuits claiming that most of their line consisted of pirated editions, including sometimes furtively reprinting other publishers' books by simply changing titles and names of authors, Full Deck Books ceased operations before the series' final installment could hit bookshops. Presumably, the shady US publisher never actually acquired the rights to *The Great Disasters* from Jameson or Vermilion Press, which, aside from that one aberration, remains the sole source of the author's books.

The original one-volume edition of *The Great Disasters* sports a cover illustration by the renowned Jake Kurtz, the prolific New York cartoonist who created comics classics such as *The Internationalist*, *The Preservers*, *The Last Boy*, *Dinosaurs on the Moon*, *Destroyer of Worlds*, and many others. The cover is split into four quarters, with a title box in the middle. Each vignette illustrates, respectively, one of the book's four sections.

The expression "The Great Disasters" usually refers to the apocalyptic hysteria of 1961, when worldwide civilization — capitalist, communist, and preindustrial — was convinced its end was imminent, first by ice, then by fire, and finally by water. Although people who were alive at the time claim to remember the mini ice age, the scorching droughts, and the great floods that successively afflicted the entire world, and certainly newspaper headlines and magazine covers from that era confirm these memories, current scientific studies point to the whole thing being a hoax — or a strange, shared fever dream — as no quantifiable evidence of any of these phenomena remains. Perhaps worldwide anxiety in that tense Cold War era had reached such a pitch that humanity collectively imagined these primal disasters as a way to cope with the looming threat of nuclear war and the consequent destruction of civilization?

Indeed, *The Great Disasters* concerns itself with this epochal moment in world history. This time around, Jameson is not a pirate but an aviator who made his fortune as a vermilion merchant and now zips around the world at the helm of his solar-powered jet in search of adventure. The book is separated into four sections: Ice, Fire, Water, and the baffling conclusion, The New World.

At the start of Ice, our intrepid adventurer witnesses a clandestine bomb test in the arctic. There is no violent explosion as such, but concentric waves of energy emanate from ground zero, forcing the aviator to crash his airplane in the snow. The damage to the aircraft is minor. While Jameson repairs his jet, a group of five scientists surrounds him, and, at gunpoint, they take him prisoner.

The scientists mean to lead him to their headquarters, but they lose their way in the arctic desert (the astute reader will notice a recurring theme). They explain to Jameson that their bomb test has inadvertently set in motion a rapid ice age and that within a few months the entire planet will be covered in ice, possibly ending all life. Soon, they forget their weapons and begin treating Jameson as one of their own. Jameson himself forgets his own past, his identity, and the group increasingly behaves like a hive mind.

The hive mind eventually reaches the rogue scientists' arctic lair. For the next ten or so pages, the action is described in a series of geometric tableaux, dense with allegory and challenging to decipher. Gradually, this virtuoso narration segues into a more conventional style, with Jameson, triumphant and individuality regained, flying his aircraft over a retreating ice age.

Both Fire and Water follow a plot structure similar to that of Ice, each time with Jameson the aviator accidentally encountering a quintet of scientists responsible for the disaster, and each time seeing him involved, always in a similarly allegorical fashion, in saving the world from its latest armageddon. Could these adventures detail the true, secret history of that apocalyptic year? Perhaps — although part 4, The New World, veers off into obvious fantasy.

The New World, which is itself longer than the three other sections of *The Great Disasters* combined, opens with Jameson flying over the receding floodwaters, providing clear continuity from the previous section, Water. Jameson spots an unfamiliar land formation and directs his plane toward it. Reaching his destination, Jameson wonders if he has discovered a new continent. Unfamiliar cityscapes appear in the distance. Intrigued by this mystery, Jameson lands his plane in a field and sets off on foot. In this strange land, Jameson encounters tribes, settlements, villages, and even cities populated by humanoid animals, but the species do not intermingle, save for trade or war.

The various animal species all possess the power of speech, and, even more startling, they all speak a recognizable human language: English, French, Italian, Japanese, German, Arabic, etc. (In the text, all the foreign dialogue is rendered in the original language, with no translation.)

But Jameson soon discovers that he has lost his own ability to speak. He can now vocalize nothing more than grunts and moans. Typically, he has lost his bearings and can no longer locate his airplane.

He sees few other humans; like him, none of them can speak. They are slaves to the most privileged animals. The dominant animals recognize that Jameson is different from their servants; invariably, the animals treat him as a guest.

This long section is marked by Jameson's predilection for repetition. Every encounter unfolds in a similar manner: as dawn breaks, Jameson wanders into the territory of a new species; he meets a guide who escorts him; Jameson is witness to activities and conflicts whose nature he barely understands; as night falls, he is invited to a ceremony; there, before Jameson's eyes, a human slave is ritually slaughtered — although the specifics of the ritual differs from species to species, even the herbivorous animals perform this act for Jameson's benefit — and the meat is offered to him. Always, he refuses to eat the human flesh; he is then cast out. He wanders until he encounters the next group.

Eventually, in a city of cats, the ritual is preceded by the intake of vermilion. When the meat is offered to him, the intoxicated Jameson enthusiastically agrees to consume the flesh before him. The sacred food is delicious. Once Jameson has chewed and swallowed, the mayor of the cat city says: "Now, speak your name."

The novel ends with the hero saying: "My name is Bram Jameson."

WHY I WANT TO LOVE (1969)

Why I Want to Love is a difficult, experimental book. Here, the author eschews such writerly conventions as chapters, paragraph breaks, sentences, and punctuation. For the entirety of its 475 pages, *Why I Want to Love* consists of one uninterrupted string of words. Set entirely in Venera, this book, unlike Jameson's first two releases, is narrated in the first person, although, paradoxically, the protagonist and narrator is never explicitly identified as Jameson and remains nameless — at least in the text itself. The introduction by Lee Williams, who also appears as a character in the narrative, namechecks Jameson as the protagonist and claims that Jameson's text is the real, accurate, and uncensored record of life in Venera, circa 1967. Jameson's text is vague on personal details, but the Williams intro mentions Jameson's Venera mansion, with its throngs of naked, young, beautiful sycophants, both male and female, as eager to sample Jameson's stores of vermilion as they were willing to give their bodies to whoever desired them.

In the 1950s, Williams was better known as the international gun-toting costumed vigilante Interzone. After the tragic death of his wife and crimefighting partner, the archer Arrowsnake, he reportedly retired to Venera, although this has never been officially confirmed. *Why I Want to Love* is the only document authenticating this rumour.

This is the first time a Jameson book is explicitly touted as nonfiction, but that claim is suspect. For one thing, despite the well-documented sexual openness of the late 1960s, especially in Venera, legendarily notorious for its history of unbridled promiscuity, the story — a nonstop hedonistic display of sexual excess, perversity, and depravity described in bluntly explicit anatomical detail — stretches credibility. For another, it's hard to believe in the parade of celebrities the three protagonists (the narrator; the now homosexual Williams; and a shockingly teenage Tito Bronze, who already displays the enthusiasm for spanking female derrieres that made his later films so scandalous) encounter on their orgiastic odyssey: Ronald Reagan, Jacqueline Kennedy Onassis, Richard Nixon, Doris Day, Sophia Loren, Audrey Hepburn, Orson Welles, Ringo Starr, Jayne Mansfield, Fred MacMurray, Federico Fellini, Nico, Anita Ekberg, Anouk Aimée, Ursula Andress, Serge Gainsbourg, Brigitte Bardot, Pablo Picasso, Diana Rigg, Salvador Dalí ...

Perhaps Jameson (and Williams) really do remember the events as described, regardless of what actually occurred. Both the Williams intro and the Jameson text mention that the three protagonists were at the time constantly under the influence of vermilion, in a state of perpetual imaginative euphoria that would certainly lend itself to hallucinatory experiences. As some studies have shown (see, for example, Jasmine Cockney's 1974 counterculture bestseller, *The Vermilion Fix*, published by Albion Pulp Press), it is possible, although not definitely proven, that prolonged communal consumption of vermilion can produce shared hallucinations. And if that is the case, then *Why I Want to Love* might be simultaneously memoir and fiction.

MOTORCRASH (1974)

Few remember Venera's brief and disastrous attempt to join the car culture of the twentieth century. Renowned for being a pedestrian haven, the archipelagic city-state has never repeated the experiment.

Motorcrash is Jameson's personal account of those events, which had transpired the year before. The book's first-person narrative has the ring of authenticity — especially given what is on the public record regarding the period in question. More tragic and affecting than anything to that date in Jameson's eclectic bibliography, *Motorcrash* opens with Jameson driving on the newly constructed elevated highways of Venera, his recent bride, Kara Hunger, in the passenger seat.

At the end of the first chapter, which otherwise describes the view of Venera from these new roads, their car collides with another automobile. In the aftermath, both Jameson and Hunger, having suffered only minor bruising, find themselves sexually aroused; every aspect of the process — the collision; the exchange of insurance information with the other driver; going to the garage for repairs — only increases the couple's sexual tension.

As the repairs cannot be finished that day, their car is kept overnight. Jameson and Hunger are compelled to break into the garage at night and have sex on the back seat of their damaged automobile, tearing their clothes and drawing blood from each other in the process. Jameson admires the various bodily fluids smearing the interior of his new but already well-worn vehicle.

Afterward, they are accosted outside by Raphael Marcus, the driver who collided with them earlier; and thus begins their journey through the underground world of motorcrashers, a cult worshipping the automobile as the trigger for the next phase in human evolution and the motorcrash as the ultimate form of prayer, the most intense form of communion with the divine force driving human existence.

Jameson and Marcus become inseparable: Jameson refuses to buy into Marcus's messianic ravings but warms to the madman because of the intensity of their conversations about the effects of the automobile on human consciousness; Marcus, for his part, cannot resist trying to convert this fervent nonbeliever. The sexual tension between the two men is thick.

Although Jameson is never convinced by Marcus's technomysticism, he nevertheless gives himself up totally to car culture. His automobile allows him the most satisfying expression of his sexuality. Jameson's text fetishistically describes automobiles, sexualizing every aspect of car culture: likening maintenance to prolonged, devoted foreplay; conversations with other drivers to public displays of mutual masturbation; visits to the garage for minor repairs to breast-augmentation mammoplasty; driving to marital relations; hitchhiking to prostitution; car-pooling to orgies; automobile parts to erogenous zones of the human body; and, most dramatically, car crashes to primal, uninhibited animal sex.

The plot comes to focus on a sort of eroticized duel between Marcus and Jameson, each of them espousing different, although not mutually incompatible, visions of automobile worship. Caught in the middle of this conflict of machismo and technotheology is Jameson's wife, who finds herself drawn both to Marcus's cult and to Marcus himself. The motorcrasher messiah welcomes her conversion but rejects her sexual advances.

Eventually, Jameson and Marcus consummate their rivalry in a brutal act of automobile sex: that chapter is written in virtuoso style, the multiple perspectives colliding violently. Meanwhile, Kara, with unbridled religious fervour, engages in a series of reckless car crashes, until her transcendent death-wish is finally realized.

The book itself ends with Jameson learning of Kara's death. In the real world, following a rash of traffic accidents, Venera dismantled its highways and permanently banned automobiles. The first car in Venera had ignited its engine on 1 March 1973, and the autoroutes closed forever on 1 December of the same year.

ICARUS UNLIMITED (1978)

Once again, Jameson is in the cockpit of his solar-powered airplane, previously seen in *The Great Disasters*. He snorts a line of vermilion, revs up the plane's engine, and takes off from Venera; thus begins *Icarus Unlimited*.

It is never stated when, exactly, the book takes place, but presumably the events follow closely on the heels of those related in *Motorcrash*. Grief-stricken over the death of his wife, Jameson decides to leave

Venera behind and fly aimlessly around the world, to wherever the sky and the winds will take him.

The entirety of *Icarus Unlimited* takes place inside the cockpit of Jameson's airplane; in fact, the whole narrative is set in his mind. Jameson's fifth book is a philosophical, stream-of-consciousness meditation on flight, travel, identity, war, mortality, love, sex, masculinity, friendship, and violence, peppered with breathtaking and often surreal descriptions of the view from Jameson's cockpit.

By the book's final pages, the vistas Jameson describes are unrecognizable as Earthly, the meditations following an increasingly inscrutable logic. *Icarus Unlimited* does not conclude so much as simply stop.

SKYSCRAPER (1981)

Skyscraper is another rare instance of a Jameson book cover sporting the work of a recognizable artist, this time paperback legend Obama Savage, well-known for his heroic and evocative covers of men's adventure novels. This cover depicts a muscular man in a ripped shirt standing with his fists clenched (presumably the iteration of Jameson described in the novel); behind him a skyscraper burns. The colours are rich, the intense gaze of the protagonist mesmerizing, the attention to minute detail captivating.

Is *Skyscraper* another descent into pure fantasy? In the heart of Venera, Jameson, now described as a chiselled, hyper-competent übermensch adventurer of near-limitless resources, inhabits the top five floors of the Venera World Trade Centre, a phallic, modernist spire piercing the lush, sensuous shapes of the Veneran skyline. (There was indeed such a skyscraper, the only one ever, built in Venera in 1978; it burned down in 1980.)

Joining him is a team of five assistants: the hirsute and muscular biochemist Hank Priest; the dapper lawyer and fencing champion Teddy Cauchon; the ruggedly handsome engineer and retired boxer J.R. "Junior" Fox; the sinuously athletic daredevil and inventor Bobby Long; the bespectacled archaeologist and linguist Billy Poderski.

Each chapter describes a densely detailed, fast-paced adventure, each with its own lurid, sensationalistic title: "The Hydra of a Thousand Heads," "The Menace of the Meteor Men," "Treasure Hunt at the North Pole," "Werewolves by Night," "Oasis of the Lost," "The Monster-Master," "Land of Terrors," "The Mysticals," "City of Phantoms." Each adventure follows a strict formula: one of Jameson's aides bursts into the group's headquarters accompanied by a person in dire straits; the problem is stated to the group, minus Jameson; Jameson then appears, having heard everything on his security system, and accepts the case; the group then goes into action, taking off aboard their "solar jet gyro" from the launch pad on the roof of the skyscraper; they encounter the menace and defeat it after exactly two of them face near-death challenges.

Only the final chapter, "The Fall of the Tower," breaks the formula. Returning from an adventure (the otherwise unreported but perhaps aptly named "The Case of the Vanishing Pulpsters"), the adventurers find their headquarters invaded by a group of men in perfectly cut striped grey business suits. With alarming efficiency, the intruders dismantle Jameson's headquarters. The intruders ignore all questions put to them and, whenever one of Jameson's band tries to grab one, the man in the business suit manages to evade his would-be assailant's grasp with snake-like suppleness.

When the power goes out, Jameson and his crew reluctantly descend into the lower floors to investigate. They find the skyscraper's inhabitants transformed, the office workers' clothes in tatters, revealing the flabby bodies beneath. The offices have become atavistic temples; desks are now altars where living human flesh is sacrificed to unknown gods. Amid the screams of the sacrificial victims, the skyscraper people chant in a cacophony of alien tongues that even linguist Billy Poderski cannot begin to decipher. One by one, the members of Jameson's team forget who they are. Jameson struggles to keep the group together, fighting to maintain his sense of identity.

The fires from the sacrificial mounds spread to the walls. As the skyscraper burns around him, Jameson takes out his knife and peels off strips of his skin, feeding it to his companions.

HELLO VENERA (1984)

In 1982, Mike Walters, the self-appointed American "Theme Park Emperor," finally unveiled his secret European project, built on an artificial archipelago in the Mediterranean: Vermilion World, which he claimed was "a near-exact replica of Venera, its facades, its streets, its mysteries." Being a privately held corporation, WalterWorlds Unlimited never disclosed the cost of developing and constructing this immense luxury attraction. Day passes went for US$1000, not including transportation, food, or anything besides entrance to the theme park. Hotel stays began at US$2000 a head per night on top of the entrance fee; vacation rentals started at US$25,000 per week for studio apartments and went as high a US$3,000,000 per week for the most upscale villas, with support-staff fees not included. Within a week of the announcement, the park was already fully booked for the next three months.

With this project, the American entrepreneur threatened to lift the veil that surrounded the mysteries of Venera. As Walters had leased French territorial waters for this endeavour, the Veneran government tried and failed to get from the French courts a quick injunction to force Vermilion World to close its doors until the matter could be settled, in or out of court. However, while the firm of Hawk, Murdock, Spencer, and Associates was still figuring out its next move on behalf of Venera, a disaster befell Vermilion World that rendered further legal action moot. The precise details of the incident never reached the press, beyond the fact that, following a number of explosions of such large magnitude they could be heard and seen everywhere along the French Riviera, the theme park sank into the sea.

In *Hello Venera*, Jameson proposes an unlikely but thrillingly recounted scenario explaining these events. Jameson is now an agent of the Vermilion Eye, Venera's secret organization of international operatives, i.e., its superspy agency. Assigned the Vermilion World case, code-named Hello Venera, Jameson gains access to the theme park as a paying guest, with false papers that identify him as Jimmy Flamingo, an American expat living in London.

In short order, Jameson confronts Walters, portrayed here as a madman whose world-domination scheme involves replicating the greatest cities on Earth as theme parks and then destroying the cities themselves, with agents provocateurs arranging for the blame to be shouldered by so-called "terrorist" groups.

Jameson fights Walters's giant automata, escapes elaborate traps, and finally physically battles Walters after having dispatched hundreds of his goons through a combination of unbelievable luck and even more unlikely prowess. The mad developer falls to his death in a vat of boiling chemicals, setting off a series of explosions that ultimately destroys the theme park, and with it Walters's megalomaniacal scheme.

To save himself from the conflagration, Jameson snorts a specially prepared vermilion concentrate, chants a mantra, and jumps one month forward into time. Finding himself adrift in the Mediterranean, he swims briefly until a submarine sporting the Vermilion Eye logo on its hull surfaces and takes him aboard.

Mike Walters has not been heard from since the Vermilion World catastrophe. His body has never been recovered, but he is presumed dead. A popular conspiracy theory propounds that Walters is being kept alive in suspended animation in a secret laboratory owned by Walter-Worlds Unlimited.

EMPIRE OF THE SELF (1987)

At age thirty, in 1984, Veneran filmmaker, pornographer, and iconoclast Tito Bronze was only beginning to have his work recognized internationally. His every movement was not yet subject to the minute scrutiny that would begin in 1989, when his fame and notoriety hit the stratosphere with the scandalous Cannes premiere of *In primo luogo, esamino il culo*.

It is then possible that he embarked on an ill-fated film project with Bram Jameson in 1984, namely *Empire of the Self*, the story of Jameson's childhood travails in Nazi-occupied Venera.

The main thrust of the book of the same name is a behind-the-scenes look at the disaster-afflicted production. On-set lethal accidents, bankrupt investors, legal entanglements about ownership and authorship of the screenplay, personal betrayals, petty pranks, sabotage by persons unknown, incendiary love affairs, the producer threatening to replace Bronze with a commercial Hollywood director ... what didn't happen to this project? Ultimately, much of the footage was lost — stolen, misplaced, maliciously destroyed? — and the film cancelled. Interspersed dreamlike into this narrative are Jameson's memories of life in Venera, circa 1941–45.

Here, Jameson reveals that his father was a Canadian botanist on contract in Venera when the Germans invaded with no warning. The young Bram's parents were captured and sent to a POW camp in Germany, but their son eluded the Nazis and spent the next four years with no permanent residence, discovering through necessity a knack for hiding in plain sight and living as a ghost in the besieged city-state. He moved with ease between the resistance and the German invaders, secretly befriending people on either side, other times playing pranks on whomever his fancy or opportunity dictated. Trickster, freedom fighter, collaborator, traitor, thief, squatter, saboteur, informant, spy ... the young boy was all of these. After the end of the war, Bram was reunited with his mother and father in northern Manitoba, Canada.

Despite Tito Bronze's celebrity, this aborted collaboration with Jameson has never been reported on outside of this book. Bronze was explicitly named as a character in three Jameson books (see also *Why I Want to Love*, above, and *Millennium Nights*, below), yet Bronze has never publicly mentioned Jameson, let alone the long friendship described in these books.

Bram Jameson: hoax? pseudonym? reality? The enigma persists.

NOSTALGIA OF FUTURES PAST (1991)

If Venera ever considered operating its own space program, it's a well-kept secret. Yet, that is the premise of Jameson's *Nostalgia of Futures Past*, which finds Jameson one of six astronauts awaiting the final countdown for the launch of Venera's first rocket, *The Nostalgia*, en route to orbit Venus. Much like in *Icarus Unlimited*, Jameson never leaves the vehicle within the timeframe of the narrative.

Whether or not the space program is factual, the majority of *Nostalgia of Futures Past* is unquestionably fiction. For the bulk of the book, while Jameson waits for the ship to blast off, he daydreams about the future. He imagines his voyage taking much longer than the projected seven-year mission. He skips over any speculation about the mission itself, and instead his thoughts linger on what will happen once he and his crewmates return to Earth.

They find the Terran population in a state of lethargy. Fossil-fuel reserves have dried up. Entertainment conglomerates have all gone bankrupt. Governments have all been dissolved. Pandemics have wiped out hundreds of millions of people. Shopping malls have become post-capitalist ghost towns. In the face of civilization's collapse, instead of chaos, there is merely resignation. Even Jameson's beloved Venera seems to have withered, its former lustre turned drab, its gardens of vermilion plant overrun with weeds.

Whenever Jameson attempts to communicate with anyone, there is no conversation, no connection. Although they speak in turn, his interlocutors talk in dull tones as though responding to another conversation entirely, lost in the dreariness of their arid inner lives. Jameson's emotional outbursts are ignored by those around him. Even his former crewmates are eventually infected by this generalized apathy.

Jameson yearns for escape. He decides to return to space. With the help of his solar-powered airplane, he embarks on a worldwide tour of space centres, now all deserted and derelict. He hopes to find one functional ship to take him back into space. But every vehicle he finds is rusted and in complete disrepair. Besides, there is no fuel left anywhere.

Returning to Venera, he resolves to push his solar-powered airplane beyond its limits and fly it into space — an escape into his own imagination ...

As he prepares to take off, the real world interrupts his reverie with the shriek of a loud siren. In his headphones, he hears the phrase "Launch aborted" repeated again and again. Thus ends the book.

THE SCHEHERAZADE MOSAIC (1997)

In the framing sequence of *The Scheherazade Mosaic*, Bram Jameson is a literature scholar researching the links between *The Arabian Nights* and the secret history of Venera. He descends into the buried ruins of the city-state and finds himself in a strange underworld of vermilion lights, where he encounters the seemingly immortal Scheherazade, who bears a small cask of vermilion wine. The two share the wine and together enter the metafictional world of story.

The book is otherwise comprised of three novellas: "Scheherazadiad," "A Phantasmagorical Odyssey of Scheherazade," and "Chimerascape."

Narrated in verse by Scheherazade, "Scheherazadiad" is an autobiographical epic reconciling seemingly contradictory traditions, myths, and speculations about the life of the archetypal storyteller herself into one story weaving through layers of reality and fictionality.

In "A Phantasmagorical Odyssey of Scheherazade" Bram Jameson provides a surreal and digressive psychoanalytical diagnosis of Scheherazade. (This section has also been published, in somewhat different form, in the Vermilion Press anthology *Three Phantasmagorical Odysseys of Scheherazade*, alongside novellas of the same title by Magus Amore and Renata Austin. Because that anthology bears no publishing date, it is unclear in which of these two books the text first appeared.)

Told in the format of a Socratic dialogue, "Chimerascape" — the longest of the three novellas — once again tackles the subject of Scheherazade's contradictory biographies, this time in juxtaposition with Jameson's own panoply of alternates lives as presented in his eclectic bibliography. Jameson and Scheherazade trade stories about themselves and about each other, questioning each other's narratives using various techniques of literary criticism. Chapters alternate, with the odd-numbered ones echoing the titles of Jameson's oeuvre (from "Pirates to Nowhere" to "Nostalgia of Futures Past") and the even-numbered ones borrowing their titles from episodes of *The Arabian Nights*.

Although the Jameson of *The Scheherazade Mosaic* is metafictionally self-aware of the different and irreconcilable iterations of himself presented in his own books, the rhetorical exchange between himself and Scheherazade fails to solve the riddle that is Bram Jameson.

THE VOICES OF CREATION: THE COMPLETE SHORT FICTION OF BRAM JAMESON (2000)

The Voices of Creation: The Complete Short Fiction of Bram Jameson displays a heretofore unrevealed aspect of Jameson's writing: Venera is never mentioned, the protagonists never bear the author's name, and, for once, there is no doubt that we are dealing completely with fiction.

All culled from obscure, defunct periodicals such as *Brave New Fictions*, *Gambit's Fantastic Quarterly*, *The Pringle Zone*, *Research and Story*, *Innerspace Argonaut*, and *Pulp Wave*, these 101 stories highlight Jameson as science-fiction writer, a genre his book-length works often flirt with. Here we find space voyages, mad scientists, adventures to microscopic universes, utopias and dystopias, apocalyptic disasters, bizarre mutations, lost civilizations, and time travel. The earliest story, "Prime Bell," dates from 1956, and the last, "The Obscure Planet," from 1997.

Vividly imaginative, composed with elegance and economy, characterized by a careful attention to unusual and troubling images, possessing arresting psychological depth, these stories linger disquietingly in the mind.

THE LOST VOYAGE OF SCHEHERAZADE THE SAILOR (2001)

In a sequel of sorts to both 1984's *Hello Venera* and 1997's *The Scheherazade Mosaic*, Bram Jameson and Scheherazade are agents of Venera's superspy organization, the Vermilion Eye. To stave off invasions from alternate realities, Jameson and Scheherazade recommission the *Esplendor Català*, a former cruiseliner designed by the Catalan architect Antoni Gaudí and acquired by Venera after being decommissioned by the

Franco regime in 1937. With a crew of Vermilion Eye agents, Captain Scheherazade and Assistant Director Bram Jameson sail the Mediterranean Seas of the multiverse, engaging in combat — surreally described in the jargons of semiotics and quantum physics — with the fleets of hostile forces, which become more fantastical in character as the book progresses and the ship travels farther and farther away from consensus reality.

These multiversal sea wars go on for decades, perhaps centuries, but the crew is kept ageless by the contents of the Cornucopia of Venera, a cask of vermilion wine that forever replenishes itself.

Their mission ended, the crew docks in Venera — yet a doubt lingers: is this the same Venera from which they set out or has the ship anchored in an alternate world that is not their true home?

MILLENNIUM NIGHTS (2002)

Millennium Nights, a return to the epic scale of 1964's *The Great Disasters*, is split into three self-contained sections: Vermilion Beach, The Velvet Bronzemine, and Supermall.

At the start of the first section, an aging yet still vigorous Jameson and his girlfriend, Victoria Shepherd, a private detective, arrive at the eponymous Vermilion Beach, a new gated community for the ultra-rich located on one of Venera's outer islands. They have bought a unit there, as a vacation home. The climate is especially clement, and the beach is stunningly beautiful. Also, the open sky provides a calming change from the dense urban settings of either central Venera (Jameson's home) or downtown London (Shepherd's home). The resort community is a boon to Venera's economy. Jameson jokes to Victoria that the elite, egocentric colonists have no idea that the "gate" is mostly there to keep *them* out of Venera itself, while the city-state gorges on their money.

The couple is soon befriended by the resort's administrator, Colin Harper, a charismatic figure who sees in Vermilion Beach the key to humanity's future, the template for life in the 21st century and beyond. In his utopian dream, everyone will live in ever-increasing isolation from the distractions of both society and the natural world. This isolation will accelerate the evolution of human consciousness as everyone will eventually achieve full self-knowledge. A skilled rhetorician, Harper deftly evades Jameson's pert socialist objections ("What about the serving staff?" etc.). Jameson finds Harper's elitist fabulations ridiculous, even offensive, but cannot deny the man's aggressive charm. Attentive readers will notice that Harper is a similar figure to that of Raphael Marcus in *Motorcrash*, albeit more refined and subtle in character.

There is a death announced on the couple's second morning there. But the deceased was elderly, and a natural passing is assumed. In the coming weeks, the deaths pile up, and eventually Harper hires Shepherd to look into the case.

Victoria's personality undergoes a progressive change in the course of her investigation. She becomes increasingly apathetic, parroting Harper's rhetoric in listless tones, accepting each new murder as inevitable, even necessary.

Soon, she is permanently entrenched in her beach chair, shielded from the sun by a parasol. When Jameson prods her on the progress of the investigation, she claims that she is solving this case in a manner appropriate to the facts: by submerging herself in her own mind. She ignores Jameson's scoffs and concerns.

Jameson takes up the case, but, whenever he attempts to question anyone, Harper is there, subtly but surely blocking Jameson's investigation.

The death toll keeps increasing. Every day, someone dies. Yet, no-one leaves. Jameson decides to grab Victoria and escape before Vermilion Beach becomes fatal for either of them. But he can't find her. Finally, he confronts Harper, who admits that Shepherd now lives with him; he even lets Jameson see her, but she refuses to leave. "Why should I?" she says. "I think I'm finally understanding this place. I'm understanding myself. It's the same thing." Heartbroken and enraged, Jameson seeks to escape Vermilion Beach, but the ferry service has been shut down. At the pier, he steals a sailboat and leaves the doomed resort behind.

The abrupt closure of Venera's short-lived Vermilion Beach resort community, amid rumours of mass suicide, was mentioned in the news in 2000. London private investigator Victoria Shepherd was listed among the deceased at Vermilion Beach.

The second part of *Millennium Nights* occurs over one night, during Tito Bronze's notorious Millennium Bacchanal, held at his Venera mansion, the Velvet Bronzemine. But the orgy that ensues is not of the expected sexual kind.

Early on in the evening the internationally bestselling thriller writer Magus Amore gathers a number of party guests into a circle at the centre of the Bronzemine's banquet hall, inviting them to participate in a renewal ritual to welcome the new millennium. He strips, revealing that his tall, thin, scarecrow-like body is covered in tattoos of sigils and lizards. He speaks a few ritual phrases in a language that sounds inhuman. Then, in English, he invites his audience to shed their own clothes, and most of them do.

Amore chants, and his tattoos glow. The assembled partygoers gawk at the writer-priest, enraptured by this strange spectacle. Luminous, ethereal snakes ripple out of Amore's body. The snakes converge on another of the guests: Bram Jameson. They orbit around him, ever more rapidly, creating the illusion of an iridescent whirlpool. Throughout all this, an odd serenity spreads through Jameson and through the rest of Amore's congregation. Jameson remains calm even when some of the snakes bind him and others slither into his body via his facial orifices. As the binding serpents drop away, Jameson starts to rip at his own flesh: emerging from inside his own decaying body is a rejuvenated version of himself in the prime of adulthood. Soon, all of his old body has been shed. The viscous gore of his discarded self covers the new skin of the reborn Jameson.

Amore gestures theatrically toward another mesmerized congregant, but then a look of panic etches itself on the writer's face. He convulses uncontrollably; his eyes become vacant. Dreadful monsters emerge from Amore's shimmering body. Soon the mansion is overrun with these beasts, who slaughter not only each other but also anyone within their reach. Only the reborn Jameson laughs through it all; barehanded he rips apart every monster in his path, eating their otherworldly flesh, their gore mingling with his own on his naked flesh. But there are too many beasts for this lone man to deal with; and, anyway, he seems unconcerned, perhaps even amused, by the carnage around him. More monsters pour out of Amore by the second.

Meanwhile, Bronze wonders if he should shoot and kill Amore, but he worries it might make matters worse. Instead, not really knowing what else to do and miraculously sidestepping the barrage of deadly supernatural creatures, he blows several grams' worth of vermilion up Amore's nose. There's a blinding flash of light, and then all goes quiet. Reality has been restored. Only the rejuvenated Jameson and the strewn, dismembered corpses of most of Bronze's guests remain as evidence of the weirdness that occurred. As for Amore, his mind is all but wiped clean, either by his own spell or by the vermilion overdose, or perhaps by the combination of both. (In 2000 Magus Amore dropped from public view amid rumours of insanity just as his latest, and last, thriller, *The Best Americans*, hit the international bestseller lists.)

Supermall was the name of the luxury "retail sanctuary" financed by an international development consortium, set to open for the Christmas shopping rush of 2001. It was built on an artificial island just outside of Venera's territorial waters. The Veneran government was not happy at this intrusion, but all their efforts to halt construction failed. Supermall's inauguration attracted thousands of shoppers, but it was shut down on the very day it opened, with no further comment from the consortium, which disbanded soon after.

According to part 3 of *Millennium Nights*, Jameson was among the patrons on Supermall's opening day. In this section, the text fetishistically deploys brand names and lingers voyeuristically on detailed descriptions of designer fashions and other luxury consumer products.

At noon an alarm sounds, and a loudspeaker announcement proclaims that Supermall has been locked down. The director of the mall, Marilyn Danvers, has been found dead in her office, and security wants to question all three thousand people at Supermall in relation to the presumed murder. But, although no-one is allowed to leave, no investigation is instigated.

After several days, Jameson confronts Rex Danvers, the head of security. Danvers makes a show of listening to Jameson's concerns: already, there have been instances of looting and outbreaks of minor violence among the imprisoned shoppers. But Danvers appears unworried. When Jameson inquires whether he was related to the deceased director, the security chief answers: "Yes, she was my wife ..."

As the weeks roll on in the artificially controlled environment of Supermall, time loses meaning. Danvers's megalomania becomes increasingly overt, as he encourages tribal rivalries among the shoppers, whose devotion to consumer goods lead them to create new rituals, to forge alliances based on allegiances to popular consumer brands. The abandoned stores become the temples of this new atavism. Wars break out between the faithful of different branded sects.

Again, Jameson confronts Danvers, who answers: "But people adore consumer goods. I'm allowing them to live out their passions to the fullest, to accept their true religion ..."

Jameson is grabbed by a group of Danvers's men. They are five in number, and they match the descriptions of the pirates from Jameson's first book, of the quintets of scientists from the first three sections of *The Great Disasters*, of the five men in Jameson's *Skyscraper* team, and of the astronauts in *Nostalgia of Futures Past*. Are these all the same men? Similarly, the captain from *Pirates to Nowhere*, Raphael Marcus from *Motorcrash*, the villains in various *Skyscraper* adventures, Mike Walters from *Hello Venera*, the meddling producer from *Empire of the Self*, Colin Harper from Vermilion Beach, and Danvers all appear to be different iterations of the same character. And what of Jameson's repeated motifs, such as getting lost, cannibalism, atavistic rituals, vehicles, escape, capitalist development projects, vermilion, and Venera itself? What of the books that stray from his typical scenario? Which are more factual, and which are more fictional? Can these enigmas be solved, to reveal the primal Jamesonian ur-story hiding behind these bizarre phantasmagorias, to understand the life of this author? What is Jameson, if he indeed exists, struggling to reveal or trying to conceal?

Back to *Millennium Nights*: in a Supermall office, the captured Jameson is tortured by Danvers and his men. When they release him, Jameson's perceptions are altered. The meaning of Supermall and its inhabitants is reduced to their geometrical shapes. Within these shapes lies the path to his escape. His mind engages in arcane calculations as he wanders through increasingly abstract landscapes ... until he finds himself in a whirlpool of light. He steps out of the whirlpool and into a garden. Readers will recognize it as the same garden previously encountered in Jameson's first book, *Pirates to Nowhere*.

Jameson reaches out toward a vine, snaps off a leaf, and smells it. His gaze returns to the luminous whirlpool as he starts to chew on the leaf. The end.

THE TERMINAL DREAM (2010)

From the back cover of *The Terminal Dream*: "Bram Jameson (1930–2009) was one of the twentieth century's most significant writers. This revelatory memoir spans the entirety of Jameson's remarkable life: his birth in Canada; his childhood in Nazi-occupied Venera; his young adulthood in Manitoba and England; his first-hand testimony to the great, sweeping changes of the twentieth century; his involvement with many of the most mysterious and emblematic events of the last century; and his meetings with some of the world's most provocative figures. With incisive precision, Jameson recalls the experiences that would fundamentally shape his writing, while simultaneously providing a lucid perspective on the latter decades of the twentieth century. *The Terminal Dream* is the captivating and definitive account of the uncommon life of an extraordinary human being." Thus I learned of the death of this enigmatic author.

The Terminal Dream is a handsome volume, the cover featuring a grainy black-and-white photograph of a very young boy, certainly Jameson, playing in the snow (presumably in northern Manitoba, before his family moved to Venera). The image evokes palpable nostalgia. Is Jameson's oeuvre a strange coded yearning for a return to that state of innocence, an attempt to map out a surreal or mythic path that might lead to his personal nirvana?

I have carefully read and reread *The Terminal Dream* many times. I treasure it with deep affection, even reverence. That it has engaged my imagination more profoundly than anything else I have ever encountered is a risible understatement. But ... it has yet to help me finally discern truth from fiction in the author's baffling body of work, or regarding his mysterious life. Every one of *The Terminal Dream*'s pages is written in a cipher that has so far resisted all my efforts at decryption, no matter how much vermilion I consume ...

Sometimes, I think the drug allows me to see a whirlpool of light. But when I reach for it the illusion is always shattered.

PART 2

ADVENTURES IN TIMES PAST

THE HECATE CENTURIA
(SPRING 109)

⌒

In the light of the full moon, her vision enhanced by vermilion, Dematria watched in horror as Hecate's changeling centurions terrorized her beloved goddess-city, Venera. The Romans had so far ignored the archipelago; in return the city-state fed the Roman capital with a steady supply of underpriced vermilion spice. As a priestess of the goddess Venera, Dematria tended to the hidden gardens of vermilion plant, tended to the sacred fires whose embers were crucial to the manufacture of the mind-altering powder.

But now the gods — or at least one goddess — had taken an interest in the insular city-state. The Hecate Centuria was only ever deployed on direct order from the goddess Hecate herself.

Yet another centurion howled in victory; from her place of concealment Dematria shuddered at the thought of what atrocity could have motivated the outburst. Already, she had seen at least seven of her sisters savagely torn apart by Hecate's lupine soldiers.

There was only one thing another god could want from Venera: the goddess's sacred fires. As long as the holy flames were kept alive and within city limits, the goddess and her eponymous city were as one, each of them an aspect of the other. The sacred fires could also infuse mundane matter with a spark of divinity, hence vermilion's potency. For someone with the proper training, for someone who knew the sacred rites of the goddess, vermilion could be much more than the simple recreational drug most used it as.

Hidden she may be among the wax statues of the Platea Theatrum, atop a slight rise that gave her an unobstructed view of the eastern shore and of the heart of city — whose most recent face had been overseen by the Pompeian exile Maria Vitruvia, outdoing by far the decadent Campanian metropolis for the gaudy eroticism of its architecture; the goddess Venera encouraged indulgence in carnal and sensual delights, and the architecture of her city reflected her predilections — but Dematria knew it was only a matter of time before the centurions caught her scent and hunted her down.

Dematria weighed her options. There was a chance she might survive if she went underground and lost herself among the layers of history and prehistory beneath the modern city of Venera; there was a hidden opening to the tunnels a mere hundred steps from where she stood ... if she could reach it without being detected. Or she could make her way to the sacred altar where burned the goddess's holy flames, where perhaps, with the proper ritual, Venera might grant her the divine attributes necessary to save the city, but that carried not only an increased risk of discovery but the potential of leading the enemy to the very secrets they desired to wrest from the goddess. Or Dematria could reveal her presence to the invaders and let herself be slaughtered by the changeling centurions, eliminating any danger that she might carelessly betray her city-goddess. Or the priestess could simply do nothing, stay hidden, and hope that she survive the carnage.

Or she could inhale the last of her stash, pray to Venera, and perhaps the plans of the city-goddess might then be revealed to her.

Choice was taken away from her: two of Hecate's man-wolves were now sniffing around the piazza, converging upon her. Quickly, she snorted the rest of her vermilion, hoping at least that it would numb the pain of the inevitable brutal assault.

The heavy dose of the holy spice made her lose control of her sensory input. Dematria could barely hold on to even her sense of self. No longer aware of the material world, she was thrust into the presence of the goddess Venera, became one with the object of her worship. Dematria hoped to fathom if the goddess had any plans to save the city, but the deity — like her Earthly alter ego, the city-state that bore her name — was under attack. Venera was locked in combat with the divine she-wolf, the goddess Hecate herself. Dematria did not so much see as intuit the conflict; the gods could not be reduced to mere visual representation. Hecate remained locked in her lupine attribute, and Dematria recoiled at the savageness of the invading deity, at the assault of ethereal claws and fangs; Dematria marshalled her courage, struggled to remain calm and silent; she dared not distract her matron goddess, lest she unwittingly give an advantage to the aggressor Hecate.

Sharp physical pain pulled Dematria back to the material world, back to the Platea Theatrum. One of the wolves had attacked her. He had gone for her neck, but even in her vermilion trance Dematria had reflexively protected herself by blocking the assault with her forearm.

They were both on the ground now, the wolf's jaws clamped on her arm, tearing it to shreds. The second wolf hung back, observing the fight and protecting his fellow centurion's flank.

Dematria's blood covered the wolf-soldier's snout, filled his mouth. Due to the divine attributes of vermilion, Dematria's consciousness extended to her shed blood. She was one with her blood as it slid down the wolf's throat, as her blood itself became one with the wolf.

Dematria herself became one with the wolf. Her desperate, vermilion-enhanced consciousness overwhelmed that of the overconfident and obedient soldier's, and she now commanded the changeling's body. With her newfound wolf senses, heightened by vermilion, she detected that the other wolf was smelling that something was not right with his fellow centurion. Dematria could not afford to wait.

Before the other wolf could be fully on guard, Dematria set upon him and tore at his throat until he lay dead before her.

With wolf eyes, she looked back at her bleeding, savaged human body. She did not have long to live. There was no time to waste.

This wolf body had escaped unscathed from that first confrontation with another wolf. She knew she could not always be so fortunate. The Hecate Centuria was a full hundred soldiers strong. She had possessed one and killed a second. That was only two.

With a last sniff at her dying human vessel, Dematria howled at the full moon and set out to hunt the 98 remaining werewolves.

THE SECRET DRAGON
OF IMPERIAL POWER
(SUMMER 1515)

⤔

The promise of vermilion acts as a powerful lure for the hedonistic Zhengde Emperor. The small sample with which I gained admittance to his inner circle has worked its predictable charms. He yearns to re-experience that elusive euphoria. Here in China, they mine cinnabar, with which they produce a dye vermilion in colour. The Chinese revere that hue more than any other and use it as decoration to garish excess. Even before I provided him with the drug extracted from the vermilion plant of Venera, the emperor had been beguiled for years by rumours of its potency.

As per your coded instructions received by autopigeon yesterday, in response to my confirmation that China does indeed plan to send a mission of some sort to Venera, I have now revealed to the Zhengde Emperor that I possess firsthand knowledge of our island nation. He still believes me to be a disgraced alchemist from Constantinople who fled to China to avoid a sordid scandal involving the effeminate son of one of the sultan's concubines and a stash of contraband vermilion spice. The Zhengde Emperor, who is fascinated by everything foreign or debauched, did not question my story of having once visited our beloved city-state as an apprentice and having been seduced by its decadence; that, at least, is only a mild distortion of the truth. As to my larger cover story ... the other Turks in the young Zhengde's entourage have given me knowing glances. They care not a whit about China or its irresponsible, childish, gullible emperor. As long as I do nothing to undermine the privileges Zhengde confers upon them, they will not betray me. But I nevertheless feel their eyes upon me. The young emperor is capricious, and I must be careful that he not grow bored with my erstwhile countrymen. The announcement that I would soon leave the imperial entourage to take part in the mission to Venera was received with obvious relief by this cadre of opportunistic and wary Turks.

I have, however, befriended someone very close to the emperor: Ibrahim Ben-Jawhar, a diminutive Moroccan Jew who every night shares Zhengde's bed after the emperor tires of his concubines' attentions. Zhengde is an indulgent sensualist; he usually plays with his concubines for a few hours after retiring to bed, but sometimes he is so eager for his little Jew that only a few minutes elapse before he summons him. The emperor babbles in bed, and Ibrahim is ever eager to share the contents of that pillow talk. The Jew craves attention, and flattery is a sure way to gain his trust. As most in the emperor's entourage dislike Ibrahim, he is even more disposed to confide in someone who offers amiable companionship.

The Venera operation is to be undertaken by the Secret Dragon of Imperial Power, the Chinese equivalent to our own Vermilion Eye. Murmurs abound that the Secret Dragon is displeased with the Zhengde Emperor, whose cavalier attitude toward ruling his empire is an obvious disgrace; Zhengde spends more time diddling his concubines and collecting exotic animals than he does administering China. Most people believe the Secret Dragon to be no more than a corps of glorified bodyguards, but I suspect that the full scope of the organization's activities is beyond even Zhengde's knowledge. The controversial ruler is prone to provoke rebellion from various factions with designs on the Chinese throne. Despite the Secret Dragon's dissatisfaction with Zhengde, it is a fiercely loyal organization; scarcely a day goes by without some would-be assassin being thwarted or news of some treasonous plot being foiled.

I am now convinced that the most important aspect of my mission to China on behalf of the Vermilion Eye is to infiltrate the Secret Dragon of Imperial Power. I believe that, in the hands of a more cunning head of state, the Secret Dragon would be a most effective weapon for Chinese expansion, posing a more serious threat to Venera than any European power, in spite of the great distance between our two lands.

Their martial skills—which I have seen in action on several

occasions, when assassins came close to the emperor — seem almost superhuman. Such talents bespeak not only rigorous training but also a tradition at least centuries old, honed by untold generations of master practitioners.

Tomorrow, we set off for the Forbidden City. Alas, my best source of information will then dry up. Ibrahim will not follow the entourage to the capital. He will stay behind in this satellite palace, this Pao Fang ("Leopard's Chamber"). Zhengde has created a number of such satellite palaces — each of them housing an abundant harem and a large collection of live and dangerous animals — draining the imperial coffers. The Venera expedition will be another drain on an already strained treasury. But the emperor's word is law, regardless of what the rest of the court may think.

Upon our arrival to the imperial palace, I am scheduled to be formally introduced to the other members of the expedition. I will then send another autopigeon, with a full report of what I will have learned of China's plans regarding Venera.

I yearn to be back home — or, more precisely, I wish to be me again. Some nights, I feel so far from my own identity and from my true life that I have surprised myself praying to Allah. I may tell myself that I have long ago left behind such superstitious nonsense, but early indoctrination has imprinted this notion of a supreme god deep in my subconscious. Do not worry, Scheherazade: my focus on this mission is steadfast, as is my devotion to our city-goddess.

May the Eye watch over Venera and keep us safe!

Your devoutly loyal agent, Karim Khalil.

The Secret Dragon of Imperial Power is even more of a potential threat to Veneran security than I previously believed. But I am getting ahead of myself. Let me recap the important details of this mission since my last autopigeon message to you, Scheherazade.

We left the Pao Fang (before my departure, Ibrahim confessed that he looked forward to having free run of the concubines in Zhengde's absence), bound for the imperial palace — the Forbidden City. Most of the retinue either walked or rode on donkeys and horses. But a select group, of which I numbered, enjoyed the luxury of the emperor's land-dragon.

This vehicle was a gift from the Secret Dragon of Imperial Power to the Zhengde Emperor upon his ascension. This was the first — and, as I shall report below, not the only — evidence of the Secret Dragon's scientific advancement, which I fear might outclass that of Venera and the Vermilion Eye. The vehicle measures fifteen by fifty feet and never touches the ground. It does not fly like a bird, rather it floats on a thick bed of steam produced by a hidden mechanism within the ornate metal platform of the vehicle. It is not a rapid vehicle — it is much slower than a horse — but it is perhaps the most comfortable mode of travel yet invented. I have not been able to establish for certain whether the impressionable Zhengde believes the vehicle to be powered by Secret Dragon sorcery — the Secret Dragon delights in nurturing this cloak of mysticism — or if he is aware of the technological capabilities of his own empire.

The insides of the land-dragon matched the emperor's usual taste for excess. (This pleasure taken in sensual excess is certainly a common trait between China and Venera, except that here only the elite enjoy these luxuries, whereas in Venera all may partake in the fruits of decadence.) There was a sealed-off section at the back where two young female servants prepared food and a tiny cabin at the front where one of the Secret Dragon navigated the vessel, while the rest of the floor was given to cushions, mats, and low tables. Ostensibly, there were open windows that could allow for a view of the outside, but they were blocked by some of the many thin curtains that arranged the space so as to give it the illusion of palatial grandeur. Somehow, diffuse light snaked its way in, augmented by oil lanterns. Aside from the servants and the pilot, a contingent of five Secret Dragons rode the land-dragon as bodyguards and another three, more high-ranking, sat with the emperor and myself.

Secret Dragons do not retain their birth names. Once inducted into the order, they abandon all other social ties and legacies and are given titles that may change as they gain prestige and seniority. Thus, my three high-ranking companions sported colourful names. Celestial Griffon

of Supreme Wisdom, a lean, stern elder who never eats in the presence
of others, speaks in curt bursts, especially by elaborate Chinese standards; and he never removes the gloves that cover his hands. Lunar
Dragon of Jade is the only woman I have yet seen among the ranks of
the Secret Dragon: she is completely bald, without even eyebrows; she
weighs her rare words with precise consideration; and her stony grey
stare is utterly devoid of empathy. Azure Tiger of the Hidden Moun-
tains displays a gregarious manner and slight plumpness that fail to hide
a keen analytical mind.

The other Turks in Zhengde's entourage did not follow us. Zhengde
had them dismissed and escorted south to Guangdong, where most of
them will probably try to find a ship bound for the Ottoman Empire.
It happened with no warning, so they did not have the opportunity to
put the lie to my cover story — at least to the emperor, whom they were
not even permitted to see once he had given his orders. I worry what
they might tell their military escort, but any accusation will, I hope,
carry the taint of jealousy.

All three of my Secret Dragon companions were hungry for information about myself and about Venera; in turn, they deftly sidestepped
any questions of my own. I revealed as much as I dared, peppering the
truth with convenient lies, while pretending not to notice their rhetorical tactics. Nevertheless, I was able to ascertain what they knew of
Venera, which is very little beyond its Mediterranean location, its
legendary abundance of vermilion, rumours of its sexual decadence,
conflicting stories about its social makeup (some close to the truth; some
comically absurd), hints about its technological wonders, and outland-
ish tales of demonic presences. Of the three Secret Dragons, Azure Tiger
especially seemed to warm to me.

I must confess that I, too, feel drawn to him. Were I in a position to
be my true self, I believe Azure Tiger and I would become as like brothers.
Already, shared laughter comes easily to us. His profound wisdom and
intelligence are tempered by genuine compassion and empathy. He strikes
me as an admirable man of uncommon ethics and integrity. I know my
mission requires me to exploit our friendship on behalf of Veneran interests, but I cannot help but wish circumstances were different.

China is a violent land; it knows nothing of the peace and security we enjoy in Venera. We were but three hours into our journey to the Forbidden City when we were beset by assassins. As I later learned, this time it was not by the usual mercenaries engaged by those with pretensions to the throne. No, this assault was staged by the Terrestrial Phoenix of Utopian Anarchy, a terrorist organization that seeks to destroy not only the rule of the Ming Dynasty but also the entire apparatus of the Chinese government and of imperial tradition.

There were more assailants than I could count. I still do not know how they entered the land-dragon, but one moment they were nowhere in sight and the next a squadron of masked, green-garbed warriors had all of us surrounded.

Three Secret Dragon guards were killed immediately, before anyone could react. Nevertheless, the response from the surviving Secret Dragons was both swift and deadly, even though they were outnumbered perhaps as much as four-to-one, or even five-to-one.

Azure Tiger's speed surprised me. One does not expect someone of his girth to move like a feline, but the high-ranking Secret Dragon earns his name. All I could detect was a red-and-blue blur, and in the blink of an eye he had repelled an attack upon himself by a quartet of Terrestrial Phoenixes (although I did not yet know that's who they were). Azure Tiger then positioned himself to guard both the emperor and myself.

In an amused tone, as if he were not really taking the situation seriously, Azure Tiger told me: "I bested our assailants with the *Swift Mist of Confounding Violence*. Now, I stand guard in the *Steel Fortress of Omniscient Vigilance*." I turned to Zhengde, but he seemed more bored than worried. To him, it was only one more among so many assassination attempts so easily thwarted by the Secret Dragon, or perhaps the emperor truly believed himself so divinely blessed that no mortal harm could possibly befall him.

Before us, Secret Dragons and Terrestrial Phoenixes fought savagely. Blood splattered on the silk finery of the land-dragon, although the combatants moved too quickly for me to make sense of the conflict. Bodies, immobile and lifeless, fell to the floor faster than I could count.

I released a strangled breath when the action stopped abruptly.

Among the Terrestrial Phoenix, there were five survivors; among the Secret Dragon, only one guard was left standing, while all three of the senior officers remained alive, although Celestial Griffon of Supreme Wisdom suffered two visible wounds: a cut in his left forearm and a gash in his right thigh. The five Phoenixes were backed against the opposing wall to where I stood with Azure Tiger and the Zhengde Emperor. Facing them was Lunar Dragon of Jade and the one remaining Secret Dragon guard.

Celestial Griffon said: "Stand down, Mighty Ram of the Eternal Day." And the Secret Dragon guardsman stepped aside from the conflict, leaving Lunar Dragon of Jade alone to face the five Terrestrial Phoenixes. Azure Tiger laughed; for several beats, no-one moved.

Still snickering and somewhat relaxing the stance of the *Steel Fortress of Omniscient Awareness*, Azure Tiger addressed me, loud enough for all to hear: "Pay attention, Karim Khalil."

The five Phoenixes took this as a cue to rush Lunar Dragon of Jade. They moved with alarming speed, while she slithered and danced in slow motion. Yet not one of their blows and jabs managed to connect, nor did any of them succeed in stepping past her.

Azure Tiger commented: "Lunar Dragon of Jade is outwitting the agents of the Terrestrial Phoenix of Utopian Anarchy with the *Elusive and Impenetrable Water Snake*." He would continue to provide commentary as the fight went on.

With no warning, Lunar Dragon lunged toward one, then another Phoenix — *"Destructive Woodpecker Kiss"* — and they slumped to the floor, lifeless.

The other three surrounded Lunar Dragon, stabbing at her with their daggers, but all of them missed their mark. *"Untouchable Sun Lizard."*

Then, she leapt in the air and kicked the heads of two more Phoenixes: *"Leaping Frog Kick of Resounding Death."* The sound of their necks snapping was like a burst of violent, echoing thunder. The two men died before having time to utter even a grunt. Zhengde clapped and hollered in delight, like a little boy at a puppet show.

Lunar Dragon landed two feet away from the one remaining Phoenix. Azure Tiger described her pose as "The *Insidious Claw of the Alert Hawk*."

Celestial Griffon, clutching the wound on his thigh, addressed our erstwhile attacker: "Young Phoenix, if you don't want to share the fate of your comrades, surrender now."

All our eyes were on the Terrestrial Phoenix as he surveyed the room. Finally, he knelt, head bowed, and laid his knives on the floor. I relaxed, relieved at the thought that the violence was over.

And then, in a flash, everything changed.

Azure Tiger, who had relaxed his defensive stance, was felled — but not killed — by another Terrestrial Phoenix, who seemed to appear out of nowhere. The assailant moved in on the emperor, but I propelled myself between the Phoenix and Zhengde. The Phoenix's dagger pierced my left wrist. I confess that I screamed at the intensity of the pain.

When I opened my eyes, Lunar Dragon's foot was crushing the final would-be assassin's neck against the ground; he was already dead. Farther back, the one who had pretended to surrender had taken up his knives again, but the wounded Celestial Griffon went into action, his fingers aimed at the Phoenix's belly. The Secret Dragon's hands shone like metal; his fingers looked like scissors. He disembowelled the last surviving Phoenix before he could attack anyone.

At that point, shamefully, I lost consciousness.

I awoke in a luxurious four-poster bed, with silk sheets. My room was opulent, with a large open window that let in sounds I could not quite identify. My personal effects had been brought here, neatly arranged by the wall to my right. I was tended to by a trio of nurses who refused to answer any of my questions or even speak to me. They were rather forceful, though, and I was not allowed to rise from bed or even peel back the sheets.

My head was heavy, and there was a throbbing ache where my wrist had been stabbed. The nurses would not let me examine or even see my wound. When they appeared confident that I was subdued to their will, one of them left the room. She returned quickly — before I could devise how to outwit my stern keepers — with my three Secret Dragon companions in tow.

Both Azure Tiger and Celestial Griffon bore evidence of the recent fight, but Lunar Dragon was as poised and immaculate as ever. Azure

Tiger winked at me as Celestial Griffon, hands concealed in his cloak and held tight against his chest, addressed me: "Karim Khalil! Welcome to the Forbidden City! The Zhengde Emperor is most pleased with you, and we are all in your debt. Had you not stepped in to save the emperor, he would have died on our watch. You have safeguarded the honour of the Secret Dragon of Imperial Power as well as the life of our emperor and the stability of the state. We are both honoured and shamed by your valour and your sacrifice, and we hope our gift will go some way toward acknowledging our gratitude and admiration."

I was confused. "Sacrifice?"

"Before I explain fully, Karim Khalil, let me show you my hands." When Celestial Griffon revealed his ungloved hands, I gasped. Both of them were made entirely of metal, with gears and buttons that hinted at multiple functions. Prior to this Chinese mission, I believed Venera to be the most technologically advanced society in the world, but I now I know that China is at least our match.

Celestial Griffon nodded to my attendants. They peeled back the silk sheets; my wounded hand was heavily bandaged. One of the three nurses took off the bandages. In lieu of my left hand was a mechanical appendage very similar to those of Celestial Griffon.

"I lost my hands saving the previous emperor's life. These hands, alas, do not provide the sensual pleasure of flesh, but they are better than a stump, by far. In some ways, they are superior to biological hands. The Zhengde Emperor insisted that you be granted this gift. When you are ready, I will teach you its use."

My mind raced with the things I had to report. I realized this was an opportune moment to gather more intelligence, but I was not in a state to trust my rhetorical skills. I feigned even more shock and disorientation than I was feeling and begged to be left alone.

"Of course," both men said in unison, while Lunar Dragon subtly bowed her head to me. They left, as did my three attendants.

I rushed to inspect my bags. As I suspected, they had been searched. I counted six autopigeons, but I knew there should have been seven. What would my hosts make of this machine? Would they believe it to be no more than an automaton, a toy? Or did they already realize that

I am a spy? That this technology — extrapolated by Veneran scientists from the secret notebooks Leonardo da Vinci smuggled into Venera, far from the intolerant eyes of the Catholic Church — allowed communication across great distances?

For a moment, I forgot about my new mechanical hand; it obeys my mental commands so naturally. I will take up Celestial Griffon's offer to teach me about this wondrous technology. If our scientists can unlock its secrets, it will be a boon to Venera.

I activated an autopigeon and spoke into it in our coded language. Once I am done with this report, I will set the bird's coordinates for the headquarters of the Vermilion Eye and activate its flight mechanism.

I will report again as soon as I learn more about the Emperor's designs on Venera.

May the Vermilion Eye be ever vigilant!

～ Much has changed in the three days since my last autopigeon message. If I have not reported before now it is because, when I returned from training in the use of my new hand with Celestial Griffon, I found that my entire supply of autopigeons had been purloined. However, there is no need to send more, as I am now en route to Venera and hope to arrive not much later than this autopigeon. How I came to retrieve the bird is a crucial part of my report.

For the entire day following the discovery of the confiscation, I was on edge, expecting to be arrested at any moment. Yet my hosts continued to treat me as an ally, and I could detect no hint in their behaviour that they suspected anything. Their gift of this new mechanical hand, for example, displayed both gratitude and trust. It is an astonishing piece of medical engineering and, even with only very little training, a formidable weapon.

I spent much time in the stimulating company of Azure Tiger. It weighed heavily on me that I could not be honest with him when his friendship appeared to be so true.

On my final day in the Forbidden City, I finally once again met with the Zhengde Emperor himself. The sun had barely risen, and a young man came to fetch me, informing me that the emperor required my presence immediately. I made myself presentable, and the court attendant led me outside, to a large rectangular building, which at first glance I took to be stables.

I was not prepared for what awaited me inside. In addition to Zhengde himself, there were over one hundred people in attendance, all of them sporting the crest of the Secret Dragon of Imperial Power on their vestments. Azure Tiger, ever jovial, winked at me. Celestial Griffon and Lunar Dragon each acknowledged my arrival with a subtle nod. Zhengde was deep in conversation with two very animated Secret Dragons, inspecting the reason why we were gathered in this building: a giant airship!

I estimate that it was forty feet high, ninety feet long, and fifty feet wide. Its design incorporated all sorts of navigational aids, such as rotors, wings, flippers, and the like. It was decorated in the usual gaudy Chinese manner, in gold and vermilion — yes, the same colours so favoured in Venera, but here in China to a more masculine and harsh effect. The cannons mounted on the deck were visible from the ground. Other cannons sprouted from portholes. There was no mistaking the purpose of this vessel: it was a war machine. Our own scientists have been working on perfecting the maestro's secret designs for various types of aircraft, but we have not attempted anything on this scale. This vessel could easily transport a military force of at least two hundred fighters, in addition to supplies and arms. Inwardly, I shuddered at Zhengde's probable plans for the Venera expedition. And me with no way to warn you of the incoming invading force!

After a few minutes, Zhengde took notice of me and signalled for me to come join him.

"My honoured and valorous friend, Karim Khalil! My household has been treating you well, I hope?" Without giving me time to respond, Zhengde pressed on: "Allow me to introduce Enchanted Fox of the Stars and Water Stone of the Infinite Ocean, the two men responsible for the marvel of Chinese ingenuity before us, the *Sky Dragon of Imperial Power*." The two men bowed as I realized that the Zhengde Emperor was perhaps not as gullible as I had previously believed.

"Come," Zhengde said, "let us tour this great vessel!"

A wide ramp, allowing up to seven persons, shoulder-to-shoulder, led up to the insides of the ship. Joining us as we scaled inside were the two builders of the *Sky Dragon* and my three companions from the land-dragon; each of these senior Secret Dragons was flanked by a retinue of five lower-ranking Dragons.

As soon as we were all aboard, Azure Tiger leaned in close to me, laughing, patting my back as if we were sharing a jest, but the words he whispered were far from comical. "Karim Khalil, my brother, I know you are a spy for Venera. I confiscated your cache of little automata to keep your secret safe. Please trust me, and hang back with my entourage. What is going to happen will be swift and confusing. But do not interfere, and you will be in no danger. I will not let any harm come to you."

Before I could fully digest Azure Tiger's unexpected pronouncement, the ship hummed, trembled, and rose into the air.

From the panicked looks on the faces of Enchanted Fox and Water Stone, I knew this was not planned. Zhengde shouted: "Explain this!"

Azure Tiger bowed his head toward Celestial Griffon's retinue. All five of Celestial Griffon's men drew their knives on him. They managed to cut him but failed to kill him.

Azure Tiger hissed, "Hang back, Karim!" I did as I was instructed, but in truth I had little choice. Azure Tiger's men blocked me from the action. Besides, I knew neither the meaning nor the stakes of what was happening — and this was not my conflict. Furthermore, I was no match for any Secret Dragon, of whatever rank. On the land-dragon, when I saved Zhengde, I had acted by reflex and survived only because of dumb luck.

Lunar Dragon, along with her retinue, moved to protect Zhengde and the scientists. She looked at me intently, and I could see her register the bewilderment on my face. She nodded at me, as if she had come to some conclusion.

Azure Tiger leapt into the brawl between Celestial Griffon and his men. Two among the traitorous retinue were already dead. Celestial Griffon was down on one knee, bleeding from several gashes. He twirled his mechanical hand: small metallic whips springing from his fingers slashed at the air, keeping his attackers at bay. Azure Tiger shouted a sharp one-word command, and the traitors stepped down. Celestial Griffon winced; he looked up at his fellow Secret Dragon. "You are responsible for this?" In answer Azure Tiger attacked the wounded Celestial Griffon, deftly evading the deadly whips, and killed him with one blow.

The emperor screamed in terror.

"Silence, you disgraceful pup!" Azure Tiger removed one layer of robes to reveal the colour and crest of the Terrestrial Phoenix of Utopian Anarchy. His retinue and the three survivors among Celestial Griffon's all did the same.

Azure Tiger shifted his attention to Lunar Dragon. "You and your men are outnumbered." On cue, yet more Terrestrial Phoenixes appeared from the halls on all sides. "I do not wish to shed any more blood, save to rid China of the disgraceful Zhengde." The emperor whimpered. "Surrender the emperor, the scientists, and the *Sky Dragon*, and leave Karim Khalil with us, and you can either join us or abandon ship with your lives intact."

Lunar Dragon responded: "It was no accident, then, that you were not killed by the Terrestrial Phoenix aboard the land-dragon."

"A cautious ruse, should the assassination attempt fail, so that I should not lose my position in Zhengde's entourage and within the Secret Dragon. Had it not been for Karim's interference ... but he acted with valour. He is a good man."

"When did the Terrestrial Phoenix recruit you, Azure Tiger?"

"You misunderstand, Lunar Dragon. I founded the Terrestrial Phoenix after this ridiculous whelp took the throne. I am the Terrestrial Phoenix."

Lunar Dragon betrayed no emotional reaction. "What do you want?"

"I no longer want China, although at one time I thought I did. Now, I will be satisfied with ridding the world of the shame Zhengde has brought upon us all. Then I want to bring this ship to Venera — we are already en route to the Mediterranean — and negotiate a good future for me and my men with the gift of this technology. Imagine! A flying ship powered entirely by the light of the sun! Able to be piloted by a single man — or woman." Azure Tiger bowed his head to Lunar Dragon.

"It can even pilot itself once its destination is set! What nation would not want this treasure! Along with its inventors. There are no equals to Water Stone and Enchanted Fox in all of China, nor, I wager, in the rest of the world!"

From behind Lunar Dragon's men, Water Stone spoke up: "What makes you believe we would collaborate with you, traitor?"

"Because you would rather stay alive. You are Secret Dragons, yes, but you were recruited as scientists, not true warriors. This is not an insult. We each have our roles to play. Accept your lot. Help prevent more bloodshed."

Lunar Dragon shouted: *"Raging Whirlwind of Tiger Claws!"* She and her men were suddenly transformed into barely visible death-dealing tornadoes. The Terrestrial Phoenixes tried to fight back, but they could not withstand such an assault.

Azure Tiger scowled. *"Unbeatable Blows of Furious Steel!"* He joined the fray.

The resulting violence was both swift and gory. I blinked and suddenly the only people left standing were myself in a far corner; the whimpering Zhengde, protected by Lunar Dragon; and Azure Tiger facing Water Stone and Enchanted Fox.

Enchanted Fox spat blood. "We may be scientists, but we were still trained as true Secret Dragons; the two of us can overcome you."

"If you fight me, you will die. Look at all the dead around us. It is too much already. Do not sacrifice yourselves needlessly. The world should not be robbed of your great minds."

In response, the two scientists converged on Azure Tiger. I did not even see him move, yet his two opponents slunk to the ground, dead.

Azure Tiger turned to Lunar Dragon. "I do not want to fight you, old friend. Surrender Zhengde to his final fate and join me in Venera. You have heard Karim's tales; it is a wondrous land, one deserving of loyalty."

"Did you not just say there had been enough death? Surrender yourself, and we shall turn this ship back toward the capital."

Azure Tiger sighed, then lunged at Lunar Dragon. The two disappeared in a blur of movement and colour. When the storm of violence ceased raging, Lunar Dragon lay on the floor, with Azure Tiger kneeling above her, about to deliver a death blow. But he hesitated for a second — enough time for me to push a button in my new mechanical hand and launch a small metal pellet that tore open Azure Tiger's throat, killing him before he could take Lunar Dragon's life.

Even now, I'm not certain why I interfered. Azure Tiger had positioned himself as a potential ally to Venera, and he had never acted as anything but a brother to me — even as he knew that I was lying to him. And yet ... Perhaps I ultimately intuited that there was a megalomaniacal streak within Azure Tiger, a charismatic zealotry that I could not trust not to bring death and destruction upon Venera. Or perhaps I'm pathetically trying to justify the most monstrous act I have ever perpetrated.

Lunar Dragon stood up. She looked at the emperor, who was still sobbing and cowering. I, too, was weeping. My gaze kept darting to Azure Tiger's corpse.

"You saved my life, spy from Venera."

I wiped my teary eyes and focused on Lunar Dragon. "You knew?"

"Yes. I always suspected, but when you were convalescing I searched your belongings and took one of your little mechanical birds, intending to show it to Enchanted Fox, but I never had the chance. I presume you use them to report back to your masters?"

"Something like that. Venera is different from China, though. I do not think of anyone as my master, or mistress."

"Can I ask what your plans are for China?"

"We are peaceful, isolationist. We heard rumours that China might be planning a Veneran excursion. I was sent to investigate."

Lunar Dragon gazed at me intently. After a moment, she said: "Twice, you have acted in China's interests, with courage and without hesitation, at great risk to yourself. We are in your debt. How can we repay you?"

"Allow me to take this ship back to Venera; I promise that we will not attack you. But then China will not be able to attack us. Without Water Stone and Enchanted Fox, China cannot rebuild this vessel. And faraway Venera shall be safe enough for now."

Lunar Dragon once again glanced at the whimpering emperor. For a moment, her contempt for him showed on her usually impassive features. "Granted. And this, too." Reaching inside her robes, she pulled out the autopigeon she had taken from me. "Farewell, Karim Khalil. You are an honourable man."

"Farewell? Are you not coming along? Where can you go?" I leaned against the hull and gazed out through the glass to the outside; we were far, far up in the sky. "You would be welcome in Venera; I believe you would find it to your taste."

Lunar Dragon picked up the still-cowering emperor as if he were an infant. "Do not worry about us any longer, Karim Khalil." I followed her. She opened a hatch. The winds at this altitude were both fierce and cold. Hugging Zhengde to her, she shouted: "*Graceful Flight of the Landing Swallow!*" and without looking back at me jumped out of the ship. Having witnessed Lunar Dragon's phenomenal skills, I have no doubt the pair landed safely.

This solar-powered ship is indeed ridiculously easy to pilot; although it is slower than an autopigeon, hence this final report. I have rid the ship of all the corpses, save Azure Tiger's, who deserves a proper cremation. The more time elapses, the more I question my judgment. Why did I kill my friend? If not for his interference, Chinese warriors might at this very moment be converging on Venera, mounting an invasion we would be unprepared to repel. May Allah, even if he does not exist, forgive me or at least grant me peace from the confusion and grief that torture me. The sun has set twice since I murdered my friend, and I still have not slept.

I yearn to be back home. I need to lose myself in decadent revelry and fall into a deep, long, forgetful slumber in the arms of a plump, ripe young Veneran who will wash away from my consciousness my time in China.

Soon the *Sky Dragon of Imperial Power* will loom over the skies of beautiful Venera.

AGENTS OF THE VERMILION EYE
(AUTUMN 1895)

THE MISTRESS IS SUMMONED

In our somewhat dilapidated suite at the Portland Hotel, the International Mistress of Mystery sat back after indulging in a pinch (or three) of vermilion snuff. The unruly mane of her majestic hair haloed her beatific yet stern visage. She darted a satisfied smirk in my direction. There were still a few loose ends to tie up in and profits to be made from "The Affair of the Shanghaied Effete," but she had caught the Chinatown culprits, collected her fee, and secured a generous bonus for the safe return of the ineffectual but beloved son of our client, the railroad magnate.

She barely had time to utter "Listen, my boy" — the usual preamble to the monologues with which she brightened our evenings when we were not engaged on some adventure — before we were interrupted by a knock at the door. I felt a sharp pang of disappointment that I might be denied this evening's words of wisdom. Her inspiration was capricious, and whatever thoughts possessed her at this precise moment might never again visit her wondrous mind.

I shouted: "One moment, please!" The Mistress found it more congenial for me to be in a partial state of undress when she relaxed at the end of the day, and also for me to be adorned with certain enhancements. Before I could open the door to this intrusion, I needed to make myself more presentable, lest I bring unwanted public attention to the Mistress's private predilections.

It was a telegram.

"Well, what does it say?" Already, her mood had shifted from proud self-satisfaction to bristly irritation.

I tried to read the missive, but I had to admit defeat. The text was rendered in a rather childish and completely ungrammatical faux Italian, peppered with nonsense words. "It's utter gibberish." I approached her, knelt, and handed her the telegram.

Her eyes narrowed and then grew wide. She silently mouthed several syllables, and then addressed me: "We must take the next train across the continent, to New York, and from there board the first boat to Europe."

"A new adventure, Mistress?"

"Perhaps, my boy, perhaps. We are summoned ... to Venera!"

Few outsiders ever visited the fabled city-state of Venera. Mapmakers rarely agreed on where, exactly, to situate it. The general consensus was that it was somewhere in the Mediterranean, not far from the coast of Italy. The Mistress had, in the past, made oblique references to some sort of connection to the exotic archipelago, but I had never imagined we would actually travel there. The city-state did not encourage tourism. I knew of no commercial boats or ferries that boasted of Venera as a destination.

"Summoned ...?" I asked, but she ignored my question. I knew better than to press her for information she was not yet ready to share. Without another word, the Mistress retired to her bedchamber, leaving me bereft of her company until sunrise.

A TRANSCONTINENTAL JOURNEY

The next morning we boarded the San Francisco train but changed lines north of Sacramento, where we took the transcontinental. We stayed on that line until Fremont, where we again changed trains, this time for Chicago. In Chicago, we boarded our final American conveyance, to New York.

I rush through this account of our railroad trip, although, it, too, was not devoid of adventure. The Mistress possessed a keen awareness of mischief, and so we were on this leg of our journey embroiled in minor cases — "The Affair of the Gilded Brassiere," "The Unexpected Tunnel and the Unwelcome Visitor," "The Case of the Duplicate Husbands," and "The Capitalist's Ethical Conundrum." The Mistress profited nicely from these trifles, in both coin and repute.

THE *ESPLENDOR CATALÀ*

At the port of New York, we boarded the most luxurious and strange of all the transatlantic liners, the *Esplendor Català*, which was scheduled to deposit us in Barcelona six days later. The Mistress and I had, by this time, crossed the Atlantic a half-dozen times — see the previously documented "A Scandal across the Atlantic," "The Adventure of the Aquatic League," "The Case of the Identical Identities," "A Veil of Mystery in Boston," "The Peculiar Incident of the Five Fruits," and "The Lips of the Woman" (all collected in *The Transatlantic Adventures of the International Mistress of Mystery*) — but never before as passengers of this otherworldly ship. Its designer was the Catalonian architect Antoni Gaudí, whose peculiar imagination was ushering in a new aesthetic, a mystical sense of wonder, a transcendent celebration of nature and the divine; boarding this ship, with its confounding yet soothing geometry, its colourful and intricate adornments, its almost biological appearance, its ethereal strangeness, its childlike blend of veneration and playfulness, left the impression of having crossed into another world and stepping into the antechamber of a fantastical heaven.

I expected the bewildering environment to leave me overly stimulated, making sleep difficult and dreams nightmarish. Quite the contrary: on our first night aboard, I slept with serene calm at the foot of the Mistress's bed, waking fully rested, even joyous, the next morning.

The voyage was not having the restorative effect on the Mistress that it was on me. The Mistress awoke scowling, pacing about like a caged animal. Throughout the day, she accosted other passengers and crew members, dispensing verbal abuse. By the time dinner was called, the captain — a tall, regal, commanding Easterner with dark skin and even darker eyes — confined her to a utility closet for the duration of the trip, lest she further disturb the quietude of the other passengers.

As her travelling companion, I was allowed to visit the Mistress in her confinement, but I asked the captain to refrain from sharing this information with her. He acquiesced, and I retired to our berth early, enjoying a rare moment of freedom and solitude. I dosed off quickly, having the bed to myself, my dreams filled with romance and wonder, inspired by the fantastical beauty of the *Esplendor Català*.

It was in the midst of one of these dreams that I was roused to wakefulness by the Mistress, who held an oil lantern next to my face. The dim light could not fully illuminate the cabin. It was still the middle of the night, as evidenced by the darkness outside the room's tiny porthole. Nevertheless, I could discern that a tall heavy-set man stood next to her.

"Get dressed and gather all our things," said the Mistress. "We're leaving."

Questions flooded my mind. How had the Mistress escaped her confinement? Who was her mysterious companion? Where were we going? What did she mean by "leaving"? Did she intend for us to abandon ship? Here, in the middle of the ocean? But I knew better than to ask, especially in the presence of a stranger.

"Hurry, young man!" The man's thick American accent rolled out like a low growl. Looking more intently toward him, I caught a reflection of light off something metallic in his hand ... a gun!

Hoping that the near darkness would allow me some decency — I was naked under the sheets — I rapidly slipped on yesterday's clothes and quietly bustled about, assembling our luggage. Meanwhile, the Mistress and the armed man whispered to each other, paying no attention to me. Although I could only catch the occasional word, it was clear to me that they were allies and that they were conversing in a language other than English.

"We're ready, Mistress," I informed the conspiring pair.

In a low voice, she said: "Follow us, and be quiet. Trust no-one. The ship is compromised. The captain and at least some of the officers are agents of the Invisible Fingers!"

Through the years, the Invisible Fingers had been an elusive foe, the unseen force behind many of the Mistress's escapades. This rivalry preceded my acquaintance with the Mistress. Was the armed man an ally in this conflict?

The corridor was lit by oil lamps along the walls, revealing the bodies of fallen men. I recoiled.

The armed man addressed me, in a surprisingly kind tone: "They're not dead." He raised his weapon, a bulky multi-chambered contraption unlike any gun I had ever seen. "Unless lethal action is unavoidable, I use miniature darts coated with a sedative of my own devising."

I guessed him to be in his mid-fifties. His hair was close-cropped, but he sported a thick unruly beard. He exuded strength, and his eyes were stern and wary. He wore a brown and red uniform of military cut, although I did not identify it as the fashion of any nation. On his chest were pinned medals, but again I failed to recognize their design.

Before I could scrutinize him any further, he led us outside. The armed man went first, gun at the ready, followed by the Mistress once he gave the all-clear. I joined them and noticed yet more unconscious bodies on the deck.

The armed man raised a small device to his face and spoke into it. He looked skyward. I, too, peered up. The night was cloudy, obscuring the stars. I could not guess what he was trying to glimpse.

Keeping an eye to the sky, he approached me and said: "You cannot carry all this. You'll need a free hand. Here, let me take these." He relieved me of two of the Mistress's bulkier bags. Then, turning to the Mistress, he commanded: "Grab one, too. Though I wonder why you require this much luggage."

The Mistress bristled. She was not accustomed to being spoken to in this manner. Yet, she acquiesced. I was careful to hand her the lightest item among our baggage.

I silently wondered why I would need a free hand.

The armed man holstered his gun and wrapped his fist around something in the dark night air. I peered intently and saw that what he grasped was a rope dangling from the sky. There were three such ropes. Where did they lead to? I peered into the sky, and still all I could see was darkness. Were there helium balloons hidden up there? If so, how did they remain so steady instead of being borne off by the wind? The armed man tied the first rope around his waist, than another around the Mistress's, and the last one around mine. He grabbed my free hand and placed it on the rope. "Hold tight!"

He tugged three times on his own rope, and after a pause I felt a tightening jerk where the rope was fastened around me … and I rose into the sky!

I had travelled upward some thirty feet when I felt a sharp sting in my leg. Another dart whizzed past my cheek. The shock made me drop our bags. The armed man, too, dropped the bags he'd taken from me. He aimed his weapon and shot at our attackers on the deck below.

Within seconds, though, we were out of reach of our enemies' weapons.

Addressing the Mistress, our armed ally asked: "I trust there was nothing of potential use to the enemy in those bags?" But the Mistress remained silent. In the darkness, I could not make out her expression. The armed man grunted with obvious disgust. In a softer tone, he said: "We'll get you help aboard the ship, young man." As he addressed me, I realized that I felt very sickly indeed. He now spoke into his handheld device: "The Fingers used silent air guns with poisoned darts in lieu of firearms, so as to not alarm the innocent passengers of the *Esplendor Català*. The Mistress's assistant is wounded. Alert the medic."

Suddenly, I was aware of a gigantic airship above us. The vehicle was almost as large as the ocean liner we had just escaped from. How could such a machine exist? Any nation that had so solved the timeless enigma of flight would possess an insurmountable military advantage over all others. My ponderings were cut short. Another few seconds, and the three of us were pulled into the impossible airship. By that time, I was burning with fever, slipping in and out consciousness, dreams, and hallucinations.

Both the Mistress and our rugged ally stood by my bedside. The Mistress held my hand, which she squeezed to the point of pain when she realized I was once again fully conscious. Her eyes were moist with emotion, a rare public display of affection that filled me with devotion for her. The man, standing stiffly in a military manner, introduced himself. "Young man, my name is Brigadier Fox. I am told that your patron has yet to fully inform you of the specifics of your employment and of this voyage to Venera." The two of them exchanged a glance. The Brigadier continued: "Your loyalty and bravery are not in question, and there is no reason to not fully initiate you into the secrets of the organization for which you have been unknowingly working these past nine years."

The Mistress and the Brigadier exchanged a glance and nodded at each other.

"I had meant to explain everything myself under less dire circumstances, my boy, during our journey to Venera, but ..." she trailed off, then assumed a solemn posture. "Welcome to the Vermilion Eye."

The Brigadier joined her, and together they intoned: "May the Vermilion Eye be ever vigilant, and may it forever keep Venera safe!"

THE VERMILION EYE IS REVEALED

I was bursting with curiosity. The Mistress and the Brigadier answered many of my queries, although I could tell that they were both adroit in deflecting questions without seeming to. There were aspects of my newly discovered situation that neither of them was ready to reveal.

The flying vessel on which we were aboard was called the *Occua inel Ciel*—which, the Brigadier told me, was Veneran for *Eye in the Sky* —and it was the flagship of a fleet six strong. Venera had possessed this technology since the sixteenth century, and, according to the Brigadier, had only ever used these ships militarily as a deterrent toward nations who threatened to invade the archipelago of Venera. Venera had no interest in becoming an imperial power, but nor did she want to become a vassal state subject to another nation's expansionist ambitions.

(Both the Brigadier and the Mistress kept referring to Venera in the feminine. It was not uncommon for people to so personalize their nation, yet I perceived the hint of something more profound in their use of the feminine pronoun, a near religious awe, an almost palpable capital H for *Her* and capital S for *She* — as if Venera were not a nation but person, a great leader, a deity even.)

Centuries ago, in the wake of a devastating Viking invasion, and with memories of an earlier Roman conquest still a painful cultural heritage, a group formed in Venera with the goal of forever avoiding any such violation of Veneran autonomy: the Vermilion Eye. Venera was by then an ethnic soup, with no indigenous population — Turks, Jews, Italians, Scandinavians, Gauls, Iberians, Africans, Asiatics — but they all shared a profound loyalty to Venera, a desire to safeguard her from future violence.

The ethnic mix of Venera made it easy to dispatch a network of spies across the world, and thus the Vermilion Eye kept watch over all nations, doing its best to discourage foreign powers of any notion regarding military incursions into Venera.

Some agents operated in plain sight, like the International Mistress of Mystery, always careful, though, to keep silent regarding their allegiance to Venera. Others, like Brigadier Fox, operated in secret. Many of the Mistress's cases were in fact indirectly in service to Venera, operating on several levels of intrigue beyond what I'd recorded in her published adventures.

During the seventeenth century, the Vermilion Eye became aware of an organization calling itself the Invisible Fingers. Its aims were, at best, obscure, but on more than one occasion it had showed itself to be hostile to Venera and to her isolationist goals. The Vermilion Eye was fighting blind, with no idea where their enemies were headquartered or what their full agenda might be. Recently, the conflict had become more open, more deadly, more urgent. And the Eye was losing.

I asked: "And what of our current mission to Venera?"

Again, the two of them spoke briefly to each other in what I assumed to be Veneran. The Mistress answered. "We were not told. Our summons included a code word that indicated the highest priority, but that's all we know."

I sensed truth in her statement, but I also gleaned there was another layer of truth to which I was not yet privy.

THE EYE'S MIND

We docked on the roof of a building the Mistress called "The Eye's Mind," explaining that it was the Vermilion Eye's centre of operations. At night, all I could see of the legendary metropolis was an ethereal rust-red illumination. Before I could discern any shapes in this otherworldly light we were met by a retinue of anonymous female guards wearing reflective globes that covered their heads. These featureless agents of the Vermilion Eye were a most disquieting sight and not at all welcoming. Their attitude was even less so. We were immediately escorted inside, to our rooms. Both the Brigadier and Mistress asked anxious questions of them in that pseudo-Italian that I presumed to be Veneran, but they were answered with curt monosyllables that only increased their anxiety, and thus my own.

The inside was unlike any building I had ever seen. Working with the Mistress, I had long ago learned to shed my modesty regarding the human body and its sexual needs, but I was unprepared for the lasciviousness of the decor, for the ubiquitous architectural adornments of semi-human beasts engaging in the most perverse activities. In addition, vegetation glowing with that same eerie rust-red tint I had espied outside grew in and out of the walls, the floors, the ceilings. Nor did I quite grasp the irregular arrangement of space, nooks, angles, open atria, arches, doorways, and stairs that divided the interior of the Eye's Mind.

Eventually, we reached a portion of the building that was almost a conventional corridor. The Brigadier was ushered into one room, and then the Mistress and I were led to our own room, three doors farther down. Once inside, we discovered that our door was locked from the outside.

The Mistress said: "This is most irregular."

But by then exhaustion overcame me. I was not yet fully recovered from the attack. Although the oil lamps were lit, revealing austere surroundings, I fell asleep in my chair.

GATHERED AT THE ROUND TABLE

The director of the Vermilion Eye was a masked man who introduced himself as Brother Nocturne, although it was clear that among all of us gathered here only I did not know him previously. He stood well over six feet and moved with the strong grace of a trained fighter but also with the arrogance of wealth and privilege. He dressed entirely in black, including a cloak that reached to his knees, and sported a walking stick that was almost certainly a disguised scabbard. Although his voice was muffled by the eyeless mask that covered his entire head, his accent was recognizably English, most certainly coastal and educated, most likely from Brighton or thereabouts. For my benefit, he led the meeting in English, although I offered him the additional options of Italian, German, Dutch, French, and Greek, to which he responded: "Your familiarity with these languages will speed your learning of Veneran. But English will do for now. We all speak it."

Emboldened, I added: "And it is your native tongue, sir."

He tapped his walking stick to the floor twice in rapid succession. "Quite so! But on to more serious matters."

Including the director, the Brigadier, the Mistress, and myself, there were ten of us gathered in the meeting room. The director stood at the ostensible head of the round table, while the rest of us had been invited to sit. Some but not all of our tablemates were known to me, and full introductions had yet to me made; the three agents I did not know were all women. One was small, dark, and spectacularly beautiful. Another was pale and gaunt, with long hair like brittle, colourless straw; she appeared too ancient to be alive. The third seemed barely there, as if she were flickering in and out of existence; there was some sort of glamour about her face, making it difficult to distinguish her features. Those agents familiar to me were, like the Mistress, renowned adventurers, revealed now to also be, as was the entire assemblage, clandestine field operatives of the Vermilion Eye. The trio I knew were called Le Nomade des Étoiles, Eule-Königin, and Sweet Honey; together they travelled throughout Europe, their often scandalous exploits never failing to be the talk of both low and high society. Our paths had crossed on five occasions, sometimes working in tandem, sometimes engaged by patrons with conflicting aims. (The first of these encounters was published as "The Adventure of the Peerless Machines," collected in *The Scientific Investigations of the International Mistress of Mystery*.) I now suspect that, whatever the ostensible conceit of the cases we were involved in, the Mistress and this trio always worked together for the interests of Venera first and foremost.

We had descended several flights of maze-like stairs to reach this cavernous room. Above, below, and around us mineral veins and plant tendrils pulsed with that eerie rust-red glow that I now associated with Venera and which provided our only illumination. The table around which we were gathered was made of glass and reflected the sinuous ebbs and flows of the reddish light, accentuating its disquieting lifelike character. At first, the room seemed too dark to clearly discern anything but soon my eyes adjusted. Or had the vermilion light grown in intensity since we'd arrived? I could not be certain.

The director continued: "Our new recruit shall, alas, endure a trial by fire. This chamber has now been sealed by both science and sorcery. There is no way out until I utter the secret command." The transparency of the table seemed, at this point in the meeting, designed to remind us all of our vulnerability.

The consternation among the gathered agents was palpable. Only one of the others, one of those three as yet unknown to me, seemed more amused than alarmed. I glanced at her again. She was indeed a great beauty, perhaps the most beautiful woman I had ever beheld. Less than five feet tall, she nevertheless radiated regal assurance. Her face was youthful, but her eyes betrayed a calm wisdom and a vast potential for mischief that such youth could not account for. Even under the reddish hue that pervaded the room I could tell her skin was as dark as any unmixed African's, but her features were more Arabian, or perhaps Indian, as was her long lustrous black hair. Her dress was simple, but also immodest by most standards. A floral frock with generous décolletage that left her arms bare and reached above her knees. The garment's rust-red pattern seemed to shift if I stared at it. Her eyes sought to probe my own, but I lacked the confidence to lock my gaze with hers.

Brother Nocturne ignored the ensuing questions and protestations. He patiently waited for his agents to regain their composure. When at last they had, he continued: "All will be explained shortly. For now, for the good of the Eye and the welfare of Venera, it is necessary for you to introduce yourselves, as not all of you are familiar with each other, and, to fulfill our agenda today, we must come to know each other as thoroughly as possible."

The Brigadier spoke up. "You overstep your position, Nocturne. Your directorship is not a mantle of authority, but merely a mandate of coordination and communication."

"Nevertheless," Brother Nocturne accentuated the word with a double tap of his walking stick, "this is how we shall proceed."

There was tentative agreement from the group. "For now, perhaps," Le Nomade des Étoiles said with a hint of northern French accent.

Brother Nocturne ordered me to go first, and I repeated to the assembled group what the Mistress already knew about me. It seemed to satisfy the director.

The Mistress was next. "You all know me. I am the International Mistress of Mystery."

There was a long pause, and when it became clear that the Mistress did not intend to continue, Brother Nocturne said: "No. That will not do. Who were you before, and how did you come to be who you are now? What is your relationship to Venera? How did you come to work for the Eye?"

Sweat ran down the Mistress's brow, although the temperature was comfortably cool. Even I, her companion and biographer, knew very little about her beyond her *nom d'aventure*, her exploits (which were, to some extent, known to the public as well), and her nocturnal proclivities, which only she and I shared. But of her past — nothing. She was a very guarded and private person. "No, Brother Nocturne. I have worked long and hard to perfect the anonymity of my persona as the International Mistress of Mystery. Why should I divulge anything now?"

The director stayed silent for a moment. Then, he tapped his walking stick twice on the ground — evidently, a quirk of his that indicated having come to a decision — and said: "One of us is a traitor. Perhaps unknowingly so. I include myself among the suspects. A high-ranking operative of the Vermilion Eye has been leaking intelligence to the Invisible Fingers, threatening the security of our beloved Venera. It has been determined that only we ten had access to the breadth of information in question. We must now cross-examine each other with complete candour, until we determine the identity of the traitor."

There were gasps around the table, although the beautiful dark woman laughed.

The Mistress bristled. "Why, then, is my assistant here? He did not even know of the Vermilion Eye before your summons." Other objections, in multiple languages, were heard from various points around the table.

The director tapped his walking stick to the ground, silencing the group. Addressing the Mistress, he said: "If what you claim is true, then he has nothing to fear. Before we commence our mutual cross-examinations, we must at the very least each of us know all the others. We must have some basis from which to interrogate each other."

The entire assemblage stayed resolutely silent. Was this kind of insubordination common at the Vermilion Eye?

Again, a double tap to the ground from the director. "Very well, then. I shall introduce each of you to the gathering, with the exception of our recruit, who has already done so himself."

Brigadier Fox objected. "No. If at least one of us is a traitor, why risk exposing our secrets? No, I vote against this course of action. In fact, I propose we put it to a vote now."

There were murmurs of assent among the group. Brother Nocturne started to reply, but the dark beauty interrupted him.

"We all know there is but one appropriate way for us to resolve this question and to discover if there truly is a traitor among us." Her voice was like a song. She did not speak English; I could not identify the language she used, or even distinguish the words she uttered, yet I understood her meaning. She continued: "Or, Brother Nocturne, are you fearful of what true sharing might reveal?"

He said: "Of course not, Scheherazade." The director now sat with the rest us, resting his walking stick against his chair. His previous show of arrogance, along with any semblance of authority, seeped out of him. He deferred to the dark-skinned beauty he called Scheherazade.

Who could refuse whatever she proposed? Her voice was more seductive than any siren call could ever be. We all fell silent. Were they all as awestruck as I was? It was my first encounter with this woman, and I presumed that they had been exposed to her charisma before. Although I could not imagine that her voice ever diminished in potency, regardless of how often one might be privileged to hear it.

She pointed to the centre of the table. Had it not been empty before? Yet, there lay a translucent decanter. Within it shimmered a liquid possessing that same vermilion glow that suffused much of what I had so far seen of Venera.

"This vermilion wine is a gift from the Goddess," she said. "Let us commune." She reached for the decanter of wine and took the first sip. Although the vessel was large and somewhat ungainly and she petite to the point of almost, were it not for her heady aura and physicality of womanhood, being mistaken for a child, she drank with elegance, her every movement beguiling and enchanting. Scheherazade rested the decanter back on the glass table. She sang, in that language that seemed to encompass all languages: "May the Vermilion Eye be ever vigilant, and may it forever keep Venera safe!"

They all repeated the oath, in a cacophony of tongues.

WE DRINK VERMILION WINE AND COMMUNE WITH SCHEHERAZADE

The decanter made its way around the table, counter-clockwise. One by one, the gathered agents drank from it — although we were not as deft with the decanter as Scheherazade. Each of us spilled some of the wine on ourselves, rivulets of vermilion fluid snaking down our chins, necks, chests, and clothing. Brother Nocturne raised his mask slightly so as to be able to drink. He did so as briefly as possible and tried to hide the small portion of his lower face that was thus revealed. I thought I saw scars around his mouth, but it might have been my imagination.

I had no choice but to join in the communion, as all eyes were on me when the decanter was placed in front of me.

All the while, Scheherazade spoke — or sang; I could not tell the difference or if, for her, there was a distinction to be made. I could discern no words or overt meaning. Rather, her voice conveyed a mood, a context. I felt myself and the nine others, including Scheherazade herself, become characters in a dream she was weaving. Doorways opened around the room-cavern, in ten different directions.

I now sat alone at the round table. Where had all the others gone? I called out to the Mistress, to anyone, but my voice was drowned out by the song of Scheherazade, which still reverberated within my mind.

I waited, but aside from the subtle variations of Scheherazade's melody the scene remained static. The song did not offer any guidance, save perhaps a yearning for exploration. There was no alternative but to follow one of the ten paths offered me, which were all equally foreboding, equally tempting. Each of them presented a similar melange of darkness and light. The vermilion radiance did not truly pierce the darkness; rather, the ten black chasms were punctuated with vermilion lights and pulses.

Whether my growing restlessness was a result of the dark woman's song, of the strangeness of my situation, of my impatience for something — anything — to happen, or of some combination of all these, I nevertheless could no longer tolerate inaction. I chose the opening nearest me and walked into the vermilion-sprinkled darkness.

I travelled only briefly on this path. Soon, with one step and without warning, I exited the dark tunnel and found myself in woodlands at dawn.

EULE-KÖNIGIN, THE OWL-QUEEN

I breathe in the pungency of greenery and decay. I am running. Not from anything, but for the rush of pleasure it affords me. The blood pulsing through me; my heart a thumping, comforting presence in my chest. Twigs and branches scratch my skin, leaving faint lacerations. I mumble-sing in nonsense sounds, peppering in the occasional German word. My thoughts, too, are in German. I think of how I can barely tolerate the presence of my five younger sisters. I wish I had a brother. My mother mostly ignores me, leaving me to my own designs as long as I do what's asked and expected of me (I don't always); she and I neither love nor dislike each other. I believe I am my father's favourite little girl. At least, that's what I see in his eyes whenever I peer into them, what I hear in his voice whenever he sings to me.

I am a little girl?

Yes, my head is adorned with long golden tresses. I'm wearing a dress that was once white and blue but is now mended with patches of disparate designs and colours and covered with the filth of farming and the stains of play in the woods.

I should be starting my daily chores. Sweeping. Scrubbing. Cleaning. Feeding the pigs and the goats and the chickens. Looking after my sisters. Instead, at dawn, I am here.

I stop. I stop running and singing. I clear my thoughts of everything about life on the family farm. And I listen.

I listen.

She is hooting: Eule-Königin, the Owl-Queen.

I close my eyes and stand absolutely still. I focus on the sound. It grows louder and louder. My body vibrates, as if tuning itself to the call of Eule-Königin.

The air swooshes around me. There's a rustle of leaves and branches. With every hoot of the Owl-Queen the ground throbs like a gigantic drum.

I open my eyes and turn around, and there she is: Eule-Königin, the legendary Owl-Queen. For one month now, since the last full moon, she has visited me every time I venture into these woods, at dusk or dawn. This past night, the moon was full once again.

The Owl-Queen stands taller than I do, taller than would a full-grown man, her owl head thrice the girth of an average person's. Her talons, so thick and robust they look like they could shred metal, dig in the soil beneath her.

Her merciless gaze envelops me. I feel fragile and vulnerable. But I do not flinch. I meet her gaze with whatever cold resolve I can muster, pushing down the awe that threatens to engulf me.

I sense her giant eyes evaluating me, looking for the fear that is not within me. As she does at every encounter, the Owl-Queen stares at me unblinkingly, waiting for the terror that will compel her to attack and devour me. Always, she flies away. Whether she is disappointed by or approving of my fearlessness, I cannot fathom.

This morning, it is different. She waits longer than she ever has before. Her gaze is static, unwavering, relentless. I, too, am static, unwavering, and relentless. I am hers to gaze upon. A living statue devoid of emotion and response.

But my body betrays me. My belly tightens and is then gripped by sharp spasms, by a rhythmic ache followed by a strange sense of release. Moistness spreads from my sex and onto my thighs.

Immediately, I know. My time has come. Womanhood.

[The illusion — or dream? — was at that moment briefly shattered, and I was myself once again, in the darkness of the narrow tunnel, my eyes teased by the sparse strands and pinpricks of vermilion glitter. I reflected that the girl — the child version of the tall, regal woman I knew as Eule-Königin, agent of the Vermilion Eye — was not quite as young as I had first surmised. Before I could formulate another thought, I was once more transported into the scenario of the young girl, or rather *woman*, being both her and myself at the same time.]

I struggle to remain stoic in the face of this transformation, this bloody farewell to childhood, to not let pain or discomfort or uncertainty tarnish the cold demeanour I present to the Owl-Queen.

But I cannot fool her.

The character and timbre of her hooting changes. She beats her wings and flutters around me with a swiftness that is surprising for such a bulky creature. Although her feathers brush against me, cutting my flesh, I do not fear the Owl-Queen. Let her devour me if she so wishes. I do not fear her.

I close my eyes, waiting to be consumed. It is a much nobler fate to become food for this powerful and ancient goddess than to become yet another anonymous farmwife bearing children I do not want — better this than a lifetime of filth and tedium and neverending chores.

But her hoot once again changes, becomes more songlike.

The flutter of wings builds like a crescendo until it becomes a rumbling of wings.

I open my eyes. The Owl-Queen is flanked by her subjects. Hundreds, perhaps thousands of birds of all kinds — more species than I am able to identify.

The birds swarm to me. They peck at the underside of my knees, and my legs buckle. I fall onto a bed of birds, and I am carried up, up, up into the sky.

Eule-Königin leads the flock. We head south. So high in the sky, the cold wind is terrible, and for the first time I am afraid. I fear that I will freeze, accidentally, the Owl-Queen oblivious to my human frailties. I do not want to die in such a thoughtless, meaningless manner.

I huddle into foetal position, or at least as close to it as my precarious carriage will allow. I rub my hands and shield my face. This I do with regret, as the view of the world from the perspective of the birds is even more beautiful than I ever imagined.

By the time we alight on a roof garden, although the air is hot and moist, my whole body is shivering. The landing itself is surprisingly gentle. It is now mid-morning, and I am the midst of a vast city, unlike anything I have ever seen. [I experienced a double vision of sorts, as my submerged true self recognized Venera.] The vegetation and the architecture meld together into one giant puzzle as far as my eye can see, broken only by a complex network of street-like canals, bustling with activity. Everything is so alive that I briefly imagine that the buildings themselves are in constant movement or transformation. Before I can examine my surroundings more carefully, I am greeted by a dark-skinned woman, shorter than I am even though I am barely not a child anymore and she has many years on me. Her long black hair —

[The sight of Scheherazade, looking exactly the same as she did in the meeting room, decades later than the scene I was experiencing, jolted me back to the dark passage and to myself. I waited, but I did not re-enter the dream. Growing impatient, I marched deeper into the tunnel, to rapidly find myself at a crossroads, with nine other tunnels offering possible paths. In the background of my mind, I could still hear faint echoes of Scheherazade's song. In equal parts fascinated and irritated, I chose the path to my immediate left.]

SWEET HONEY

In this second tunnel I encountered a simulacrum of the woman I knew as Sweet Honey — petite, dressed to emphasize her disproportionately ample feminine voluptuousness, brazenly wearing her shoulder-length hair loose. Always, the Mistress and I had met her in the company of Eule-Königin (or, rather, according to what I had just learned, she who grew up to assume the owl goddess's name) and Le Nomade des Étoiles. The three of them travelled the world under the guise of adventurers-for-hire — what better way to serve the Vermilion Eye and the international interests of Venera than to hide in plain sight? After all, the Mistress operated under similar pretenses.

The simulacrum, which hovered a few inches off the ground, was not entirely solid, as I could detect faint traces of the wall beyond its faint vermilion glimmer. And yet it seemed alive, more so than a ghost (or at least than the ghosts the Mistress and I had faced in "The Strange Case of the Ghosts of the Dog-Men," published in *The Weird Adventures of the International Mistress of Mystery*).

I murmured to myself: "What is this eerie apparition?"

In Sweet Honey's voice, the simulacrum answered: "I am the sum of all the stories and memories and dreams that make up Sweet Honey's identity. I am the oracle of Sweet Honey. Ask me anything about her, and I will answer."

Startled into silent awe, I circled the floating oracle, as if observing it from different angles could somehow explain how any of this was possible. Was this a projection of some sort? Was Sweet Honey somehow casting her voice from afar, perhaps using some variation of Alexander Graham Bell's telephone invention? Or, more likely, was I under the spell of the vermilion concoction Scheherazade had us all imbibe, suffering a series of bizarre hallucinations? Perhaps all this was an initiation ritual into the Vermilion Eye and, while I was under the suggestible mental state induced by the glittering potion, Scheherazade or Brother Nocturne or even the Mistress or perhaps the entire gathering was using the techniques of mesmerism to make me experience these unreal encounters. Yet, in the wake of my initial disorientation after drinking the vermilion wine, none of this, no matter how bizarre, felt unreal. Despite the strangeness of my circumstances, my mind was entirely awake and alert, my body fully tangible, all my senses active and taking in whatever evidence they could gather.

I essayed a query to test the simulacrum: "Is Sweet Honey herself aware of your existence and of our conversation?"

"Sweet Honey will encounter me as you are encountering me now. She will only be aware of our encounter and its particulars if she enquires about it."

"Have you spoken to others, besides myself?"

"Yes." Without further prompting, she enumerated: "Brigadier Fox, the Snow Fairy, and Brother Nocturne."

The Snow Fairy had to be the name of one of the two women I had not yet identified. Was she the old crone or the shimmering semi-presence? I pushed aside that question for now. "How did Sweet Honey come to know Eule-Königin and Le Nomade des Étoiles?"

The simulacrum answered as if she were Sweet Honey herself. "We were all of three of us already agents of the Vermilion Eye. We met here, at the Eye's Mind. I was returning to report on the death of my parents, who were also agents. According to their last report to me, they had traced a cell of the Invisible Fingers to a secret underground compound in southwest Texas. Fearing my parents might be in danger, I left the New Orleans whorehouse out of which I had been operating and set out to join them. The day before I reached El Paso, the local sheriff had stumbled on their bodies in the desert. Their corpses showed no sign of violence, but they were nonetheless dead. For seven weeks I tried to retrace their steps and locate the Invisible Fingers compound, but I failed. I made my way back to Venera rather than report by autopigeon, as I felt I needed time to recover in Venera's embrace. Upon my return to the city-goddess I met The Nomad of the Stars and the Owl-Queen. The two of them were already lovers, but they welcomed me to their bed. Afterward, I changed my assignation, no longer an undercover prostitute in the brothels of the North American continent, but a companion-in-adventure to the Nomad of the Stars and the Owl-Queen."

I realized this was my chance to learn much about Venera, the Mistress, the Vermilion Eye, and its myriad agents. And to do so more easily than I had ever thought possible.

Before I could formulate my next question, a shiver ran down my spine, as though the ambient temperature had fallen precipitously. I twisted to look all around me, a reflex that saved my life. Something sharp sliced my right cheek. It was only a superficial cut, but the wound stung and bled.

Something large, fast, and vicious had swooped past me. Had I not moved, my neck might have been fatally slashed open.

I turned to face my attacker. The vermilion glow of the tunnel and of the simulacrum was bright enough for me to make her out: it was the old crone from the meeting table. Despite her decrepit appearance, she radiated menace. Her eyes shone blood-red; her fingers ended in long gnarly claws; her posture was like that of a predator about to pounce; her mouth was open, revealing a pair of three-inch-long fangs in lieu of canines.

The mistress and I had faced such creatures before, in "The Gory Affair of the Successful Vampires" (collected in the aforementioned *The Weird Adventures of the International Mistress of Mystery*). Despite the title I gave to the case, we had defeated the monsters. Having established the nature of the danger in which I found myself, I wasted no time and took the initiative before my foe pressed her advantage. I tackled her with my left shoulder, crushing her against the stone wall. Most of her torso and parts of her arms shattered into dust, but already she was regenerating. I kicked her head with my boots — again and again. When I was certain her skull had been fully pulverized, I stopped. With her head destroyed, she could no longer regenerate.

The trick to defeating vampires was to conquer whatever instinctual fear they provoked. Yes, they were fast, bloodthirsty, violent, physically strong, naturally armed with sharp claws and fangs, and able to regenerate almost any wound, but they were also incredibly fragile, their brittle flesh and bones easy to shatter into dust. They depended on fear and surprise to overcome their prey. But with proper knowledge and courage, anyone could defeat a vampire, even if it meant suffering a few cuts and maybe even gashes. This time, I'd been lucky. I would need to wash the cut on my cheek, though, lest it get infected. When we last faced — and defeated! — such brutes, the Mistress and I had, upon her frantic urging, quickly retreated to our accommodations in Portsmouth, where we treated each other's wounds with a mixture of water, soap, witch-hazel, and Irish whiskey.

Recovering from the rush of action, I noticed that the tunnel was darker now. The simulacrum had vanished. I called out to it, but there was no answer. I did not wait for it to reappear, doubting it ever would. I needed to tend to my wound. If my only way out of this maze was to go through the entire circuit of pathways, then I should make haste and not tarry in any one location.

I wondered as I walked deeper into the tunnel: was the old crone, too, a simulacrum, or had I faced her true self? Was the attack merely an illusion, or was I truly wounded? Perhaps even already infected? Before my mind entirely lost itself in such futile entanglements about the levels of reality I was experiencing, I again found myself at a crossroads of ten paths. To solve the riddle of what was happening, there was only one way: onward. I entered the tunnel to my left.

BRIGADIER FOX

[It took me a few seconds to realize that the faint flickering illumination did not come from vermilion glitter and that the walls surrounding me were not those of the tunnel.] It is nighttime. In a small log cabin, a single candle burns. I am kneeling on the floor, my hands joined together as if in prayer. Although my father, Ignatius Fox, is a preacher, I no longer believe in his God, or perhaps in any god. I am beseeching the universe.

My name is Linus Fox. I am a deserter. Until yesterday afternoon, I was a soldier for the Union, fighting for the secession of the South from the American federation. I no longer believe that is a cause worth killing for. I question whether any cause is worth killing for, save perhaps self-preservation.

I fought because my father ordered me to. I fought because I believed I was protecting my family, my neighbours, my countrymen. But I have come to understand that the cause I was fighting for was more tarnished and complex than I was told by those with authority over me. I want no part of the corruption and duplicity of either the South or the North.

Running through my mind is a chaos of images and sensations: the stench of human waste, gore, and decay; broken men bleeding out into the soil; a cacophony of screams, cursing, weeping ...

I was lucky. I was never wounded, nor did I suffer from the ailments that struck many of my compatriots — typhoid, tuberculosis, measles, malaria, pneumonia. But I have killed dozens of men since the outbreak of this war.

I no longer want to kill. Although I understand that the fundamental savagery and selfishness of men makes killing a sometimes unavoidable outcome, I nevertheless vow to henceforth try to avoid being a killer myself.

For some reason, I recall one of my father's sermons, from six years ago, following the passage through our town of a strange Negro freewoman, claiming to be from a European land called Venera. At the time, I was only ten years old but she stood shorter than I did, shorter than many children, yet her bearing exuded the confidence of adulthood. She was radiantly beautiful, and her skin was darker than that of the darkest of slaves.

My father railed against that Negro woman, called her the bride of Satan, warned against listening to her deceitful, sinful words, warned against her lies and about her devil-worshipping nation.

Once, I had met her on the street, coming back from getting yarn for my mother at Dumont's Supply Store. Despite my father's interdictions, I was drawn to this foreigner, who seemed both harmless and kind. She said her name was Scheherazade and she described the wonders of her homeland. Her words were too strange for me to comprehend her descriptions, but I was nevertheless left with the impression that Venera was a place more beautiful and more just than anywhere else on this Earth. She gave me a piece of candy, a confection from Venera. She told me to hide it until bedtime. Then, I should plop it into my mouth and suck on it gently, letting it melt. I did so that very night. My only expectation was that it would be the most delicious candy ever. Its taste, however, was more spicy than sweet. I nevertheless savoured it, relishing, in the manner of little boys, the secret that it represented. As more of the candy's juice flowed down my throat, the exotic spicy flavour grew strangely soothing. Soon, I had segued into sleep and dream, but my dreams were neither pleasant nor welcome. I was visited by visions of savage eroticism, disturbing to a prepubescent boy raised by a preacher for whom the lure of women was the lure of sin.

Now, the savagery of eroticism seems like a welcome lure indeed, even a salve against the brutality of war.

I take an additional vow: to find Venera. If it is a land filled with women such as Scheherazade, I believe is a land I might want to call home. A better home than what I know. Perhaps, should I still yearn for action, as maybe all red-blooded men do, to their probable downfall, it is even a land I would fight for.

[A gust of wind blew out the candle, and I was once again myself, once again in the third tunnel. The gash on my cheek burned. I was afraid to touch it, lest it worry me even more. Quickly — onward! On to the next nexus of tunnels and through the next opening to my left.]

THE SNOW FAIRY

There was snow in every direction, as far as I could see. The unrelenting wind bit into my bones. I melted some of the snow by rubbing it between my hands and gently daubed the wound on my cheek with freezing water. At first it hurt more than ever, but then it felt numb. Whether that was a good omen or a bad one, I had no clue.

I walked on, trying to keep warm, but I could not help but shiver. There was no shelter in sight, no end to the unchanging snowy landscape.

After a while, I could no longer move. The only option left to me was to let the snow take me. Of all the ways I imagined I might die, this one had never occurred to me. I stood motionless, like an ice sculpture, waiting to die. After a while, I came to notice that a buzzing sound had been nagging at the edge of my consciousness.

At that moment, a small winged woman, no taller than the length of a hand, fluttered like a hummingbird right in front of my face. Her wings beat so rapidly that I could not tell if they were like those of a bird or an insect — or of some other nature entirely.

She grew to full human size and stood in the snow. I recognized her as the flickering agent of the Vermilion Eye; although she seemed a little more substantial now, making it possible to discern some aspects of her features; her narrow and long face was pointy and angular, with not even a hint of the curves that make up a human face.

She said: "Welcome to the land of my dreams. It is desolate, because, as far as I know, I am the last of my people, the last snow fairy. And even then, I barely exist, my tether to the world growing ever fainter. I yearn for the snow and ice of northern Scandinavia, the land of my ancestors, but I know I would die there, as did all of my people. I do not know what caused their extinction or their disappearance. As a youth, I was plagued with wanderlust and, unlike other snow fairies, who were sedentary and always huddled in groups, I craved for solitary adventure. I flew across the globe — seeing, tasting, experiencing the flavours of the world. One day, feeling homesick, I returned to Scandinavia, but my people were nowhere to be found. I scoured the entire north, and there was not a trace of them. Then, I noticed that I was growing less and less solid, as if I were fading from existence. I had all but vanished entirely, but I could still perceive a song, a faint melody that pulled me back into the world. I followed the song, and it led me to Venera and to the singer: Scheherazade. Her song keeps me in the world, but for how much longer I do not know."

The Snow Fairy shrank back to the size of small bird and flew away.

And the world went from white to black. For a moment, all that remained was the faint echo of Scheherazade's song in the back of my mind.

My eyes readjusted to the darkness. I walked farther ahead and found myself once again at a crossroads. I shivered one last time, and the chill seeped out of me. My wounded cheek felt tender to the touch; there was nothing I could do about my predicament but see this strange odyssey to its end. I ventured into the next tunnel to my left.

LE NOMADE DES ÉTOILES (THE NOMAD OF THE STARS)

An image appeared on the tunnel wall; it took me a few seconds to realize that it was a moving image. Against a slowly changing backdrop of planets, suns, stars, comets, and other celestial bodies, there was a name in bold golden letters: *Le Nomade des Étoiles*.

I was by then so accustomed to the constant hum of Scheherazade's song that it took me a few more seconds to realize that the images were accompanied by loud music from a string orchestra; the tune was garish — overly dramatic and dripping with sentimentality.

I had met the Nomad on a few occasions — most notably when he, Eule-Königin, Sweet Honey, the Mistress, and I joined forces to unravel "The Adventure of the Extraordinary Rogues" (from *The Daring Exploits of the International Mistress of Mystery*) — yet, despite his celebrity (some would say *notoriety*), I knew very little about him. A tall man with flowing blond hair whose features somehow managed to convey both Aryan strength and effete grace, the Nomad provoked in me an odd mixture of fascination and revulsion.

The Nomad's name faded, and both the parade of celestial bodies and the tempo of the music increased. Then the music came to a crashing halt as the image focused on a planet of blue oceans and green continents, partially draped in white clouds. A voice said: "La planète Terre." The music resumed, more softly than before, as we moved closer and closer to the surface of our planet, until settling on the wide panorama of a city I instantly recognized. On top of the scene, its name and a date faded into view: *Paris, 1866*— information that was repeated by the French narration. Where and when the Nomad made his first known appearance — defeating and apprehending a terrorist calling himself Le Sabre Algérien who was planning to set Paris ablaze in a series of well-planned arsons.

The presentation of words and moving images then went on to recount what was publicly known about Le Nomade des Étoiles: that the newspapers circulated many conflicting rumours about his origins, all billed as "exposés"; I knew from personal experience, having questioned the Nomad myself regarding some of these rumours, that the Nomad revelled in all this attention, never fully confirming nor denying anything that was said of him.

Framed from the torso up, a series of people appeared to explain or espouse these many stories regarding the origins of Le Nomade des Étoiles. Their names were spelled below their heads. Some were unknown to me, but a few were famous indeed. A man in priestly vestments explained that a small though fervent religious cult worshipped Le Nomade des Étoiles as Adam, the first man of Biblical mythology, returned from Heaven. The French novelist Jules Verne mistrusted the Nomad vehemently, accusing him of being a spy from another planet, from an otherworldly civilization, gathering intelligence in preparation for a conquest of the Earth from the stars. Another speaker agreed that he was of extraterrestrial origin but instead believed that he was stranded here due to some kind of interplanetary shipwreck. Yet another believed him to be the last survivor of another world, one that had suffered cataclysmic destruction. An elderly woman described him as a guardian angel, sent to Earth to protect us from evil. An obese man with thick spectacles claimed that the Nomad was not a living being at all but a sophisticated automaton. A disapproving Orthodox priest explained that in Greece a cult proclaimed the Nomad to be the sun god Apollo. An aged Charles Darwin (seeing the living image of man deceased more than a decade ago reminded me viscerally of the wondrous improbability of this spectacle of moving images) advanced the theory that the Nomad heralded the next stage in human evolution, further hypothesizing that any woman mating with the enigmatic personage would birth more of this new breed of human beings. H.G. Wells, a young British author, championed a similar though even more fanciful theory: that Le Nomade des Étoiles was, yes, an evolved form of human being but that he hailed from the future and had travelled through time to reach our era. (Verne was shown once more, to accuse Wells of fabricating that theory merely to help the sales of his book *The Time Machine*.) Another British author, the renowned Arthur Conan Doyle, was adamant that Le Nomade des Étoiles was in reality a fairy creature. A Parisian police inspector detailed the futile official efforts to discover the true identity of Le Nomade des Étoiles. One of the most popular theories, claimed the anonymous French narrator, was that the Nomad was a French explorer who had stumbled on the legendary Fountain of Youth.

Among what fuelled these fanciful scenarios was that, in the three decades since he had made himself known, the Nomad had not aged a day. He still looked as youthful and handsome as ever, his features classically flawless, his body perfectly toned. He seemed entirely impervious to harm or decay. Some even claimed that they had witnessed him float off the ground and fly into the sky. (I had never seen him perform such a feat.)

The date 1914 was stamped over a map of Europe. The future! The music swelled to melodramatic heights. The narrator described a war of horrific proportions, a conflict he called "la Grande Guerre." Political unrest within the Austro-Hungarian Empire somehow escalated beyond its borders, igniting long-unaddressed international tensions between the great nations of Europe. The conflict grew to involve Russia, the Ottoman Empire, parts of the Near East, Japan, and the United States. As I wondered what this had to do with the Nomad, I could only hope that the whole thing was mere speculation.

The scene shifted: the Nomad was piloting a strange winged vehicle outfitted with propellers and firearms. The view expanded to show an entire squadron of such manned machines. One by one, the vehicles started rolling, faster and faster, until they took to the skies! Would flying machines become so common two decades from now? I was informed that in 1915 the Nomad offered his services as an air pilot to the United Kingdom against Germany.

The Great War ended in 1918, to the staggering cost of ten million lives. The political map of Europe and the Near East was completely redrawn as, by then, among other changes, Russia had been swept by revolution and the Ottoman and Austro-Hungarian empires collapsed and fractured into smaller independent states or protectorates of the surviving powers. I was especially disturbed when the narrator called the conflict by yet another name: "la Première Guerre Mondiale" — the First World War. Were there yet more such horrific conflicts to come?

The moving image now showed two older women. They sat outside, at a small café table. In Paris? The French Riviera? Rome? Venice? But soon my eyes picked out peculiarities such as the erotic demonic carvings next to the door behind them and the reddish veins pulsing on the ground. This was Venera. From beyond the image a male voice asked them questions in Veneran, and they answered in the same language. I did not recognize them at first, but as they spoke and moved I realized I was looking upon Eule-Königin and Sweet Honey in their elder years. Although from the lines on their faces I guessed them at around the age of sixty or seventy years, they moved and spoke with the poise and vitality of much younger women. Was I now seeing the even more distant future of the 1920s or even the 1930s?

I did not speak Veneran, but the Owl-Queen occasionally peppered her answers with a bit of German. That, combined with those Veneran words and expressions that closely resembled Italian or French, enabled me to understand that the subject of the interview was Le Nomade des Étoiles and that his two former companions now seethed with loathing for him. I noticed that Eule-Königin, whether expressing herself in Veneran or in German, was always careful to use the German version of the nomad's name: der Nomade der Sterne. In my memory of our previous encounters, regardless of the language we spoke, she had always used his more common original French appellation. The reasons for the two women's estrangement from him escaped me, and soon the scene again changed.

The image now showed a city that it identified as Berlin, but it was much changed from the Berlin that I knew. The accompanying music took on the air of a military march, but with a pretentious operatic grandeur. The year was 1933. In the back of a motorized carriage stood a dark-haired man with a tiny moustache. He was dressed in military garb and saluted the thousands of people lined in the streets to see him with a rigid gesture, his right arm extended in front of him.

Sitting next to him, also in militaristic garb, was Le Nomade des Étoiles. I could no longer follow the narration. Previously it had been in French, but now the voice spoke in Veneran and I struggled to make sense of the words, even with the images as a guide.

The music took on tenebrous tones as what looked like a flag took up the entire image. Its body was red, and in the middle was a white circle with a black swastika in the centre. On top of that image the date of 1939 was superimposed, and the background image shifted to a massive rally, with the dark-haired moustached leader speaking to a crowd of thousands. The swastika logo was reproduced both behind him on a giant flag and on banners hanging from every possible vantage. A little behind him stood Le Nomade des Étoiles in a garish uniform that echoed the design of the swastika flag: heavy black leather boots and gloves; a skintight red bodysuit; a white circle with the black swastika in the middle of his chest; a black cape fastened over his shoulders with gold stars.

Although I understood German, I could only make out a few words that were in equal parts spat and barked by the moustached leader. Partly because of his oratorical style, partly because the sound was faint, as if coming from a great distance, partly because of static distortion that garbled some of the words, and partly because of the Veneran commentary that sporadically drowned out the leader's speech. The words *reich*, *übermensch*, and *der Nomade der Sterne* were often repeated during his oration. Finally he gave that stiff salute, which was echoed by the crowd as they chanted "Heil Hitler!" Behind the leader, der Nomade der Sterne rose off the stage. Higher and higher he floated, with his arm extended in salute and a severe gaze fixed on his face.

The crowd exploded in applause and cheers. A wide smile spread across the face of the moustached leader.

There followed, again with Veneran commentary I could not quite understand, a montage of images showing monstrous, fantastical warfare, with armoured mechanical behemoths spewing destruction from long cannons that jutted out from their tops, sleek airships dropping explosive shells on civilian and military targets, soldiers equipped with guns far more deadly and efficient than the soldiers of my era. There were images of gaunt prisoners, including women and children, being tortured and executed in prison camps. Was this the future of warfare? The future of international relations? Was this another of the "World Wars" of which "the Great War" had been — or, rather, would be — the first?

Then, under the gaze of the flying Nomade der Sterne, who directed the operation, troops bearing the swastika symbol invaded Venera, with the insular state surrounded on all sides by a naval armada. Rapid-fire guns thundered through the metropolis — a gory massacre that left at least hundreds, perhaps thousands, of Venerans dead in the streets of their city.

The image faded to black and then showed *1945*. There followed an aerial view of a city; it was identified as Berlin as letters replaced digits. The city was in ruins, many of the buildings having caved in on themselves, with rubble littering the streets everywhere. Armed foot-soldiers and armoured mechanical behemoths advanced through the devastated city facing no resistance. The music was still sombre, although in a cloying, syrupy manner.

The narrator, now speaking English with a Canadian accent, described how the European front of "the Second World War" was drawing to a close, with "Nazi Germany" (I remembered now that the Veneran narration had used the word *Nazi*, too, but I still did not understand exactly what it meant) having been defeated by the "Allied Forces." But one important conflict remained. The view rose into the sky above Berlin and it came closer and closer to two flying figures fighting each other: the Nomad of the Stars and ... the Nomad of the Stars! There were two of him!

One of them was stark naked, his perfect body reminiscent of the idealized sculptures of Classical Greece. The other bore the uniform that I had come to identify with the Nomad's German appellation, der Nomade der Sterne.

The two Nomads struggled with unbridled ferocity. But they seemed equally matched, unable to cause any visible damage to the other. Yet every punch, kick, strike, and collision caused a burst of sound and light. The harder they came at each other, the bigger the bursts became.

There was no music, no narration. Only the furious struggle between the two airborne Nomads. I was glued to the scene, observing every manoeuvre of the fight between the superhuman doppelgangers.

There came a point when the unnatural light caused by the Nomads' conflict covered the sky, the sound growing so loud that the tunnel from which I was viewing the scene seemed to tremble. The two Nomads were indefatigable. Der Nomade der Sterne's uniform had gone from pristine to tatters to nothing. The two Nomads were now both naked and thus indistinguishable from each other. And then there was a burst of almost blinding and deafening intensity. When the image of the sky was restored, neither Nomad was visible.

The view descended back to the ground. Below there was a crater of gigantic proportions, the aftermath of a devastating explosion. The narration resumed, explaining that, in the aftermath of the fight between the Nomad of the Stars and der Nomade der Sterne in the skies over Berlin, the German capital was completely obliterated, presumably killing "Adolf Hitler" (whom I assumed to be the moustached German leader), along with all Germans and Allied Forces occupying the city at that moment.

1961. The planet Earth as seen from space once more appears in the background. Then the words *The Great Disasters* replaced the year.

"In 1961," the narrator explained as the background music took on a mechanistic quality, characterized by drone-like repetition and eruptions of discordant cacophony, "the world suffered three subsequent global disasters whose causes have never been fully explained or understood. First, as March drew to a close, an ice age swept the entire planet. Continents blanketed by snow storms. Cities beset by devastating ice storms. Waterways frozen over. Glaciers advancing from both poles at the rate of dozens of metres per day." Moving images supported these pronouncements, depicting a wintery world where civilization and life itself were supplanted by endless frozen wastelands. "The sudden ice age lasted three weeks, retreating as mysteriously as it had blanketed the world. It was soon followed, in mid-June, by a drought of unprecedented severity, as global temperatures rose to nearly ten degrees centigrade higher than peak of summer averages in both north and south hemispheres with no precipitation to relieve the arid heat. Desertification advanced with alarming rapidity. Crops failed worldwide. Water reserves dried up. Diseases spread." Again, gruesome images accompanied the narration, as did more of the alienating mechanistic music. "The drought lasted twice as long as the ice age, finally breaking after six weeks, but the cure was perhaps worse than the affliction. The rainwaters finally came, but they would not stop. Water levels rose by several centimetres a day. Rivers overflowed, cities flooded, some becoming entirely submerged. The whole world was covered in rainclouds so thick that day and night became meaningless abstractions. After a full month of this onslaught, average water levels had risen by more than two metres. One of the few signs of hope during this watery apocalypse was the re-emergence of the mysterious man known as the Nomad of the Stars. He now sported a skintight black uniform upon which a panoramic starscape was in constant motion. It covered his entire body, except for his head." The Nomad's flying form was shown. "A white cape fastened to his uniform by red metallic stars completed his new attire."

I was shown scenes of the Nomad rescuing people from flooded buildings, bringing food to starving families, igniting fires to keep huddled survivors warm.

"Without explanation, the rains finally stopped in early September. The clouds parted. And water levels dropped precipitously, returning to their normal state. Around the world, people braced themselves for the next disaster, but as 1961 rolled into 1962 and then a normal cycle of winter, spring, summer, and autumn followed, people everywhere warily came to believe that the Great Disasters had come to an end. During this period, the Nomad of the Stars continued to provide relief and rescue to those in danger. Even more, the Nomad healed the sick and the infirm everywhere he went." There was a scene of the Nomad among a refugee camp. He raised his palms toward the sick and an unearthly light enveloped them, after which they were restored, healed.

"By early 1963, the entire world was embarked on a collective re-construction project. It was around that time that the Nomad once again vanished from the public eye. There was no event to mark his departure. But after a while it was noticed that he was no longer active. In part fuelled by his disappearance, the Nomad became a pop culture icon and an international sensation. He was the subject of comic books, movies, and television shows. Replicas of his uniform were top-selling novelty items. Department stores could not keep up with the demand for toys and dolls bearing his likeness." Although the language was Eng-lish, there were many words and notions I could not understand, and even the images, cascading far too quickly for me to analyse, were too alien to fully grasp. It was less than a century into the future, and I could no longer recognize or understand the world.

"By the early 1970s, the Great Disasters were almost forgotten, as if they had been nothing more than a collective nightmare, and interest in the Nomad of the Stars died completely. He was not seen again for more than a century. When he finally returned, as ageless as ever, some hailed him as a returning hero, but others saw him as a villain." *2084*. "In the 2080s, the world was visited by another strange costumed char-acter with superhuman abilities. His name was the Ultimate." There was an image of another flying man; he, too, wore a skintight uniform. Its colours were various shades of gold, from near-white to deep yellow; on the chest was a bizarre crest with a somewhat mystical aspect. His face was strangely anonymous, more like the idea of a human face rath-er than the real thing. "And his stated mission was to bring utopia to the Earth. Not everyone shared his vision of what utopia meant. Many colourful adversaries opposed him." The moving images showed strangely costumed characters with equally bizarre names, among them: Captain Thunderflash, Gameboy and the Legion of Boytoys, the Laser Leech, the Radioactive Heart, Submarineman, the Supremacist of Love, the Anti-Ultimate League. "But the only one who nearly defeated the Ultimate was the Nomad of the Stars. For more than a year, they were trapped in a stalemate, neither being able to gain the upper hand, as one or the other thwarted the other's plans, as every battle ended in a draw, as every strategy failed to resolve their conflict. Unlike the Ultimate's other enemies, the Nomad of the Stars did not merely combat him, but he also faced him in the arena of public opinion, campaigning against the Ultimate's utopian agenda, claiming that the Ultimate's plan was not a solution to humanity's problems and warning the global populace to be wary of anyone claiming to be a prophet of utopia. Both the Ultimate and the Nomad of the Stars were charismatic figures, and the odds were even as to which of these two would eventually prevail and fully capture the collective imagination of the public. But the Nomad's past as der Nomade der Sterne — as a super-soldier for the Third Reich — was used against him, shattering his credibility. And so the Ultimate defeated the Nomad of the Stars, who once again vanished, this time for nearly a thousand years."

By then I had entirely given up being able to fully understand what was being related. Too many words, too many concepts were completely unknown to me, and the narrator assumed a familiarity with cultural and historical information that was entirely foreign and incomprehensible.

3057. In the background, a map of the world. Although I recognized the shape of the continents, the political boundaries were unfamiliar, which was not surprising given the amount of time that had now elapsed since my own era. The narration continued, still in English.

"When the Nomad of the Stars resurfaced, humanity was once again on the brink of global conflict. The world was divided into four spheres of influence. The Americas, along with most of the small islands in both the Atlantic and Pacific oceans, were ruled by the High Aztec Empire. Africa was under the aegis of the Dynasty of the Pharaoh of the New Sun. Western, Northern, and Central Europe, as well as the islands of the Mediterranean, were now called the Community of Venera. Most of Asia, along with Russia, the Arabian Peninsula, the Antipodes, and the archipelagos of the Indian Ocean and the Pacific Coast, and parts of Eastern Europe fell under the dominion of the Caliphate of the Trimurti Buddha, the largest and most populous of the four superpowers. Although the Dynasty, the Aztecs, and Venera were not formal allies, they had no designs on each other's territories. The Caliphate, however, was an empire predicated on religious conversion to Zen Islam, and there were tensions along many of its borders. The Aztecs had ceded the circumpolar territories from Alaska to Greenland to the Caliphate at the end of the Northern Wars of the 2880s, and there had been global peace ever since. But there was a feeling that under the new caliph, Vladimir XI, the Eastern superpower would now once again seek to expand its borders and political and religious influence. The Caliphate fortified its military presence in the Circumpolar Territories of North America, under the wary gaze of the High Aztec emperor, Ernesto Águila. The stretch of Egyptian land that once linked Africa to the Arabian Peninsula had been destroyed in the Jihad Wars of the 23rd century, but the Caliphate eyed Egypt and Sudan greedily across the expanded Red Sea. However, the borders the Caliphate shared with the Community of Venera were in more heavily populated areas and were more contentiously defined. The Veneran province of Turkey was surrounded to the East by the Buddhist provinces of Greater Persia and Russia. The province of Scandinavia jutted against the Russian north. The Veneran provinces of Deutschlandia, Hungary, and Romania shared uneasy borders with the Buddhist provinces of Poland, United Czechoslovakia, and Greater Ukraine. The Avatar of Venera wanted to avoid war and feared she would be the caliph's first target should armed conflict erupt."

The image presented a view of the island city Venera, where, even in the distant future, vegetation and architecture were oddly confused in unsettling shapes and configurations from the dreams and nightmares of deranged artists, where ethereal lights pulsed to the beat of the fantastical city-state's heart.

"A meeting was held in the capital of the Community of Venera, at the Eye's Mind, the headquarters of the Veneran secret service, the Vermilion Eye. In attendance were: representing the High Aztec Empire, Emperor Ernesto Águila and his military advisor Paloma Moreno; from the Dynasty of the Pharaoh of the New Sun, the First Queen Fatima Isis and the Pharaoh's official ambassador to Venera, Inira Suez; and, standing for Venera, the Avatar of Venera herself and Director Magus Amore of the Vermilion Eye."

In procession, the six of them entered a meeting room and sat at a table. Emperor Águila was a short white-haired man with an easy smile. His head was adorned with a bejewelled eagle crown; he was dressed in a sleeker version of a gentleman's dinner jacket, but its colours were flamboyant, like the plumage of a brightly hued bird. Advisor Moreno sported military garb heavily laden with gold and effigies of eagles; her head was shaved bald and a dark band fit snuggly against the circumference of her skull and completely hid her eyes. Queen Isis and Ambassador Suez were distinguishable from each other by the number and size of the jewellery that adorned their otherwise entirely naked bodies, the First Queen being more copiously decorated than the ambassador; they resembled each other like sisters, or at least cousins. Magus Amore looked ancient beyond words, every inch of desiccated skin that peeked from his simple robe intricately tattooed, his hair so long I wondered if it had ever been cut. In a lotus position, the Avatar of Venera floated and rotated a few inches off the surface of the meeting table, having positioned herself at its centre. She shone brightly of vermilion, making it difficult to look directly at her or clearly distinguish her form.

The narration ended, replaced by the sound from the meeting. The six dignitaries spoke in a cacophony of languages, none of which I could understand. At least an hour went by, if time meant anything in this dreamlike labyrinth. Unable to understand the proceedings I was witnessing, my attention wandered back to the throbbing of my wounded cheek.

Just as I decided to leave, Le Nomade des Étoiles walked into the meeting room, looking in this far future exactly as young as he did in my era and still wearing the same uniform as when he'd reappeared during the Great Disasters and when he'd opposed the Ultimate. He addressed the dignitaries in a language that I assumed to be some future form of Veneran. They all continued to talk in their various foreign tongues. I presumed at this point that the Nomad was immortal and that his story would never end. The narrative had progressed so far beyond my own era that I could not see what useful intelligence I might glean from it. So I walked away, deeper into the tunnel, to once again find myself at a crossroads of ten paths.

Again, I chose the tunnel to my immediate left.

SISTER BLOOD

The noise hurt my ears. This sixth tunnel was filled with phosphorescent spectral monsters: intangible screaming vampires, which I recognized as such by their fangs, talon-like fingernails, and leathery wings. They wisped through the air, passing through me and in and out of the vermilion-flecked walls. Although their physical shapes could not harm me, their screeches stabbed into my brain like sharp needles.

I would not linger in this tunnel. I ran forward, expecting to soon exit at the next crossroads, but this tunnel went on farther than any of the previous ones. It became too hard to breathe; the muscles of my legs were sore, my stomach cramping. I collapsed on the ground and pressed my hands against my ears, which barely muffled the painful wails of the ghostly vampires.

A vampire ghost huddled in front of me. I recognized her: the old crone who had attacked me and whom I had killed in self-defense.

Unlike the others, she did not scream. Instead, softly, she spoke in a Russian accent. "I know who you are."

Not wanting to linger on the subject of my identity, I asked her: "And you — who are you?"

"To the Vermilion Eye, I was Sister Blood. My human name ceased to matter a long time ago. Now you have destroyed me; no name matters anymore."

She moved swiftly, her ghostly fangs digging into my wounded cheek. Startled and terrified that I could feel this ghost's touch, I sprang up and bolted deeper into the tunnel. This time, I was successful and found myself at the next nexus of tunnels.

My cheek throbbed more painfully than ever. I reached up to probe the wound, and fresh blood stained my fingers.

THE INTERNATIONAL MISTRESS OF MYSTERY

The seventh tunnel was even longer than the sixth. I walked for what seemed like days — long, monotonous, unchanging days punctuated only by my need to relieve myself. My grey urine stank of decay.

Although this tunnel was as dark as any other, I found that I could now see quite well. All my senses seemed sharper, as if they were now actively analysing my surroundings with predatory keenness.

Eventually, I spotted a figure standing in the distance at the mouth of the tunnel, blocking the entrance to the next crossroads. No matter how far I walked, though, the figure grew no closer. I broke into a run — this time it did not exhaust me. I ran faster and faster, with uncommon strength and vigour.

The distant figure still did not grow any closer.

I ran faster and faster. Faster and faster. Faster ... until my feet left the ground and I flew toward the figure. I batted my arms and leathery wings sprouted from my sides, shredding my clothes.

Finally, I neared the figure. I stopped before we collided and landed on my feet in front of her — the International Mistress of Mystery. She held a simple unadorned wooded box to her chest.

She said: "Is it really you, my boy? You've changed so much." Her voice was sadder than I'd ever heard it, with not a trace of the impatient sternness that usually peppered her every inflection. She said: "I know who you are." Sister Blood had said the same thing. Did they all know?

I said: "I don't know what's real and what's not anymore. Is it really you, Mistress? Or are you simply an illusion or a simulacrum?"

She ignored me. Instead, she continued: "Within this box is everything there is to know about me." She extended her arms and offered me the box. "Take it. Open it. Learn everything you've so yearned to uncover."

Her posture looked resigned and defeated, but her gaze — she looked directly into my eyes — was suffused with tenderness.

Without warning, rage erupted within me. I moved faster than I believed I could. I slapped the box away; it shattered, empty, against the walls of the tunnel. I dug my fangs into the Mistress's neck. I drank her. I drank all of her.

BROTHER NOCTURNE

I staggered, weeping, along the next tunnel.

I became gradually aware of the repetitive sound of a walking stick striking the ground. A little boy of roughly eight to eleven years, judging by his height, walked at my side. He was dressed in a miniature version of Brother Nocturne's costume.

With his free hand he grabbed mine, and we walked together in companionable and oddly comforting silence.

I avoided looking at, or acknowledging, what my hands had become.

Soon, there appeared at our feet faint spectres of bloodied corpses; judging by their wounds, they'd been savaged by a blade of some sort. There were adults and children of various ages. After all I had witnessed and experienced so far in these tunnels, this gory apparition was not enough to evoke more than a mild curiosity. Somewhat perfunctorily, I asked my companion if he knew who these people had been.

He replied with the voice a young British boy: "Yes. They were my family. Parents, siblings, uncles, aunts, cousins, grandparents. And the house staff. It happened at my mother's birthday. I am the only survivor."

There was something dead and unforgiving his tone. I had no choice but to ask: "Did you kill them?"

"That's what I told the police. They believed me. But, in truth, the only one who died at my hands was my twin brother. He left me no choice. I loved him more than anything or anyone in the world." It was too easy to deduce what he carefully left unsaid.

I asked one final question: "What was his name?"

"Robert." He volunteered more information. "Mine was William. But no longer. Now, I am only Brother Nocturne."

We stopped talking as we continued our walk, our hands still clasped. Eventually, the litter of corpses faded away.

With the voice of the adult Brother Nocturne, my childlike companion broke the silence. "Now, this current situation has become far messier and bloodier than I'd expected, although I suspect Scheherazade knew exactly how this would turn out. Even I can't always follow the layers of machinations behind her plans for Venera."

I said: "Aren't you going to fight me?"

"Why should I do that? Either I kill you or you kill me. Or maybe we both wound each other gravely. What's gained with any of that? Nothing. You've already killed two agents of the Vermilion Eye."

"So that was the real Mistress and not an illusion? Despite every-thing, I truly loved her. She meant more to me than anyone."

Brother Nocturne answered swiftly, his tone dismissive. "We all tell ourselves the stories we need to believe. Regardless, I want no further casualties. You need to speak with Scheherazade. You need to hear which story she has in mind for you." At the mention of her name, I realized that I could still hear, in the back of my mind, a faint echo of her melody.

He let go of my hand. I looked at him. He waved goodbye with his walking stick as he vanished into the shadows. I had not moved but I was now standing at the next crossroads. There was an explosion, and the entrance to the tunnel behind me collapsed, sealing off that path. Instead of the customary ten tunnels, this junction offered only two remaining doorways.

REFLECTIONS

I did not want to continue, to choose either of the two offered paths. I was weary and bereft, unsure, despite what Brother Nocturne had claimed, if anything I had experienced and learned was real and true. Was my journey through this labyrinth some cruel confinement of lies and illusion, a trap I had not anticipated and had naively fallen into?

I sat on the ground with my eyes closed. If I waited long enough, if I refused to go on and play this game, the Vermilion Eye would come to me on my own terms, to whatever extent I was still able to determine my own fate.

But Scheherazade's song nagged at me, spurred me to action, despite my resolve. I struggled against the impulse to get up and resume my jour-ney through these tunnels of the mind. There were only two paths left. I presumed one was a tunnel through my own memories, and the pros-pect of being forced to confront myself felt unbearably odious. The other path no doubt led to Scheherazade herself — a prospect even more unsettling than facing myself, though I did not understand why the idea of this diminutive woman provoked such anxiety in me.

I waited with all my will. I waited until I could tolerate it no longer, until Scheherazade's relentless song left me no choice but to stand and walk into the next tunnel.

One step was in darkness, the next in nearly blinding brightness.

Mirrors. All around me were mirrors. As my eyes adjusted, I tried but could not locate the source of the intense light. I avoided looking at the image that was reflected from an infinity of angles. The image of who I had become. Of what I had become.

There are those vampires who may ambulate among the human population; yes, they all look gruesome to some extent, but not all are so bestial at a casual glance. I had not transformed into one of those vampires.

My clothes were in tatters, revealing that my entire body was now covered in dark grey fur. My features had become ratlike, with only the faintest resemblance to the human face I'd once borne. My ears were like those of a giant bat's. My canine teeth had grown into three-inch-long fangs. Leathery wings sprouted from the sides of my torso, attached to my hands, which ended in six-inch-long gnarly fingernails.

The reflected images changed from showing the one thing — my new monstrous self — to depicting a mosaic of scenes from my past. My bland unexceptional childhood as the son of an unambitious government clerk and a doting mother in London. My first meeting with the Mistress, when she solved the brutal murder of my younger sister at the hands of a police inspector. My recruitment at the service of the Invisible Fingers, in the Paris catacombs, in the midst of my third adventure with the Mistress, "The Seduction of the Romanian Beauty" (from *The Continental Cases of the International Mistress of Mystery*). The riches the Invisible Fingers had promised me! But those paled beyond my sense of indignant self-righteousness. The Mistress, to whom I had freely given my complete devotion, had lied to me, the Parisian representative of the Invisible Fingers revealed. She was not loyal to the United Kingdom; she secretly served the nefarious nation of Venera as an agent of the Vermilion Eye. The Invisible Fingers — a cabal of private businessmen from Great Britain, France, Belgium, the Netherlands, Germany, and Italy — sought to counter and halt the insidious operations of the Vermilion Eye inside the borders of unsuspecting nations. I knew very little about the workings of the world, but I knew I wanted to avenge this betrayal. I began to doubt the veracity of anything she had ever told me, including the identity of my sister's killer. Continue to play your role as the Mistress's assistant, I was told. And report to us. You will play an essential role in safeguarding Europe.

Scheherazade's song prompted a host of self-examining questions. I rebelled against this intrusion into my psyche. I lashed out, jumped into the air, and flew into the mosaic of mirrors.

THE STORY CONTINUES

I was back in the meeting room where the ten of us — myself, the Mistress, Brigadier Fox, Brother Nocturne, Sister Blood, Le Nomade des Étoiles, Eule-Königin, Sweet Honey, the Snow Fairy, and Scheherazade — had initially gathered.

I sat in the same seat I'd occupied at the outset of this strange journey. However, I was not the man I had been; I had truly become a vampire. My flesh was lacerated by shards of broken glass, with blood oozing onto my fur. I remembered how fragile we vampires were, surprised that the collision with the mirrors had not damaged me more severely. Already my wounds were healing. Fragile, yes, but ever so resilient.

Most of the agents were no longer here. Next to me lay the corpse of the Mistress, her head twisted unnaturally, showing the wounds my fangs had inflicted on her throat. Across the table, sat the headless remains of Sister Blood. That left only one other agent of the Vermilion Eye here with me: Scheherazade.

Her song had ended. The silence was both soothing and oppressive.

Scheherazade sipped more of the vermilion wine, looking at me impassively.

Finally I said: "Who are you?"

She said: "I am the story, and the teller of story."

What did that mean? Sensing that it was a futile avenue of inquiry, I said: "What now?"

She inclined her head toward the entrance to the room. The door was open. She stood up and held her hand to me.

I rubbed my palms to get rid of any lingering shards, then I broke off the ends of my ridiculously long fingernails. I rose and took hold of Scheherazade's tiny hand. Her grip was astonishingly strong, like that of a burly workman. Its touch was cool, like the hands of women often are, but it also pulsed with a feverish heat that left me dizzy.

Hand in hand, we climbed the stairs. We encountered no-one. During our ascent, my sense of unease increased. I did not feel safe in the company of Scheherazade, even though I physically towered over her childlike body, yet I dared not take back my hand. We reached the roof of the Eye's Mind. It was nighttime, and all around us Venera shone with ethereal beauty, seductive, alluring. Scheherazade also shone with that same seductive and alluring beauty. Yet, despite that glamour, both the city and this woman — both of them at once too real and too unreal — filled me with dread.

I would not fight or attack Scheherazade. I suspected that my will was no longer my own in this matter. My fate was in her hands. I no longer knew which cause I believed in, if any. The Vermilion Eye. The Invisible Fingers. The British Empire. What was the purpose of the existence of such impersonal entities? What good could come of such enterprises? With the Mistress, I had led a life of adventure and, yes, of love — however odd and uncomfortable the Mistress's expression of love might have been. That was the only truth that mattered to me now.

Scheherazade addressed me in that language of hers that seemed to transcend all languages. I hunched low, to look her in the face. "Your story here is ended. There is another story awaiting you. But it is not here, not in Venera."

She kissed me, licking my lips and my fangs. This intimate contact was not sensual but threatening. Into my ear she whispered a brief melody — a set of coded instructions my conscious mind was not meant to understand? — then let go of my hand.

I leapt into the sky and flapped my wings. Was I fleeing or following the path Scheherazade had decided for me? Was there a difference? I flew away from Venera, across the Mediterranean, having no idea what would come next.

THE SURREALIST LANTERNS
(JUNE 1982)

❧

I. OCTAHEDRON: AIR

The Octahedron lantern pulses in the dark, interrupting Dalí's mournful prayers. Who would be so callous as to call him tonight of all nights? The guests have left; Dalí has dismissed even the house staff. He wants to be alone — alone with his God and with the memories of his beloved Gala, his muse, buried here at their home, the Castle of Púbol, a few hours ago.

But the incessant pulse of the lantern nags at the 78-year-old surrealist. Dalí has produced only a handful of each of the five geometric lanterns, and few people know how to access their properties — for example, that the Octahedron allows for the instantaneous transmission of light and sound not only anywhere on Earth but anywhere across time and space in all possible universes. Propping himself up with his cane, he resigns himself to the intrusion.

He touches one of the lantern's eight faces, which causes a V of light to emanate, forming a shimmering window from which a voice issues.

"Dalí, my friend! I have now just heard the sad news. I wish I could have been there for you, been there to pay my respects to Gala. I was on a shoot, cloistered, finishing my new film — our film, I should say. We will dedicate the film to Gala. Together, my friend, we have created a masterpiece, brought forth by your masterful script and storyboards. The world has never seen the like of *Visions in Vermilion*. Never!"

The usually garrulous Catalonian cannot bring himself to respond to his friend. Behind Tito Bronze, Dalí can perceive just enough of his caller's surroundings to know that Bronze is sitting in his study at the Velvet Bronzemine, the filmmaker's decadent Veneran mansion, which Dalí himself designed, with the help of the young architect and inventor Hemero Volkanus.

Bronze continues: "My dear friend, I apologize. Forgive my unseemly enthusiasm."

Dalí nods, wiping tears from his eyes. He cannot imagine that he will ever stop mourning. Well, he has not long left on this mortal plane. His health has been poor these past few years. Soon, God will call him.

"Dalí — are you alone in that huge, desolate Spanish castle of yours?"

"Tito, I am in no mood for company, nor for conversation. Leave me be. I will call you in a few days. When I am at least a shadow of Dalí, for I doubt that, without Gala, and with my faculties failing, I will ever be more than that again. But now, tonight, I am less than a smudge."

"Of course, my friend." But Tito does not break the connection.

"Your tone does not match your words. Please, leave me be for now." The surrealist pleads.

"I want to object, to implore you to seek the closeness of those who love you, to not isolate yourself, but I won't. I will leave you with this: my home is your home, always, and I would be honoured if you were to come stay at the Velvet Bronzemine. Venera is the only city in the world that is a match for Dalí. It is where your home should be; here, among those who share and understand your passion for art and imagination. I could show you the rushes of our new film. Show you that Dalí will once again startle, shock, and amaze the world!"

"Your enthusiasm and friendship are dear to me, my young friend. But tonight there is no Dalí — there is only Salvador Domingo Felipe Jacinto Dalí i Domènech — a tired, bereaved old man who knows that death is near and who will graciously welcome it whenever it finally chooses to visit. Goodnight, Tito. Goodnight." Dalí breaks the connection and shambles to his bedroom.

But the surrealist cannot sleep. His old, aching body cannot settle into comfort or repose. His mind is besieged with nightmarish distorted memories of his life with his beloved Gala. As the night progresses, he grows more restless, his disquieting visions growing more disturbing, more vivid. Finally at the first, faint hints of dawn, after hours spent tossing and turning, his heart growing ever heavier with grief, Dalí lugs himself out of bed, grabs his cane with his left hand, and slowly makes his way to his study.

There, his left arm shaking as he struggles to retain his balance with his cane, he pauses before the niche where rests his personal set of the five surrealist lanterns: the Tetrahedron, its four triangular faces evoking the flames of fire and the mathematics of architecture; the Hexahedron, the perfect cube representing the tactility of earth, the substance of the real world; the Octahedron, the aerodynamicism of its eight triangular faces evoking the classic element air; the Dodecahedron, the whole of its twelve pentagonal faces being a portal to the wilds of art and creation; and the Icosahedron, its twenty identical equilateral triangular faces symbolizing both the intricacies of structure and the fluidity of water.

There are four other sets of these lanterns, scattered among friends, patrons, and collectors around the world. Few are cognizant of the lanterns' surrealist properties, thinking of them as merely decorative. Even among those, like Dalí's friend Tito Bronze, who are aware that the lanterns are much more than they appear, only a fraction of the lanterns' true attributes are known. Sometimes Dalí worries at having created such dangerous artefacts. Only God should wield such power. But the call of art and creation cannot and should not be denied or suppressed. He imagined the lanterns, therefore he created them.

As the sun rises, Dalí feels a faint optimism seeping into his dark mood. His thoughts turn to Tito Bronze, whom, it is true, he misses. Dalí does not expect to have much time left before his body expires. It is also true that Venera is one of the greatest wonders of the universe, and he would be deeply saddened should he never see it again.

As dawn gradually gives way to morning, Dalí collapses into his armchair, contemplating his brief future.

... Until the house staff returns promptly at eight o'clock; Dalí instructs his manservant to pack his bags and bring them to the stables. Dalí is going to Venera, after all. He almost calls Tito to inform him, but a dribble of the mischievous remains in Dalí despite the darkness of his waning years and he decides to surprise his old friend.

Dalí trusts his man to pack his clothes and other necessities, but the artist wants to bring his lanterns; those, he encases himself. The artist will bequeath the lanterns to Tito, along with all their secrets. More, he will task his friend with the recovery of the remaining surrealist lanterns, lest their power fall into the wrong hands. Dalí has to think seriously about his legacy, and there is no-one living he trusts more than the extravagant filmmaker.

Besides, the power of the surrealist lanterns would not disrupt or destroy the decadent city-state: Venera is already suffused with more surrealist energy and creativity than the rest of the world combined. The lanterns should be safe there and not attract undue attention.

Dalí's manservant lugs the case, as he did the rest of the artist's baggage, to the stables, but this time under Dalí's watchful eye.

Dalí can sense that the house staff thinks he has lost his mind, but they all obey him nevertheless. The door to the stables is five storeys tall, built onto a stone frame. It is a door that seems to lead to nowhere. The stone frame juts out of the earth amid the castle grounds, a door on one side, a blank wall on the other. The artist knows they all believe this to be a sculpture, but as is the case with much of Dalí's art it contains secrets few know or even suspect.

Dalí, dressed for travel, his luggage by the door to the stables, takes out a large bronze key, which he himself sculpted, from an inner pocket of his coat, and unlocks the giant, gilded door.

The door opens inward, into Dalí's imagination. Dalí sings in melancholy tones, calling his favourite animal.

Immediately, the space elephant steps out from the door to the stables; Dalí chants his instructions to the massive beast with the impossibly long and thin legs. With its trunk, the elephant loads the artist's luggage into the carriage on its back. Then, it picks up Dalí and delicately deposits him in the rider's seat.

Off they go! First, south — from the shores of Catalonia to the waters of the Mediterranean. The space elephant steps into the deep waters; its legs are so long that its bulky pachyderm body is still hundreds of metres above sea level. Rider and beast continue eastward at the speed of Dalí's imagination. Within seconds the Italian mainland,

Sicily, and the Venera archipelago are all within sight. The travellers slow down as they near the port of Venera. But as they approach the city-state the surrealist notices that something is dreadfully wrong. The garish beauty of the metropolis, its lush biomechanical architecture, its mazelike streets that confound visitors have given way to a drab grey grid bereft of greenery, mystery, and sensuality, as if another city altogether — a dead one — had crushed and then superimposed itself on surreal, fantastical Venera.

And worse: scattered on the ground are the bullet-ridden corpses of hundreds of people, their clothes as ash-grey as the rest of the city, the pools of their dried blood the only colour in the urban landscape.

2. HEXAHEDRON: THE WORLD

Still atop the space elephant, Dalí turns to his lantern case. He opens it and takes out the Hexahedron, the perfect cube that encompasses all that is real in linear spacetime. He points the lantern toward the mundane dregs of what was once the most resplendent city on Earth, and he twists it so that the time-image will move backward. He fast-rewinds until the view of Venera is restored to its customary glory, from twelve hours ago, mere minutes after he last spoke to his Veneran friend Tito Bronze.

Dalí lets the scenario play out …

3. TETRAHEDRON: FIRE

In the moonlight of the previous evening, a group of five men parachutes down into Venera. Dalí zooms in to get a better view. The men are all wearing identical dark grey business suits, cut to the latest in Italian fashion. Their heads are shaven, and their features are hidden behind black facemasks in the Venetian style. Each man carries a black briefcase. On each briefcase is emblazoned a golden eagle clutching a bundle of wooden sticks in which is embedded an axe blade, the fasces — together, the symbol of Italian fascism.

During the Second World War, Hitler's Nazis and Mussolini's Fascists together occupied Venera — one of the darkest eras the city-state's history ... Dalí wonders, are these neofascists with a decades-old grudge against Venera for never supporting Mussolini?

A crowd of Venerans — mostly women, as the population is reputed to be at least seventy percent female — begins to gather around the five men.

One of the five neofascists walks slightly ahead of the other four, who flank him and shield him. These four men pull out miniature assault rifles from their jackets and start mowing down the Venerans. Amid this carnage, the first man crouches and opens his briefcase; he pulls something from it and stands up, holding high in his hands ... a Tetrahedron lantern. A Tetrahedron lantern created by Dalí.

The neofascist chants while manipulating Dalí's sculpture; surreal fire erupts from the lantern and engulfs the whole of Venera.

When the flames subside all the beauty of Venera has been burned away, and there remains only the drab, ash-grey husk Dalí witnessed when he arrived at the shores of Venera. The five neofascists are nowhere to be seen, but Dalí is under no illusion that they perished. They are at large, wielding the power of at least one surrealist lantern. Dalí dreads what those other four briefcases might contain ...

Dalí weeps that his art could be responsible for such devastation, such ugliness. More than ever, he knows that all the surrealist lanterns must be recovered — and maybe even destroyed.

4. ICOSAHEDRON: WATER

But first things first: Dalí must repair the damage; he must call upon all his creative energy to restore Venera. He is old and tired and ready to give up mortal life whenever God should decide to call him to Heaven, but for now he is still alive — and he is still Dalí!

The artist carefully puts away the Hexahedron into his carrying case, then he pulls out the Icosahedron, which symbolizes water and structure. With its help, Dalí hopes to achieve his goal.

It is rumoured that Venera is not only a city but a goddess, that the city and the goddess are two manifestations of the same divine entity. It is said, too, that Venera is a water goddess: at every gibbous moon the waters of Venera flow red with her menses. Or at least it did when she was alive. Yes, alive. Because the city, whatever its true nature, was alive. She bled like a woman. She was sensuous and beautiful, like a woman. But now she is all but dead, a shadow, a smudge of its true self. Will she still bleed with life come the next gibbous moon?

The artist instructs his space elephant to crouch down below the surface of the sea. As beast and rider submerge, the Icosahedron lantern envelops the pair inside an air bubble in the corresponding shape of an icosahedron. Following Dalí's commands, the space elephant circles the main island of Venera, the capital of the archipelago. The Icosahedron — the water lantern — siphons whatever divine spark might linger in the waters of Venera.

Around and around they go, until the lantern glows, indicating that is charged and ready.

How long were Dalí and his space elephant underwater? Hours? Days? Longer? The artist does not know, but as the beast surfaces he notes that it is now past nightfall and that the moon is gibbous. Dalí despairs momentarily, as the waters of Venera are not, as they should be, flowing red with the menses of the goddess. Can Dalí truly restore to life this divine city?

When he was a young man, yes, of course ... but he is so old now, and so tired. And his muse, his wife, his Gala, has died. The aged surrealist sighs, the aches of his 78-year-old body reverberating in the outtake of breath.

Nevertheless, the septuagenarian musters his will, his energy, his creativity, his lust for art. The world needs him to be Dalí — who but Dalí can save Venera?

The surrealist wields the Icosahedron lantern; torrents of blood-red waters — the waters of life — flow from the lantern and wash over the moribund city-state. The waters are so voluminous that the island nation is submerged. The vermilion-red waters glow in the light of the gibbous moon. The waves wash over Venera all through the night. Relentless and determined, Dalí focuses his creative will through the Icosahedron, breathing art and life into Venera.

5. DODECAHEDRON: CREATION

As the sun rises, the vermilion-red waters recede; Venera is revealed, reborn, as strange and beautiful as it should be. The whole city glistens in the sunlight, still damp from its watery rebirth.

At first, the resuscitated Venerans wander the vias in a dazed stumble, but then some of them catch sight of Dalí atop his space elephant. A crowd gathers and grows by the water. The Venerans whisper and chatter among each other. The voices are too dim and too far away for Dalí to decipher what is being said; besides, Dalí has always struggled to make sense of the Veneran dialect.

Then one voice booms over the rest: "Dalí! Dalí has saved Venera!" It is his friend Tito Bronze, wielding a handheld camera, filming the surrealist and his space elephant.

The crowd takes up the chant: "Dalí! Dalí! Dalí!"

The aged surrealist soaks up the adulation, almost forgetting the pain in his bones, almost forgetting how profoundly exhausted he is, almost forgetting the grief at having so recently lost his beloved Gala. If only he could revive her as he has revived Venera ... But, no, Gala was mortal, whereas Venera and all who inhabit her exist beyond the mundane world.

Dalí's thoughts are interrupted by his lanterns. All five of them rise from their casings, blinking and ringing in alarm. Other surrealist lanterns are active in close proximity ...

Dalí's five levitating lanterns form an X, with the Dodecahedron in the centre. A beam of surreal light issues from the Dodecahedron, locating the source of the other lantern activity: the five neofascists stand in a circle on a Veneran rooftop, each of them wielding a different surrealist lantern. A dark roar of energy builds around the quintet ...

There is no time to lose; Venera is again in deadly danger. Dalí grabs the Dodecahedron lantern and dons it as a helmet, its stand reversed, pointed antenna-like on top of the artist's head. The other four lanterns congregate and attach themselves to the makeshift helmet. Dalí becomes imbued with the faculties of all five lanterns, as filtered through the most powerful of them all, the lantern of creation, the Dodecahedron; Dalí is transformed into the Surrealist Lantern, courageous and relentless protector of madness, beauty, and art.

The Surrealist Lantern speeds through the sky toward the neofascist usurpers of the lanterns' powers.

On the ground, Tito Bronze shouts: "Lights! ..."

The Surrealist Lantern glows with the power and intensity of Dalí's imagination.

"... Camera! ..." Bronze points his camera toward the rooftop where the neofascists are assembled as the Surrealist Lantern confronts them.

" ... Action!"

And the fight is on, with the fate of Venera in the balance. The fate of madness and art and beauty. The stakes for which Dalí has always fought and will always fight, to his dying breath.

INTERLUDE

THE PHANTASMAGORICAL ODYSSEYS OF SCHEHERAZADE

THE PHANTASMAGORICAL ODYSSEY OF SCHEHERAZADE: A CRYPTOMYTHOLOGICAL BIOGRAPHY
by Jane Zacks

[from the Albion Pulp Press catalogue]

MOST SCHOLARS BELIEVE SCHEHERAZADE to be nothing more than the fictional storyteller of *The Arabian Nights*, nothing more than a narrative device that enabled the gathering of fantastical tales from various cultures across North Africa, the Middle East, the Indian sub-continent, and parts of Asia as far as China. The genesis of *The Arabian Nights* itself is complex and tangled — is the original prototype Persian, Indian, or ...? — but Scheherazade's story is even more multifaceted, reaching far beyond the confines of *The Arabian Nights* scholarship. Anthropologist Jane Zacks traces the origins of Scheherazade to the dawn of language and religion and ties the creative energy of a young Ethiopian woman from 300,000 years ago to the development of human art and culture. Most controversially, Zacks claims that Scheherazade's history and that of the enigmatic, isolationist city-state Venera are profoundly entwined and that Scheherazade might still be alive today, engaged in a secret civil war with its current rulers, the Venera Church of Mother Earth.

Prologue: The Lure of Vermilion
Zacks recounts her initial visit to Venera and her first taste of vermilion spice in the underground ruins of the city-state — the event that led to the study of Scheherazade becoming her life's work.
Chapter 1: The Primordial Days and Nights of Scheherazade
The life of a female child in prehistoric Ethiopia.
Chapter 2: The Invention of Story
The young Scheherazade invents storytelling.

Chapter 3: Gods and Demons and Fantasy, Oh My!

Did Scheherazade create all the gods and demons and fantastical creatures of the world, or were they drawn to the magic of her story-telling?

Chapter 4: The Storyteller within the Story

Becoming herself a character in her own stories, Scheherazade tours the world, leaving in her wake a wealth of myths, legends, fantastical beasts, and sacred rituals. Her time in China and India provides glimpses into the early precursors of The Arabian Nights.

Chapter 5: The Epic of Scheherazade

Scheherazade spends centuries in the Near East and Asia Minor of antiquity, the so-called "cradle of civilization." Her many contributions to that seminal time in history include creating the earliest version of The Epic of Gilgamesh; *assuming the identity of the poet-priestess Enheduanna, the "daughter" of King Sargon; being involved in the Tower of Babel incident; and planting more story-telling seeds that would eventually grow into* The Arabian Nights.

Chapter 6: A Girl and Her Goddess

The early friendship of Scheherazade and the goddess Venera.

Chapter 7: The Lure of Vermilion

On an island in the Mediterranean, Scheherazade and the goddess Venera discover the properties of vermilion and found a city unlike any other.

Chapter 8: The Arabian Nights of Scheherazade

As the Goddess Venera becomes increasingly preoccupied with the city, religion, and archipelago that bear her name, she and Scheherazade grow apart. For centuries Scheherazade travels throughout the area from North Africa to China, further fuelling and cementing the literary tradition that will one day coalesce into The Arabian Nights.

Chapter 9: The Vermilion Eye

Scheherazade returns to Venera. During her absence, the city-state was twice invaded, first by the Romans, then, centuries later, by the Vikings. The goddess and the storyteller resume their alliance, founding the Vermilion Eye to protect the archipelago from further military incursions.

Chapter 10: Agent of the Vermilion Eye
Scheherazade's covert involvement with world affairs and history as an agent of the Vermilion Eye.
Chapter 11: The Bondage of Scheherazade
The Vermilion Eye is betrayed by its agent Le Nomade des Étoiles, leading to the Fascist invasion of Venera and the capture and imprisonment of Scheherazade.
Chapter 12: Bram Jameson
As a child, the future author Bram Jameson ran free in occupied Venera, as chronicled in his 1987 book Empire of the Self, *but there he fails to mention how he singlehandedly freed Scheherazade from Nazi bondage, leading to the liberation of Venera and to young Jameson's recruitment as an agent of the Vermilion Eye.*
Chapter 13: The Venera Church of Mother Earth
In the aftermath of the Second World War, a religion calling itself the Venera Church of Mother Earth seizes control of the city-state, redefining the identity of the goddess Venera and driving Scheherazade underground, among the labyrinthine ruins of subterranean Venera.
Postscript: Scheherazade as Cultural Icon
A look at the cultural impact of Scheherazade as a fictional character from her classic portrayal in The Arabian Nights *to her depiction in fine arts, film, architecture, comics, television, music, and more.*

THREE PHANTASMAGORICAL ODYSSEYS OF SCHEHERAZADE

[from the Vermilion Press catalogue]

Three Phantasmagorical Odysseys of Scheherazade is an anthology of novellas by some of the most notorious writers of the Venera arts scene. Each story bears the same title: "A Phantasmagorical Odyssey of Scheherazade."

- In a rare new text since his self-imposed exile to Venera, Magus Amore provides a surreal parade of erotic perversions, body modifications, exquisite torture, and disquieting rituals.

Entirely devoid of plot, the novella follows Scheherazade's escapades through a relentless orgy of shock, sex, and horror.

⊚ Bram Jameson probes the inner world of Scheherazade's imagination. Using the language, tropes, and conventions of psychotherapy, he recounts the adventures of the archetypal storyteller trapped in her own mind, navigating the labyrinth of story that makes up her identity.

⊚ In the lyrical and poignant version of the story by Renata Austin (two-time recipient of the Venera Fantasy Award), Scheherazade wanders an infinite road, encountering the characters and settings of her own tales. One by one, she sheds and forgets these fabulations, until all that is left of her is a young Ethiopian girl in the world before civilization, before fiction.

THE DARKBRIGHT BOOK OF SCHEHERAZADE
edited by *Sanderson Grecko & Bettina Easton*

[from the VFC 50 promotional mailing to members of previous years of the Venera Fantasy Convention]

To coincide with their stint as Guests of Honour at the fiftieth Venera Fantasy Convention, Sanderson Grecko and Bettina Easton, publishers of Darkbright Books, which is also celebrating its fifth anniversary, have commissioned Scheherazade stories from their eclectic stable of authors. The anthology will be a free giveaway to all paid members and attendees of VFC 50.

⊚ "Duels with Scheherazade," by Daniel Dimes. A political allegory in which the High Countess of the Venera Church of Mother Earth and Scheherazade engage in a series of ritualized and violent duels over the fate of the city-goddess Venera.

⊚ "New Vermilion World," by Brad Blue. Scheherazade is an artificial intelligence plotting to overwrite the source code of reality with the virtual game universe of Venera.

⊚ "Space Whore Scheherazade," by Chas Roberts. A philosophical space opera narrated by the star-travelling Scheherazade, courtesan-ambassador from the planet Venera.

- ◎ "Sex with Monsters," by Elaine Sherman. In the aftermath of an orgy with fantastical creatures from her own imagination, Scheherazade sits at her vanity table, staring at herself in the mirror, brushing her hair, and contemplating her tattoos.

- ◎ "The Kiss of Scheherazade," by Barbara Fitzpatrick. Scheherazade is a vampire who travels the Earth preying on writers and other artists, in order to populate the island utopia of Venera with immortal, undead bohemians.

- ◎ "The Arabian Nights Plague," by Anthony Meredith. Anyone who hears or reads Scheherazade's stories is turned into a zombie.

- ◎ "The Queer Hex of Kid Scheherazade," by Jewel Gumm. In a Venera reimagined as a frontier town in the mode of spaghetti westerns, the ambiguously gendered gunslinging mystic Kid Scheherazade shoots bullets of pansexual lust and love at those who preach against the pleasures of the flesh.

- ◎ "The Saga of Scheherazade," by A.A. Miller. A young Scheherazade is taken prisoner on a slave ship; she escapes and becomes a stowaway on a pirate vessel — until she sets foot in Venera.

- ◎ "The Lost Pages of Scheherazade," by Lucas Rafael. A metafictional odyssey in which a young homeless Montreal girl nicknamed Scheherazade steals a book about the classical Scheherazade at a strange bookshop called Lost Pages; fantasy bleeds into mundane reality as her life begins to mirror that of the fictional Scheherazade ... until the two merge into one character existing simultaneously across multiple realities.

- ◎ "The Horror of Womanhood," by Christian G.Q. Mitchell. In New York, a drag queen with the stage name of Heherazade and an Arabian Nights routine is inexplicably and irrevocably transformed into a biological woman in the middle of a performance.

- ◎ "Talking to Doctor Scheherazade," by Bobby Who. Scheherazade is a Veneran psychotherapist whose sessions with patients reveal more about her own self-obsession than about the problems of those she is ostensibly treating.

- ◉ "The Star of Scheherazade Strange," by Cat Watts. Teenage Torontonian Scheherazade Strange falls into the fantasy world of Venera, where she follows a sentient vermilion star that beckons her every night.
- ◉ "The Case of the Really Mean Haunted House," by Peter Ian Trembles. On one of the outer islands of the Veneran archipelago, supernatural detective Scheherazade Jones investigates the mystery of a haunted house with a peculiar grudge.
- ◉ "Ghosts and Tall Tales," by Kevin Angel. Scheherazade is visited by the ghosts of her alternate selves, who haunt her with stories of the life paths she failed to pursue.

THE ODYSSEY OF SCHEHERAZADE: A PHANTASMAGORICAL OPERA

[from the website of the Venera Fantasy Convention, vfc.venera.web]

The premiere of this opera for solo singer by Venera Fantasy Grandmaster Award winner Neal S. Palmer will be held at the concert hall of Tito Bronze's Velvet Bronzemine. The music will be performed the Arabian Nights Orchestra, featuring singer Mandy Gay as Scheherazade. The sets, designed by Belinda Gerda and built by Hemero Volkanus, are a reproduction of the long-lost *Esplendor Català*, the legendary cruise-liner designed by Antoni Gaudí that from 1920 to 1936 — the heyday of Veneran tourism — travelled the Mediterranean between Barcelona and Venera. Neal S. Palmer wrote the music and the libretto and is the director of this first staging of his new opus.

The story: abandoning modern-day Venera, Scheherazade boards the *Esplendor Català* and travels through time, sailing the seas of the Mediterranean of antiquity, reliving and narrating the adventures that inspired *The Arabian Nights*.

The premiere of *The Odyssey of Scheherazade: A Phantasmagorical Opera* is an off-season special event sponsored by the Venera Fantasy Convention.

A SCHEHERAZADE PHANTASMAGORIA

[from the Tito Bronze website, velvetbronzemine.venera.web]

To promote the release of his new film, *The Phantasmagorical Odyssey of Scheherazade*, Tito Bronze has curated *A Scheherazade Phantasmagoria*, which will be on display for the entire month of June at Bronze's opulent Veneran mansion, the Velvet Bronzemine. Admission is free, and the doors will remain open 24 hours a day for the duration of the exhibit. The show includes:

- A gallery of 99 new photographs of the city-state Venera by photographer Petra Maxim (author of *1001 Days and Nights in Venera*). Hidden in every picture is the actress who portrays Scheherazade in Bronze's new film — can you spot her?
- Classic paintings and sketches of Scheherazade by Leonardo da Vinci, Pablo Picasso, and Salvador Dalí.
- A gallery of framed and enlarged reproductions of the covers painted and designed by Obama Savage for the nine-issue run of the 1937-38 American pulp magazine *Spicy Scheherazade Stories*.
- Original comics art by Jake Kurtz for the never-published thirteenth issue of *Scheherazade, Agent of the Vermilion Eye*, a story titled "The Shield of the Black Cat."
- Sketches by Edward Gorey for a never-produced Broadway production of *The Arabian Nights*.
- The plans for Antoni Gaudí's suppressed Arabian Nights-themed apartment building, which would have been built near the port end of La Rambla in Barcelona.
- A new series of seven paintings by Belinda Gerda, the notoriously disgraced former Painter Laureate of Venera, depicting Scheherazade in legendary scenes from Veneran folklore.
- *The Harem of Scheherazade*: in the lush roof garden of the Velvet Bronzemine all the current sycophants and apprentices in residence, wearing masks of characters from *The Arabian Nights*, perform a month-long ongoing orgy of vermilion-fuelled sex

and art. The public is invited to join in; consumption of vermilion is mandatory.

◉ On continuous loop: a video of Jane Zacks (author of *The Phantasmagorical Odyssey of Scheherazade: A Cryptomythological Biography*) and Tito Bronze discussing the adaptation of the author's classic scholarly work into a surreal adventure film.

◉ Wandering throughout *A Scheherazade Phantasmagoria* at the Velvet Bronzemine are automata created by Hemero Volkanus; meet Dunyazad, Sindbad, Aladdin, Ali Baba, Prince Ahmed, the Barber of Baghdad, Princess Badroulbadour, and other favourites from *The Arabian Nights* as reimagined and brought to mechanical life by Venera's most eccentric tinkerer.

SCHEHERAZADE, AGENT OF THE VERMILION EYE
by *Jake Kurtz*

[from the Shrugging Atlas Comics fan wiki,
theworldsofshruggingatlascomics.web/wiki]

A short-lived American comics series about the adventures of Scheherazade as an agent of the Vermilion Eye was published by Shrugging Atlas Comics to very low sales in 1969-70. However, in the mid-1970s, the series was translated and repackaged in both Mexico and Italy and was a huge success in both those markets. From the date of the original English-language publication, the series was banned by the Venera Church of Mother Earth; nevertheless, throughout the 1970s contraband copies in both English and Italian flooded the city-state. The ban was never officially lifted; by the time of Jake Kurtz's death in 1994 copies of the comics were so ubiquitous in Venera that the Church had stopped trying to enforce it.

#1: "The King of France"
Scheherazade races to discover the mythical King of France, an energy statue that gives whoever is in possession of it control over

the destiny of France. Competing with secret agents from all the world's major nations, will Scheherazade secure the King of France for Venera?

#2: "Six Million Years Past and Future"
A time-traveller from six millions years in the future travels back to twelve million years into his past — six million years before the present day — to prevent the birth of the goddess Venera. Scheherazade's mission is to stop him before he succeeds, which would wipe the city-state of Venera from history.

#3: "Chaos of Time"
Scheherazade is trapped in the time stream. But the King of France comes to her rescue. What is the true nature of the energy statue?

#4: "Friends and/or Foes?"
Having been rescued from time, Scheherazade randomly flitters between alternate realities. Which alternate iterations of the goddess Venera, the King of France, and various agents of the Vermilion Eye are friends and which are foes?

#5: "Quest for the Cornucopia of Venera"
Who has stolen the Cornucopia of Venera, the goddess's own sacred cask of vermilion wine? Scheherazade is on the case!

#6: "Who Will Drink from the Cornucopia of Venera?"
Scheherazade's investigation into the disappearance of the Cornucopia of Venera takes her to the City of the Secret Samurai deep underground in the bowels of the island of Hokkaido in Japan.

#7: "The Drums of Doom!"
In Ethiopia, a percussionist is composing a song that will destroy the world ... unless Scheherazade finds and stops him!

#8: "The Black Cats"
Scheherazade uncovers the secret agenda of Venera's population of black cats.

#9: "The Black Mice"
Scheherazade and all of Venera are caught in the middle of a war between the city-state's black cats and black mice.

#10: "The Death of the World"
Who has taken up the drums of doom? Scheherazade believed that

she had prevented that menace from ever again threatening the world. Can she stop the lethal rhythms before the final beat?

#11: "The Cruelty of Nayadaga"

Can the city-state Venera survive a civil war between the merciless secret underground society of the fish goddess Nayadaga's half-human followers and the insidiously oppressive regime of the Church of Mother Earth? Will Scheherazade and the Vermilion Eye side with either of these factions?

#12: "The Code"

It's all-out war in Venera, with Nayadaga, the Church of Mother Earth, and the Vermilion Eye each moving against the other two ... unless Scheherazade can decipher the code that will bring peace, or at least equilibrium, to the city-state.

THE PHANTASMAGORICAL ODYSSEY OF SCHEHERAZADE

a Tito Bronze film

[review by Jack Yeovil for The Fantastic Film Reader's *annual Cannes edition]*

Tito Bronze is well known for keeping a tight lid on the production of his films; nevertheless, usually some advance details inevitably leak to the press. Not so with *The Phantasmagorical Odyssey of Scheherazade.* Between the announcement that Bronze had acquired the film rights to Jane Zacks's controversial scholarly book on the secret history of Scheherazade and the scheduling of the premiere at Cannes no information about the film itself could be uncovered; not a word about the screenplay, the cast, the crew, the shoot, the music — nothing.

Even once the Festival de Cannes published its schedule, only very minimal information was made available to the press or the public: "*The Phantasmagorical Odyssey of Scheherazade.* Written and directed by Tito Bronze. Adapted from *The Phantasmagorical Odyssey of Scheherazade: A Cryptomythological Biography,* by Jane Zacks. Music and performance by Scheherazade. 218 minutes. All languages. (Country: Venera.)" The description only added to the questions of curious cinephiles. How could a film be in "All languages"? Who was the performer hiding under the pseudonym "Scheherazade"? Who were the rest of the cast?

The Phantasmagorical Odyssey of Scheherazade is deceptively minimalistic, yet also the lushest and most extravagant adventure story ever filmed. Even within Tito Bronze's eclectic filmography, it stands as profoundly original. It is perhaps his greatest accomplishment.

The film opens with an animation of the film's title cascading in multiple languages. A female voice gradually fades in, sublimely beautiful, chanting the name of the titular character, reiterating it in the different ways it is pronounced across the globe. The typographical animation gives way to a blank whiteness; the song stops. One moment, there is nothing to see or hear, and the next a woman we can only assume to be Scheherazade is on the screen. The camera zooms in on her, until a closeup of her face fills the image. It is then that she starts singing again.

The language in which Scheherazade sings is not in any way distinguishable; yet as the song unfurls so does the story. The song is the story.

It is impossible to be certain whether, for the next three and a half hours, the image projected is nothing more than the face of the singing Scheherazade or a fantastical montage of stories within stories — of adventurers and merchants and thieves and farmers and beggars and hunters and spies and kings and queens and princes and princesses and whores and clerics and mercenaries and demons and wizards and gods and monsters and warriors and demigods and ghosts and lovers; set in a mythic past that could never have been, in a time before cities, at the dawn of human civilization, in the time of the great empires, in times of war, in times of peace, throughout history and throughout the world. Or perhaps the unfolding narrative is superimposed on the face of the storyteller?

This mosaic of stories does not follow any chronology. It would be difficult, if not impossible, to summarize or even pick out specific moments from the narrative. But what is told encapsulates the whole story of Scheherazade and of the tales she has birthed.

Eventually, the singing stops. The only image left is that of Scheherazade's face, in such tight closeup that no surrounding element is visible.

After a pause during which the image is static and the film mute, the camera zooms out to reveal that Scheherazade is standing within a labyrinth of otherworldly ruins. Subtle and eerie echoes pepper the soundtrack. The only light comes from glowing rivulets of vermilion water and pulsing veins of the same colour in the stone walls.

A whirlpool of iridescent vermilion forms next to Scheherazade. Solemnly, she steps into it. The whirlpool engulfs her and then disappears, taking her along with it. The camera lingers on the ruins. It zooms out as it fades to black, then fades back in to a starry night sky. The camera pans downward, revealing the cityscape of Venera.

End credits.

PART 3

THE SECRET HISTORIES OF MAGUS AMORE

THE SUBTERRANEAN ODYSSEY
OF MAGUS AMORE

⤸

His mind saturated with vermilion, Magus Amore bends down to the basement floor and lifts a metal slab, revealing a dark chasm. He slides into that darkness, downward into the bowels of Venera, while upstairs, in her home and studio, which had once been, in the hands of the previous occupants, a boutique selling artisan vermilion aphrodisiacs, his lover, the artist Belinda Gerda, paints the first tableau in what he already knows will be a series inspired by his ecstatic visions of the world's goddesses.

Amore descends through the mysterious and inscrutable vestiges of past Veneras. The air in this underground universe is moist yet not at all dank. Amore breathes deeply, lets the uncannily fresh atmosphere fill his lungs, his belly, his head, his crotch, his entire body. It's like breathing in the conceptual ideal of spring water instead of any earthly, mundane matter; the effects are purifying, cleansing, bracing. But Amore is also aware that it might affect his sensory perceptions, perhaps even his perception of time and of himself. Mixed in with that brightly flavoured air are particles of vermilion dust; his mind is by now so attuned to the divine substance that he can detect its subtle intrusion.

At the edge of his sight he sees her: his guide through subterranean Venera, the dark-skinned feminine psychopomp of the Veneran underworld, the story within the story. She turns her head, and her eyes meet his briefly. And then she begins to sing. Softly, so softly that her song is barely a hum. She sings in the language of the gods.

Unknown even to most Venerans, this subterranean world offers a consciousness-altering spectacle of architecture, geology, history, myth, and divine lights. Once again, Amore considers forever abandoning the glittering decadence of the modern city-state of Venera and instead lose himself in the contemplation of these mysterious, forgotten, improbable iterations of the city that serves as his refuge.

Magus Amore the Mad. Magus Amore, former writer of international repute, whose every bestselling thriller has been adapted into equally successful films. But that was before. Before Venera. Before vermilion, the delicately aromatic Veneran hallucinogenic, had opened his mind. Magus Amore now spends his days whispering incantations dedicated to strange deities, engaging in atavistic rituals of brutal eroticism, surrendering his illustrated flesh to the passions of otherworldly monsters, despoiling himself like an infant as he babbles incoherent nonsense. Magus Amore, now the butt of jeers, rumours, slander, and parodies.

Magus Amore cares little for what others say or think of him. It is here, in the subterranean world of the main island of the archipelago of Venera, that he has been able to explore the ineffable mythologies of his imagination. The deeper Magus Amore descends, the closer he comes to grasping his own primordial ur-story. To experiencing the archetypal narrative through which he perceives the world. In all his novels and stories, the writer had tried in vain to achieve such transcendent self-knowledge. Then, his life's quest took him, here, to Venera. To vermilion, and to the deities, creatures, and realms the drug and the psychopomp have revealed to him.

Downward still goes the mad visionary. The tunnels lead in infinite directions, but as always he follows the trail of Venera's psychopomp. She smells of spice: of cinnamon, nutmeg, cloves, tinged with vermilion and the brine of the female sex.

The entombed Veneras of the past are not shrouded in absolute darkness. A rusty gold-red glow emanates from veins in stone and sediments, from rivulets of unknown origins that flow through some of the most decrepit ruins, from cracks on the surfaces that surround Amore in this underground universe, from the invasive roots of the World Tree Yggdrasil, reborn, from a desiccated shoot brought by the Viking invaders, as a vermilion plant — omnipresent, serpentine, and carnivorous.

The psychopomp, too, glows subtly of vermilion. As Amore descends he gets closer and closer to her, but she never lets him quite catch up. The vermilion sheen accentuates the deep darkness of her naked skin. Onward she leads him, with song, with the promise of story and the lure of the Goddess herself.

This labyrinth of past civilizations leads to colossal architectural works that sometime dwarf the bio-architectural wonders of the surface Venera. These past civilizations ooze unfettered grandiosity and sublime vulgarity. These the ruins tease achievements relegated to secret histories.

The subtle melodies of the psychopomp enrich Amore's vermilion-enhanced perceptions of subterranean Venera.

Amore stands within the remains of a structure decorated with brutal frescoes depicting demons devouring live humans. This sacred place is the Casa Tenetrarum, a sanctuary dedicated to the Thrikathian god of cannibalism, Terrutala. Downward still he travels. The song of the psycho-pomp continues to whisper to him, bestowing upon him knowledge of the lost languages and forgotten cultures and myriad histories of Veneran antiquity.

Every one of Amore's journeys into the subterranean yesteryears of Venera has revealed different and contradictory pasts. The tunnels, ruins, and chambers undergo perpetual metamorphosis. Venera's past, present, and future are all equally fluid.

The barracks and storehouses of the Thrikathian, Clumbarian, and Hyppogean eras tell stories of possible past Veneras. Etched into stone are records of colloquial languages, corruption, superstitions, everyday life, and hidden rites — such as the cruel rituals depicted in the pan-orama of Sumod's lavish Insuleaa Sanctuary.

Within the Hyppogean Maxias Kirras dwells the sacred images of one of the most ancient Veneran cults, that of the fish-goddess Naya-daga. Amore is bestowed visions of Nayadaga's half-human faithful tak-ing part in orgiastic rituals, dancing to the rhythms of forgotten musics, testing their mettle in savage initiation ceremonies.

Amore reaches never-excavated levels of subterranean Venera; these civilizations that once thrived in the world above are now buried by the deposits of the infinite iterations of Veneran history. Having reached a dead end, the psychopomp's path now takes Amore upward, back toward the surface.

Walking among the broad arcades of a Domuskian stadium, Amore relives the excitement of ancient spectacles. The Clumbarian Sylla Pompios evokes a long-forgotten vision of the afterlife tinged with aspects of Orphic mysteries, hinting at a connection to the Hellenes of Ancient Greece; its graceful, colourful, and joyous depictions of the netherworld portray the realm of the dead as a playful setting.

The Via Venza speaks of the death throes of Veneran Christianity. The small basin at the end of the hall used, at first, for the meek ablutions of these early Christians and later for the gory immersions of the debauched Baptistas, the orgiastic mystery cult that supplanted the short-lived Christian sect of Venera.

The Paollo Regola district retains the smells and arrangement of a lively commercial area interspersed with decrepit apartment blocks and lavish private villas. At Traverstera, the barracks of the Excubirotium once housed, during the Roman occupation, militia and civic guards, its walls defaced with contemporaneous graffiti — voices and images of ancient daily life. Along the deserted vias: extinguished torches, dry water pumps, desecrated altars.

On this brief picaresque journey, Amore has far from exhausted subterranean Venera's vast panoply of wonders. Murmurs from an infinity of unlikely pasts still snake within Magus Amore's mind. Already, he yearns to follow another downward path among these buried ruins and relics.

But for now the Goddess calls.

The psychopomp stands still, now silent, and extends a hand toward Amore. His fingers link with hers. He breathes in her pungent, spicy aroma. Scheherazade stands on tiptoe, her lips reaching for his. He bends his head and kisses her, tastes the complex spiciness of her mouth.

He kneels before her, smells the bouquet of her dark cunt, and then drinks from it. Her juices smear his face and flow into his mouth, up his nose, and down his throat.

Scheherazade tastes like a fountain of pure vermilion. She is addictive, irresistible. His thirst for her can never be quenched.

The psychopomp sings her orgasm. After, she grabs his head, lifting him back up.

Before them forms a whirlpool of iridescent vermilion, the gateway that leads to *Her*, to the Goddess.

Holding the psychopomp's hand, Amore waits for her to guide them both into the whirlpool, as she has done at the conclusion of all his previous subterranean odysseys. But Scheherazade stands still.

She whispers a song in the language of the gods. The words are ineffable, but the meaning unfurls in his mind: Scheherazade's story has reached its conclusion. Nothing is eternal. Not Scheherazade. Not anyone. Not any story. Perhaps not even the Goddess. Scheherazade has finally exhausted her well of stories. Venera requires a new story, a new storyteller. Magus Amore is now Venera's psychopomp.

Briefly, Amore wonders why he was chosen. Amore is aware that he is not the only one who wanders the subterranean Venera in erotic communion with Scheherazade and the Goddess; he knows of at least five others: the tinkerer Hemero Volkanus, the pornographer Tito Bronze, the Canadian expat author Bram Jameson, the celebrated Veneran writer Renata Austin, the Slavic photographer Petra Maxim. But, without pride or modesty, Amore knows that none of them abandon themselves as fully as he does to the Goddess or to her sacred spice, vermilion. He is hers, forever — or, at least, for as long as she will have him. Even his devotion to his lover Belinda Gerda is a manifestation of his adoration of the Goddess. His insatiable lust for Scheherazade is a reflection of his desire for the Goddess.

Within moments, the seeming eternal youth of Scheherazade gives way to age and decay. Seconds ago, her body had been that of a ripe young woman. And then the brittle shell of an elder nearing death. And then nothing but dust — vermilion dust that swirls around him, brushing against his eyes, his ears, his nose, his lips, his cock ... before vanishing into the sacred whirlpool.

Magus Amore follows her trail and descends into the glittering eddy, downward into mystery, subject to the inscrutable whims of the goddess Venera herself.

ADVENTURES IN CRYPTO-ALCHEMY: THE GOLDEN CRYPTOGRAPH

⤝⤞

Welcome, dear readers, to another installment of *Adventures in Crypto-alchemy*. Today's offering is "The Golden Cryptograph": a three-part serial by that literary alchemist of cryptofiction, Magus Amore, renowned author of *The League of Anarchy*, *The Best Americans*, *The Miracle Family*, *Swamp Sex*, *Who Watches the Goddesses of Lust?*, *From Bacchus*, and *The Secret History of Sacred Wines*.

Witness the genesis of the golden cryptograph in "The Quest of the Crypto-alchemist"! Follow its unlikely path in "The Exploits of the Detective of Desire"! Decipher its meaning in "The Ultimate Adventure of the Golden Cryptograph"!

⤜

PART I: THE QUEST OF THE CRYPTO-ALCHEMIST

It had taken him more than three decades, but finally the crypto-alchemist attained the goal of all those who plied the alchemical arts: he had transmuted lead into gold. Not the gaudy gold that fuelled mundane dreams of greed — no. But that elusive substance, the mystical grail of alchemists, whose golden luminescence was purer than sunlight, whose very existence held the potential to forever alter reality.

Carefully, while the gold was still in liquid form, radiating such intense heat that the crypto-alchemist nearly fainted from exposure, he poured it into a mould. Not one drop could be wasted; according to his calculations, he had transmuted exactly enough lead to fit into the receptacle. The mould was in the shape of a pen, and with that pen the crypto-alchemist intended to write, and thus record and safekeep, the arcane secrets the gold would impart. Precision was essential; he had calculated to the minutest fraction the exact volume of both the mould and the gold. Had he produced either too much or not enough gold the pen would not function. All the alchemical gold from this transmutation had to be contained within a single vessel, and that gold had to fill the vessel to saturation.

Slowly, the gold flowed into the pen. The crypto-alchemist's entire body was covered in sweat, from his long hours of labour transmuting the lead, from the unbearable heat generated by the alchemical process, from the strain of handling every instrument with superhuman dexterity. Finally, the last drop fell from the cup and into the pen. Success! His calculations had indeed been as precise as required. The crypto-alchemist sealed the top of the vessel; he held the pen in the palm of his hands, marvelling at how quickly the gold cooled once it settled into its receptacle.

The crypto-alchemist was tempted to surrender to sleep — he had been awake for sixty hours — but he knew that, should he succumb to such mortal weakness, all his travails would be for naught.

He uncapped the pen. The gold nib glowed like a miniature sun, blinding him. The crypto-alchemist remained calm; he knew that he was not blind, but that the light of the gold, now that it had moved into semi-solid state, was of such purity that it overwhelmed all other colours. That brightness would not last, however. In too short a time, unless it were crafted into a form that would maintain its alchemical properties, the alchemical gold would decay, either reverting to lead or, if the alchemist had transmuted it with especial skill, becoming indistinguishable from mundane, mercantile gold.

The hand that held the pen started to work as if of its own volition. The still-blinded crypto-alchemist surrendered to the gold.

⁓ The crypto-alchemist, his sight restored, woke up in his workshop, still holding the pen, which was now hollow, all the gold having flowed from it through the nib to create the object before him: the golden cryptograph!

He had no memory of fashioning it. As the gold had started to guide his actions through the vessel of the pen, the crypto-alchemist had slipped into a trance, from which he had segued into sleep once his task had been completed.

The golden cryptograph was composed entirely of alchemical gold. His mastery of the crypto-alchemical arts had not failed him: the golden cryptograph shone with a subtle inner luminescence. In shape and size it resembled a greeting card — a rectangle folded vertically in the middle — the gold sheet so thin and pliable that it could open and close like paper. The front-cover frame was illuminated with embossed decorations, enhancing the beauty of the object. In the centre of the design were three words, each on its own line. For now, the crypto-alchemist could not decipher those words, as he could not recognize either the language or the characters. The two inside pages were filled with text in the same esoteric script, with the occasional embossed illumination. The artful layout of text and images instilled in the crypto-alchemist, despite the as yet impenetrable meaning of the words, a sense of profound serenity. The centre of the back cover sported a small round image — concentric circles whose rings contained delicately minute swirls and designs. The crypto-alchemist suspected that within this circle there hid the key to unlocking the mysteries of the golden cryptograph.

✑ What secrets had the gold revealed to the crypto-alchemist? What was the key to unlocking the sacred alchemical language in which those mysteries were encoded? How would his life — and perhaps all of reality — be transformed once he deciphered the golden cryptograph?

These questions now consumed the existence of the crypto-alchemist. Every waking second of every day was spent trying to decode the golden cryptograph. Even his dreams were preoccupied with this alchemical riddle. Alas, the efforts of neither his reason nor his subconscious were rewarded with success.

He would not admit defeat, however. Within his grasp, he knew, there resided the knowledge of ultimate transcendence, the alchemical formula with which the ecstasies of divine knowledge and physical reality could be forever wed. Once he felt he had exhausted his own skill, knowledge, and resources, he studied under other crypto-alchemists. He didn't care if they were his elders or his juniors, if they were more or less experienced than he was — his pride was of little concern. The only thing that mattered was the quest: deciphering the mysteries of the golden cryptograph! He approached his colleagues with as much humility as he could muster and sought to expand his command of the crypto-alchemical arts, opening his mind and imagination to whatever knowledge or inspiration these other crypto-alchemists could impart.

But there was one thing he held back with selfishness, one thing his pride would not allow him to share. Never did he reveal the existence of the golden cryptograph to any of his fellow crypto-alchemists. Thus, none of them understood the precise nature of the knowledge he sought.

He toiled and studied in vain for years, until his body could no longer withstand the rigours of mortal life, and he died, never having solved the riddle of the golden cryptograph.

PART 2: THE EXPLOITS OF THE DETECTIVE OF DESIRE

The crypto-alchemist's workshop was located in the basement of the home he shared with his spinster sister, a spacious house in the suburban Libida borough of Venera, on an island of the Veneran archipelago not far from mainland Europe. The house had once belonged to their parents, where he had lived for the whole span of his life, never having succeeded in finding gainful employment, so wrapped up had he been in the arcane and unremunerative pursuit of crypto-alchemy.

The crypto-alchemist's sister grew apprehensive when he failed to emerge from the basement for more than two consecutive days. She steeled herself to make the unprecedented move of trespassing into her brother's underground sanctum. Considering her brother's advanced age and poor physical condition, she was not altogether surprised to find him dead. She felt neither relief nor grief; she was and had always been practical-minded. She made all the proper arrangements for the disposal of the body — the crypto-alchemist had donated his corpse to the Venera Hospital, so there was very little fuss, which suited her just fine.

She had no idea, however, what to make of all the strange apparatus and paraphernalia her brother had amassed in the sixty-odd years since he had claimed the basement as his own. She didn't have the will or the energy to sort through it all. Consulting the local newspaper she spotted an ad for Tomorrow's Yesterdays, a "vintage shop" (she wasn't quite sure what that could be) that claimed to buy en masse and on site the possessions of the departed. She liked the idea of getting rid of everything in one swoop instead of having to dispose of her brother's clutter piecemeal. She telephoned and made an appointment for a house call.

Patricia unloaded her van from the private parking lot behind her shop. She made a bit of extra money renting out the five extra parking spaces, reserving the one adjacent to the back door for herself. Although the streets of the island of Venera did not allow for automobiles, it was possible to drive in Libida, and many Venerans kept vehicles in the suburb to indulge in their driving vice, especially as there were no driving regulations whatsoever on Libida.

What a bizarre haul! Not even the books could help her figure out what all this stuff was. There were thirteen books in all — each of them hand-bound and -crafted, each of them hundreds of pages thick, each of them written in a cipher that combined familiar letters of the Roman alphabet, letters from the Cyrillic and Greek alphabets, Arabic and Hebrew writing, numerals and other mathematical symbols, Chinese pictographs, hieroglyphs, runes, and other completely unrecognizable characters. Some of the pages contained graphs, tables, diagrams, and other illustrations, but nothing that made any sense to her.

Some of the paraphernalia was clearly lab equipment, but it had been oddly customized. The haul also included machinery that looked straight out of a steampunk photoshoot. Was it in some way functional, or purely decorative? Regardless — her clientele included a coterie of steampunk fashionistas and fashionisters; they would eagerly jump on some of this merchandise. Another subset of her clientele, which overlapped somewhat with the steampunks, were LARPers — live action role players — the most involved of whom would certainly buy some of the books for some elaborately staged mystery/adventure. And then there was *Dovelander*, the supernatural detective series that was shooting on location right here in Libida; that show had become her best customer, constantly scouting for weird props — and as the sign read below the shop name Tomorrow's Yesterdays was "Where the Weird Is Always in Fashion."

One item struck Patricia as particularly beautiful: a golden greeting card, gilded with intricate illuminations. On its cover were three words spelled out with odd characters — although noticeably different from the cipher used in the books. This text looked utterly alien, unlike anything Patricia had ever seen. The material of the card was smoother than a girl's inner thigh, so thin it was almost immaterial. Yet, it was in perfect condition, unmarred by even the slightest nick, scratch, or tear — in such perfect condition that it seemed to emit a subtle glow.

A movement caught her eye: had the text on the cover shifted? It appeared stable now, but was it the same as it had been only minutes ago? She stared at it; the characters shimmered and danced. It was too elaborate to be merely an optical illusion, like those trick pictures that changed depending on the angle from which you viewed them.

She opened the card. There was more writing inside. The characters moved as she tried to read them. The card glowed brighter and brighter. The text settled into place, and Patricia read it — or, rather, it read itself to Patricia — and all at once she understood.

⌒ What the now-deceased crypto-alchemist had never grasped was that the key to unlocking the golden cryptograph was not knowledge: it was a person. In fact, there were, at any given time, several keys in existence, and each one of them, presented with the golden cryptograph, would unlock it in a way that was unique to that particular key, that particular person.

For Patricia, the owner and founder of Tomorrow's Yesterdays: Where the Weird Is Always in Fashion, the golden cryptograph was a sacred formula that alchemically transformed her into the Detective of Desire.

✍ Shopkeeper by day, superhero by night. Within a week of adopting this new double life, Patricia's relationship with her beau, an expat Texan named Charles, which she'd always been somewhat lackadaisical about anyway, not so much ended but petered out. Even before, they barely managed to have sex even once a month, but it had been an undemanding and companionable affair that allowed her to devote her passion to Tomorrow's Yesterdays. Still, even Charles, who needed so very little from her, had his limits. When she failed to come home for five nights in a row, he simply moved out whatever personal items he kept at her house and returned to the apartment he shared with two other Americans. He'd wanted to give it up within a few weeks of when he and Patricia started seeing each other, as he was never there anymore, but she'd always insisted that he keep it. In Patricia's mind, Charles had only ever been visiting.

Her daytime routine remained the same, but instead of working past her posted hours, as she had often done before unlocking the golden cryptograph, her late nights were taken up with her new calling as the Detective of Desire.

All she needed to do to effect the transformation from Patricia Alexandria to the Detective of Desire was to close her eyes, recall the sacred message encoded within the golden cryptograph, and let its ineffable meaning permeate her consciousness. No matter what she was wearing at the time, her mundane clothes — well, not that mundane, Patricia did pride herself on her eccentric yet timeless sense of style — altered themselves into the uniform of the Detective of Desire: knee-high dark grey leather boots with wide two-inch stacked heels; lilac wool hot pants with deep purple piping; a chain-link belt with a large buckle in the shape of the same crypto-alchemical symbol found on the back of the golden cryptograph; a gold necklace with an amulet also in the shape of the crypto-alchemical emblem; a loose white silk blouse cuffed at the elbow and with moderate cleavage; a black shawl/cape thing that fluttered like slow wings regardless of whether there was any wind; a black mask that covered her face, from her forehead to the tip of her nose, leaving only an oval opening for her to breathe and speak. Her lips were adorned with sparkly amethyst gloss, and her hair — normally brown and cut to have bangs and to fall just below her nape — became a rainbow of long strands of purple, blue, gold, and scarlet, reaching the middle of her back.

Every night, Patricia climbed onto the roof of her shop to transform into the Detective of Desire. She then flew off into the starry sky of the Mediterranean.

She patrolled the Veneran archipelago in search of lost or stolen objects. She didn't actively seek them out, but she was drawn to them. Once she found whatever object it was that the amulet directed her to that evening — it could be a clay statuette or a Pop Art necktie or a pulp magazine or a vintage purse or Victorian pipe or a set of American baseball cards or a torn envelope with a rare postage stamp or a wooden toy or a 1950s evening gown in need of repair or antique jewellery, anything, really — she would see an ethereal thread that sprouted from it. She would collect the object and then follow the thread. Always, it led to a person. She would give the object to that person, in full knowledge that, in some way that might not yet be evident, the item in question, which may have belonged to them before or may have been hitherto unfamiliar, would transform their lives in profound and wondrous ways.

The stories of the people to whom she surrendered these objects sometimes made the news — never a lead article, but low-key character pieces about eccentric collectors, crackpot inventors, reunited family members, bizarre coincidences; all these stories had in common that the object recovered by the Detective of Desire played an essential role in the related events. Some articles even mentioned the Detective of Desire by her *nom d'aventure*. Once, *Vermilion Times* — the English-language monthly magazine on Veneran life sold to the international market — ran a feature on the legend of the Detective of Desire. The reporter tracked down more than a hundred of the people Patricia's alter ego had bequeathed found objects to. The story made the cover, with an artist's interpretation of the Detective of Desire — with (unsurprisingly) bigger breasts; the uniform was mostly accurate, although the shape of the amulet was simplified and the shawl wings were all wrong, looking more like a traditional superhero cape. Still, she pasted the cover of the issue onto the front of her scrapbook that collected the media reports of the Detective of Desire's exploits.

The Detective of Desire was only incidentally a crimefighter, although Interpol, the French *Police Nationale*, and the Italian *Polizia di Stato* officially considered her simultaneously a myth and a wanted vigilante, refusing to take a clear stance. But she was safe: no-one knew that the Detective of Desire's secret identity was Patricia Alexandria. Anyway, as she never stole anything from the innocent and never resorted to violence, she was considered a minor nuisance, and the mainland European authorities, in the odd instances when they didn't dismiss the Detective of Desire as an urban legend, pursued her with a mix of bemusement and nonchalance.

Sometimes she recovered stolen objects from thieves (that's where the crimefighter tag came in) — but only a fraction of those times would the thread lead back to the previous owner of the item. Most times it would lead to someone else in the Veneran archipelago, the French Riviera, Malta, or the coast of Italy (the amulet only occasionally led her as far as Morocco, Spain, or Turkey).

Sometimes the thieves would try to fight the Detective of Desire, but her amulet protected her from harm. No blows or weapons of any kind could penetrate its force field. Although lead bullets would be let through and delicately land in her hands, transmogrified into small trinkets of alchemical gold that she would later sell at Tomorrow's Yesterdays.

Most often, though, the objects the amulet would lead her to would simply have been lost or discarded, with no-one to fight against to gain their possession.

Once, several weeks after the *Vermilion Times* article, the amulet led the Detective of Desire underground, into the labyrinth of ruins buried below the modern city of Venera. She was startled to discover that veins and rivulets of phosphorescent vermilion pulsed through the ancient walls and sediments of rocks and soil. Was this the source of the element that fed Venera's vermilion plant, itself the source of the psychotropic vermilion spice? The closely guarded secret of the crop's cultivation had never leaked past the borders of Venera.

The amulet led her downward through a maze of antiquity, of past iterations of the fabulous city-state, until finally its beam of light settled on a statuette adorned with vermilion jewels. Approximately twenty centimetres high, carved in ebony, the piece depicted a black woman with huge breasts, hips, and buttocks, one arm pointing upward, the other downward. Patricia guessed it to be an ancient fertility goddess, or perhaps an early depiction of the Goddess Venera herself. Were she to sell this, Patricia would make a fortune. The rare vermilion gems alone were priceless!

This was the first and only time that thoughts of personal gain crossed Patricia's mind in the course of her duties as the Detective of Desire. The instant this hint of greed entered her mind, the Detective of Desire transformed back into her mundane identity of Patricia Alexandria. Patricia immediately recognized her error. Had her moment of weakness forever taken away the Detective of Desire? Would she ever be able to find her way out of subterranean Venera without the abilities of the Detective of Desire?

Patricia fought her mounting panic. She calmed herself by thinking of all the happiness the Detective of Desire had brought to the world. She recalled the secret message of the golden cryptograph and contemplated its beauty.

... And the Detective of Desire returned.

Holding the vermilion-adorned statuette, the Detective of Desire followed the pull of her amulet. She flew out of the underground maze and into the sky of Venera. That night's journey took her to a notorious house: the Velvet Bronzemine. Its front doors opened, heeding the amulet. The Detective of Dreams floated inside. Throughout the mansion, naked people of all ages danced and fucked and painted and played music and sculpted and sang. They ignored her passage — not because they would not have been curious had they seen her but because the amulet made her invisible to all but her target for this mission.

She floated up the stairs and through another doorway that opened before the glow of the amulet. It was the house's master bedroom, and Patricia recognized the principal occupant of the bed: Tito Bronze himself — filmmaker, pornographer, and Venera's premier patron of the arts.

With him were a half-dozen sycophants — male, female, and ambiguously gendered — each of them his junior by at least twenty years. All were asleep, their limbs entwined in a sensual lattice.

The Detective of Desire whispered, "Tito Bronze ..." and the man woke up. He leered at the Detective of Desire with undisguised lust, but a beam of light from the amulet diverted his gaze to the statuette. Bronze shook his bedmates awake and gestured them out of the room. They complied submissively. He closed the door and turned back toward the Detective of Desire.

He took the statuette from her and fondled it with a charming combination of childlike glee, reverent awe, and perverse lust. He clutched it to his chest and looked at the Detective of Desire. He mouthed more than uttered: "Thank you."

At that moment Patricia became aware of the notorious filmmaker's tremendous erection. It was both fascinating and alarming. Then, she noticed that he had noticed her noticing. He smiled predatorily and cocked his head toward the bed.

Patricia laughed and started flying away toward the open window. But the filmmaker cried out: "Wait!" She turned back and he said: "Stay. I will make a film of your exploits. With you as the star! Stay, Detective of Desire, and I will make you the object of everyone's desires!" Patricia laughed again and flew out the window as Bronze shouted after her.

The following year, Tito Bronze's *La Détective du Désir* premiered at Cannes. When she heard about the film, Patricia did not know whether she should be irked or flattered. She settled on feeling both and travelled to Cannes to see the film. She had never before attended the famous film festival, and this seemed like a good incentive to finally experience it. *La Détective du Désir* featured an all-French cast, with the protagonist's centre of operations changed from the Veneran Archipelago to the French Riviera. A pornographic romp mingled with pulp adventure, *La Détective du Désir* was altogether silly and wonderful and had nothing to do whatsoever with the real Detective of Desire, her abilities, or her activities. Patricia loved every second of it. The lead actress even resembled Patricia a little bit. When the video came out the following year, Patricia was proud to purchase a copy.

Patricia kept the golden cryptograph in her office safe at Tomorrow's Yesterdays. One morning, she came to work to find her shop had been burglarized, the merchandise ransacked, the safe broken into, left open and empty.

Immediately, she closed her eyes and brought to mind the secret message of the golden cryptograph. To her surprise and relief, the transformation succeeded. She tried to focus the power of her amulet on the golden cryptograph, but now, as before, she had no control over which object the amulet directed her toward. Every night for the next month, she mustered all of her willpower, but the amulet resisted her efforts to locate the golden cryptograph. In time, her attempts grew less frequent and then petered out altogether. Her enthusiasm for her life as the Detective of Desire also waned.

Still, she soldiered on, but the exploits of the Detective of Desire had lost the sheen of glamour and adventure that had so thrilled her while the golden cryptograph was still in her possession. What did she care if a pair of vintage Italian heels found the perfect drag-queen feet? If a hand-carved backgammon set led a lonely man to the person who would become the most steadfast and caring friend of his life? If an out-of-print guide to nonexistent birds, with nearly half of its pages torn out or damaged, fuelled an in elderly woman a newfound passion for cryptid ornithology that filled the rest of her years with wonder?

One night, eight months after the robbery, she found she could no longer recall the alchemical cipher of the golden cryptograph. The space in her mind formerly occupied by that memory was now a bland emptiness. The Detective of Desire was no more. She wondered for a moment if she should feel sad for the loss, but the truth was that she no longer cared.

Tomorrow's Yesterdays had also lost the charm that had once fulfilled her so. Since the robbery, her attachment to it had been damaged. For years now, a friendly competitor had been dropping hints that she would like to acquire Patricia's business.

So Patricia sold the shop for a hefty sum. At the age of 36 she retired to a modest rural home in Portugal, where she spent the rest of her days in comfortable solitude, painting surreal scenes populated by animate objects involved in strange rituals.

PART 3: THE ULTIMATE ADVENTURE OF THE GOLDEN CRYPTOGRAPH

The thief who stole, among other things, the golden cryptograph from the office safe of Tomorrow's Yesterdays was not specifically seeking the alchemical treasure. Also, the thief did not want to tarry. Once he cracked the safe, he crammed all of its contents into a gym bag and was quickly away to his next target.

Ensconced in his apartment he examined the haul from his raid on the businesses of Bohemia Avenue. The thief made out well that night, but the golden cryptograph presented a conundrum. In the course of his versatile career the thief had dealt with stolen art before; although he had no clue what the strangely luminescent object truly was, he recognized that the golden cryptograph was a unique piece made of gold of uncommon purity, its value inestimable. Experience taught him, however, that the uniqueness that made the golden cryptograph so valuable would also make it difficult, perhaps impossible, to sell. By tomorrow, the theft would be reported and the police would immediately be on the lookout for the art treasure. Unless ...

What if the vintage shop had itself acquired the piece through less than honest means? The theft would then go unreported, and he would be free to profit from his acquisition.

Over the next few weeks, the thief scanned the news with meticulous care. Not one word about the golden greeting card appeared anywhere. His one-night raid on Bohemia Avenue was only ever covered for the two days following the event on the local news, and no report made any mention of the art object.

The thief was a patient man who lived modestly. With his profits from that one night's work, he could subsist comfortably for two or three years. He would wait a few months before deciding what to do with the golden cryptograph. Melt it? Fence it? Sell it directly?

Finally, six months later, satisfied that there was no alert in regards to the object, the thief contacted a collector in Genoa he'd dealt with before and offered him the piece. The transaction was concluded to each party's satisfaction.

The collector, like the thief, was not a key who could unlock the golden cryptograph; however, someone in the collector's household was: his teenage daughter.

⌒ As soon as the collector's daughter unlocked the mysteries of the golden cryptograph — approximately eight months after its theft — the alchemical formula vanished from the mind of Patricia Alexandria and she lost the abilities of the Detective of Desire. The collector's daughter decrypted the golden cryptograph in her own way — everything and everyone she touched turned to gold: her house, her cats, her father, her mother, her collection of antique dollhouses. She could not turn the power off. She fled her father's country estate, now a house of gold inhabited by golden statues. She cursed the golden cryptograph and tried to destroy it. But it was resistant to her efforts. Finally, she simply discarded it as she ran in the woods — every tree she brushed against turned to gold. Even without the golden cryptograph in her possession, the power did not leave her. Within a week, she was dead of dehydration and starvation, as nothing could come into contact with her without transmuting into gold.

Over the next few years, the golden cryptograph changed owners frequently — sometimes lost and found, sometimes discarded and discovered, sometimes stolen, sometimes bequeathed — and every so often would find itself in the hands of a key. Always, once a new key decoded the golden cryptograph, the previous key (should they still be alive) would forget the alchemical message that had been revealed to them and lose any power, abilities, or curse that knowledge had conferred upon them.

Thanks to the golden cryptograph: archaeologist Carter Adams grew wings that allowed him to fly; attorney Barbara Grey learned the languages of every animal on Earth; at every sunset, taxi dispatcher Isabel Vega changed into a fox (and back to her human self at sunrise, always naked and often in embarrassing situations); farmhand Hugo Philips gained omniscient knowledge, but his mind was unable to cope and he became quite insane; nightclub owner Ken Gibson adopted the identity of the Savage Shadow and fought crime with a variety of exotic weapons fashioned alchemically; botanist Reed Hughes was transformed into an amnesiac centaur who roamed the great deserts of the American southwest, until he was killed by a shotgun-wielding drunken widower; department store manager Steve Drake enjoyed a brief career as the world's greatest stage magician; chiropractor Max Tanaka was granted the ability to control any motor vehicle with his mind; librarian Kimberley Lee's body dissolved into a wisp of near-nothingness, and her ghostly self eventually dissipated when she had been forgotten by all those who had known her.

⁄☙ The golden cryptograph wound up in a thrift store in Newfoundland, where it caught the eye of an elderly man who thought it would make an attractive gift for his equally elderly wife. He purchased it, along with some tools and kitchenware, and got in his pickup truck to drive back to his house. He never made it home.

En route, his truck was hit by what witnesses would later call a meteor. The impact resulted in a glow of golden light that shone like a miniature sun. Federal investigators did nothing to contradict those reports of a meteor being responsible for the accident, although they concluded from the wreckage that what had killed the old man and destroyed his vehicle was not a chunk of rock, but a spaceship. A small spaceship.

The investigators, whose real findings were kept from the public, detected no trace of a pilot or other occupant. All the remains that were found at the crash site belonged to the old man. No connection was ever made between that incident and the superbeing who would, in later years, forever alter the course of human history.

The vessel from the stars had brought a visitor to Earth: a baby boy — an alien infant whose original shape and form were discarded upon impact, when the golden cryptograph reacted to coming into contact with its ultimate key. This key — the baby from the stars — was perfectly attuned to the golden cryptograph. This time, for its ultimate decryption, the golden cryptograph did not simply grant a revelation of power to the key; it merged with the key.

The alchemical gold of the golden cryptograph enveloped the infant and moulded the alien into human shape. The cryptograph took on the appearance of a skin-tight uniform in various shades of gold, from near-white to deep yellow. The uniform's cape was gilded with the same flourishes that the golden cryptograph had sported on its front page; embossed on the chest of the uniform was the circular crest that had adorned the back page.

For twenty years, the golden cryptograph and its ultimate key floated invisibly in the sky, orbiting the Earth, feeding on sunlight. For twenty years, the golden cryptograph, whose tendrils of alchemical gold had melded with the key's anatomy, uploaded into the alien's mind every bit of information it contained.

Once the key had learned all he could from the golden cryptograph, he floated down to Earth. He called himself The Ultimate. Unlike the previous keys, he was not merely a conduit for this or that aspect of the knowledge gleaned from the golden cryptograph. The Ultimate was the incarnation of everything the golden cryptograph could be, as perceived by an infinite number of consciousnesses. He mastered all the powers of every previous key and all the powers of all the keys that could be. And all that power was tempered by the compassion that came with ultimate knowledge.

The Ultimate possessed, of course, ultimate charisma, ultimate might, and ultimate wisdom. It would have been within his power to reshape the world in a single day and to bend the population of the Earth to his utopian vision, but he sought to recruit everyone to his cause of their free will. After all, he was blessed with ultimate patience.

Most were easily convinced, but a few were immune to the lure of utopia, those for whom the light would never be a source of comfort and joy but something to fear and loathe. The Ultimate's enemies took on gaudy identities in their struggle to thwart his utopian dreams: Lord X, Big Brain Boy, the Laser Leech, the Radioactive Heart, the Anti-Ultimate League, the Vampire Family, the Nomad of the Stars, the Rainbow Squad, the Amazon Dominatrix. He defeated them all and banished them to a parallel version of the Earth, one that forever revelled in dystopian misery.

After a decade of The Ultimate's unerring guidance, Earth achieved utopia. His task accomplished, The Ultimate left the planet. His goal was not to rule; his only desire was to transform the crypto-alchemical message of the golden cryptograph into utopian reality. The mistakes of human history and development had been corrected and Earth had been granted utopia, but it was up to its people to sustain it.

And so The Ultimate, in his eternal wanderings through the cosmos, spread the word of the golden cryptograph to every inhabited planet he encountered. And he saw that it was good.

THE THIRTEENTH
GODDESS

～⌇〜

I. THE BLOOD OF THE EARTH

Come the gibbous moon, the waters of Venera start to flow red with the blood the Earth. By the time of the full moon, the water coursing through the city's waterways is of a burnt-red hue. As the moon begins to wane, so does the colour of the water. By the next day — today — all traces of Mother Earth's monthly cycle have vanished. Such are the tenets of the Venera Church of Mother Earth, which has held power in the city-state since the aftermath of the Nazi occupation.

Sister Agnes takes off her shoes and, pulling up her skirt, walks down three steps on the stairs by the Via Gaia. The now-clear water caresses her toes, her feet, her freshly shaved calves. She delights in the briny smell of the salt water now that the pungency of the blood of the Earth has been washed away. Not for the first time, she dreads rather than welcomes the thought of having to bathe in the menses of the Goddess when next they flow. Not for the first time, she questions her life in the inner circles of the Church.

As Agnes begins to climb back up to the street, something bumps against her leg. At first, she can't identify what she sees. But then her mind starts to make sense of the bloated, sickly object: it's a severed arm, cut — no, torn — at the shoulder and the wrist.

She steps out of the water and stares quietly at the gruesome piece of flotsam.

2. GODDESSES OF LUST

Naked, the sweat and ichors of sex drying on her skin, Belinda Gerda applies paint to the canvas before her. The thirteenth and final canvas in her current project. She paints in watercolours; she rejects oils as too garish, too harsh. For this series, which is scheduled to hang in ten days at Tito Bronze's Velvet Bronzemine, the nexus of the Venera arts scene, the artist has perfected a solution to add depth and texture to her hues. Red is the dominant scheme throughout the *Goddesses of Lust* tableaux; every colour must also possess a hint of red — and so she has blended the watery menses of the Goddess into her colours. Included, too, to give the paint a fecund texture, are her own vaginal juices, blended with the spunk of her mad lover, Magus Amore, who is at this moment lying on the floor of her studio, writhing in a post-coital fit of delirium.

As he rubbed his engorged cock all over her body, as he repeatedly penetrated her every orifice until she could not tell where she ended and he began, he described the thirteenth goddess. By fucking her, he worshipped at the altars of the goddess's body.

And so it had been with every previous goddess in this series: Magus's insane, lustful ravings inspiring Belinda to bring her lover's erotic visions to life. But Magus had revealed to her the names of the others, all of them goddesses of antiquity: Ninlil, Inanna, Ishtar, Astarte, Kali, Isis, Aphrodite, Athena, Hecate, Demeter, Venus, Gaia ...

This strange, anonymous goddess of Magus's is unlike any deity Belinda has ever beheld. She has decided to call this painting *The Thirteenth Goddess*. There is no doubt in Belinda's mind that this thirteenth goddess is in all ways a creation of her lover's demented genius. The pomp and garishness of the goddess's clothes remind Belinda of a superhero costume, but her body, although mostly humanoid, is disquietingly alien in many subtle details. She sits on a throne of organic technology, surrounded by glowing technovegetation. The goddess holds a picture frame against her chest. In that embedded picture, the naked goddess, her skin tattooed with the same patterns as Magus himself, is attended to by monstrous multi-limbed creatures who lick and caress her face, her breasts, her feet, and her dripping cunt.

Belinda loses herself in her work. She does not notice when Magus rises from the floor and peers behind her shoulder at her work, his eyes gleaming with fascination and admiration.

After a while, he turns away, though, and leaves the room. Through the door that leads to the basement of Belinda's apartment, he climbs down the stairs. He lifts a metal slab from the floor of the lower level, revealing a dark chasm. He slides into that darkness, downward into the bowels of Venera.

The Goddess calls; Magus Amore descends, through the mysterious and confounding vestiges of Veneras past. Ancient, buried Venera is not draped in absolute darkness. A rusty gold-red glow emanates from veins in the walls, from rivulets of unknown origins that flow on and off through some of the most decrepit ruins. Here, in the subterranean world of the main island of the archipelago of Venera, he has been able to explore the ineffable mythologies of his imagination. The deeper he descends, the closer he gets to the core of his own primordial ur-story. To the archetypal narrative through which he makes sense of the world. Book after book, the writer had tried in vain to achieve such transcendent self-knowledge. Until his life's quest took him, here, to Venera. To the drug vermilion, and to the deities, creatures, and realms it has revealed to him. Climbing down through the ever-changing ruins of Veneran history that hint at a panoply of divergent and improbable timelines, he reaches the whirlpool of iridescent vermilion, the sacred portal that delivers him into her presence. Never in the same location, the whirlpool appears to him at the end of his every subterranean odyssey. Magus Amore enters the glittering eddy, downward into mystery, and surrenders himself to the inscrutable whims of his most beloved and terrifying deity.

3. THE UNVEILING OF VENERA

The sun rises, and Venera slowly, teasingly reveals itself, sensuously slipping off one thin layer of dawn mist at a time. It is as if it were freshly born this very morning, complete and perfect, like Venus from the half-shell. This is Detective-Inspector Pietro Dovelander's first trip to the city-state, and, despite himself, he is awed by the otherworldly sight of this notorious metropolis. None of those ubiquitous photographs do justice to its weird magnificence.

First, there are the rows of lights emerging from the water: markers to guide the archipelagic city's heavy boat traffic. Their glow, made ambiguous by the mist, imbues the air with an ethereal atmosphere. With precise determination, the gulls fly through this ether, miniature angels single-mindedly performing ineffable duties. The countless small boats busily but unhurriedly navigating the waters seem like phantasms of long-dead vessels floating on a ghostly sea. Then a few buildings can be vaguely discerned — bizarre apparitions of utterly alien architecture to the detective's gaze. Suddenly, the cityscape is visible: breastlike domes and serpentine elevated walkways; bulbous walls and strangely sinuous towers; vegetation suggestively entwined with wood and masonry; bright, childlike colours; pagan ornaments and monuments, at once playful and terrifying; giant sculptures of mythic beasts, voluptuous women, and intimidatingly endowed men, often engaged in prurient acts; gargoyles jutting out from walls and roofs at unexpected and menacing angles; numerous staircases leading down from the streets to the waterways that crisscross the city; tendrils of seaweed crawling up the masonry from the water to the surface; dogs trotting through the narrow streets, crossing the ornate mossy bridges, or simply staring out at the passing maritime traffic; cats and birds calmly perched on or nestled in the various nooks and ledges offered by the architecture that refuses boxlike construction and eschews right angles.

Unsettling beauty, tantalizing opulence, unfettered imagination, unabashed eroticism ... wild nature enmeshed with sophisticated civilization ... Venera, Pietro surmises, is the woman every man secretly yearns for and even more secretly fears.

Regardless — he did not request this assignment, nor does he want it. Venera is not in his jurisdiction, and the detective resents being taken away from his own city to deal with someone else's problem. But celebrity has its costs. Credited for the safe return of the triplets in the Sanangelo kidnapping and with the collar of two serial killers, Pietro is uncomfortable with his fame. It hinders his work that his face is so well-known now, and he resents that simply doing his job and doing it well is somehow newsworthy.

And now this! The High Countess of the Venera Church of Mother Earth has personally requested that he — and only he — be assigned to the macabre case besetting the insular city-state, and his government, sensing a diplomatic coup, did not give him a choice. Not if he wanted to continue working as a detective.

The boat bringing him from the mainland to Venera is the High Countess's own official state vessel. The domelike interior of the cabin forms one continuous fresco: a sea of naked women of all shapes and sizes with limbs entwined like vines, the women's nipples ripe like succulent grapes, menstrual blood flowing from between their legs into a rust-red backdrop. The joints, cabinets, doors, and window frames are all adorned with totemic gilded sculptures of exaggeratedly voluptuous women.

From the outside, the boat is black and sober — an anomaly in this city that celebrates excess — with only the gold crest of the Church on each side. Despite the rain, after a cursory examination, Pietro shunned the inside and trusted his grey raincoat to protect him from the weather for the three-hour journey.

What he really wants to do is smoke his pipe, but the Countess's eagerness to engage his services did not include permission to light up in her vessel. In fact, he would not be able to smoke for the duration of this investigation: tobacco is strictly prohibited in Venera.

Whatever it takes, Pietro will wrap up this case quickly.

4. THE HIGH COUNTESS OF THE VENERA CHURCH OF MOTHER EARTH

The High Countess of the Venera Church of Mother Earth spreads the sheets of paper on her desk, making a show of examining them, but Detective-Inspector Dovelander can see that she is not truly reading. In fact, he's certain that she knows that he's noticed this, that, furthermore, she wants him to know. She's decided to make him wait; although he resents her attitude, he is trained to respect the chain of command, and for the duration he will be reporting to her. But her lack of respect irritates him. The day before, their appointment was cancelled at the last minute, with no explanation. And now, these silly head games.

The Countess's attire jars with her portentous title. A woman of 58, the Countess looks almost twenty years younger and dresses to flatter her relatively youthful appearance. Her skin is smooth, the colour of cream into which are diluted a few drops of dark wine. Her long hair reaches down to her breasts, which are squeezed tight, still noticeably ample, by a push-up bra. Her black dress, with low décolletage but long sleeves, reaches to just above the knee. The dress is garlanded with gold, some strands of the soft metal dyed red. Her legs are otherwise bare, and her feet shorn in high-heeled evening sandals that show off her elegant feet and vermilion-painted toes. Her fingernails, however, are not painted, nor is she wearing any jewellery. In newspaper photographs, Dovelander distinctly remembers, the High Countess is always copiously adorned. This room disturbs Pietro. In fact, every room and corridor he's seen since his arrival in Venera yesterday has left him unsettled. For example, there are no corners as such in this room, nothing he can properly identify as a wall, no clearly defined ceiling. Pietro can discern no pattern to the network of arches and bulges, and he cannot even guess at the function of the various nooks and niches, or the purpose behind the division of space. Through stained-glass windows, from confounding angles, and reflected on haphazardly scattered mirrors, the sunlight wafts through the room like a heavy fog, challenging his sense of balance. The rainbow of bright colours, the ubiquitous decorative flourishes, the alien geometry, the way the light filters through the room — all of this combines to short-circuit his powers of observation. More than ever, he is convinced that this assignment is a mistake. He will not be able to pursue any kind of worthwhile investigation in this environment. He lacks the required knowledge and familiarity, which only a local or an expert could possess.

At least the floor is flat, although it, too, is heavily decorated, every tile handcrafted with intricate designs, flourishes, and symbols.

Everything is overwhelming in Venera. All of his training and experience — useless. How is he expected to know how people living in such an environment think? Or understand enough of their behaviour and customs to know how to question them? Without any frame of reference how can he possibly see the truth hidden in their lies? He'll bungle this job, create a diplomatic mess, and his career will end just as certainly as if he'd outright refused to take the case.

"You're a Christian. A Catholic."

Her gruff voice startles him. He'd expected her to speak in a smoky voice. Instead, she barks. Not in a menacing way, but, regardless, hers is a voice that insists on being heard. Under his shirt, the crucifix hanging around his neck seems to sear his skin, as if the High Countess could see through his shirt and burn the pendant with heat vision, like an American superhero.

It occurs to him, though, that she's sensed his discomfort and might be offering him a graceful way to bow out. "I regret that poses a problem, Your Highness. I'm sure my government can assign another — "

"No. You'll do. We need your skills. Crime is rare here, and violent crime even more so. We do not have the appropriate resources to deal with the current situation. We need this resolved before the next gibbous moon. I only bring up your religion to mention that, although Venera does not officially permit proselytizing faiths to congregate, services are held in various embassies, including that of your government. We tolerate it as long as such activity remains private, with no missionary agenda."

Pietro is surprised by the courtesy. His own government, undoubtedly aware of the services, never bothered to inform him. Neither did anyone at the embassy yesterday. "Thank you, Your Highness."

Is that almost a smile on her face?

"Also, I hear one of the attachés at your country's embassy has a profitable sideline procuring black-market tobacco for the diplomatic community ..." — Dovelander tries but can't contain the sigh of relief that escapes from his gut — " ... however, do make sure to contain your filthy habit to embassy grounds." Her tone is censorious, but she makes sure that Pietro sees her grin and nod.

Pietro jumps at the sound of someone clearing her throat behind him. He hadn't even been aware that anyone else was in the room with them. He can't remember the last time someone successfully snuck up on him; has it, in fact, ever happened before? Again, a disquieting feeling of inadequacy gnaws at his usually imperturbable confidence.

The new woman, an Earth Sister, looks shaken. Despite her height —she is taller than Pietro and wearing flats—she holds herself to look small and meek, digging her shoulders into herself, her back tightly constricted. "Pardon the intrusion, Your Highness, but there have been new developments." Her voice, at odds with her body language, is steady and emotionless, neither cold nor warm. The flash of anger on the High Countess's face is not directed at the newcomer but at what she expects her to say. "New body parts, Sister Agnes?"

Sister Agnes swallows before answering. This time, her voice betrays a hint of fear. "The question is, Your Highness—from what kinds of bodies?"

5. DETECTIVE-INSPECTOR DOVELANDER INVESTIGATES

"Isn't anyone going to arrest that man?"

"Why?" Sister Agnes responds to Detective-Inspector Pietro Dovelander. In a stationary boat on the Primadonna Canal, the duo is supervising the work of collecting the body parts from the water. Nine Sisters, three per boat, are doing the grunt work with nets.

Earlier, a squad of Earth Sisters had scattered the crowd of curious onlookers, but now a tall man walks along Via Bellarossa, which borders the waterway. His gait is punctuated by random fits and starts. In a loud voice, he grunts unintelligible words and phrases, gesticulating wildly. Occasionally, he bumps into walls, or trips and falls, immediately picking himself up as if nothing had happened.

"For one thing, he shouldn't be here. Is no-one guarding the perimeter?" But that's not what really bothers the detective. The intruder is entirely naked, all body hair shaved off, save for his unruly mane of dark hair and his long, wispy charcoal beard. His whole body is covered in tattoos of occult symbols. Both nipples are pierced. His long semi-erect penis flaps against his thigh; the tip of the stretched foreskin almost reaches his knee. "And for another ..."

Sister Agnes raises her eyebrows and looks the detective in the eye, the hint of a smirk crossing her features. Dovelander feels challenged, tested. Under his shirt, the small crucifix drags on his neck and shoulders like a heavy burden.

"Never mind," he says, defeated, turning his attention back to the monstrous body parts of disquieting morphology the Earth Sisters are pulling in from the water.

☞ Doctor Sam Tuturo is not a medical examiner, but there is no ME to be found anywhere in Venera. Tuturo is a surgeon working at the ER of Venera's only hospital. Unlike every other hospital Dovelander has ever visited, this one is remarkably quiet. "Where are all the patients?"

"There are a dozen or so on the third floor. Doctor Mandola is in charge of resident patients. Doctor Landau is supervising the ER in my absence." Tuturo has been assigned to assist Dovelander for the duration of the investigation. The doctor doesn't seem overly pleased by this.

Samuel or Samantha? Tuturo, like everything else in this damned city, confounds Dovelander. At first glance he'd assumed the doctor to be a man, but that was partly because Sams are usually men. The cut of the doctor's eyeglasses seem unquestionably masculine, yet the doctor's delicate wrists and smooth, fey jawline hint strongly at femininity. The doctor's androgynous voice offers no definite clue.

Dovelander estimates the doctor's height at 165 centimetres, shorter than the detective by a hand. Short for a man, but not necessarily so for an Asian man, and Tuturo is at least partly Asian, probably Japanese. The doctor sports an expensive-looking trim haircut and a slick, artfully unkempt metrosexual style that, again, betrays no specific gender identity.

The handshake, though, is female, or perhaps simply effeminate. The doctor's hand lies in his like a cold, limp, dead fish. And the doctor has made no move to remove it; they've been clasping hands for nearly a minute now. Dovelander can't tell if it's passive-aggressive flirtation or passive-aggressive, well, aggression. Maybe both. Anyway, again, it feels like a challenge. Like he would lose face if he were the one to let go.

You can tell a lot about a man by his handshake. Men learn to express their entire personality in the way they clasp another man's hand. In women, though, handshakes can be misleading. Women don't reveal their identity through their handshakes but more from their posture, including the tilt of their heads — a few degrees of angle can tell entire life stories.

This overlong and clammy handshake, though — Dovelander can't conclude anything from it, save for the already obvious fact that he himself is an alien here and, apparently, an unwelcome one.

Forcing his thoughts back to the subject of the near-empty hospital, the detective comments: "But the population of Venera exceeds five hundred thousand."

The doctor doesn't respond, which further irritates Dovelander. He tries not to show it, but he's exhausted. Having to put up with passive-aggressive cooperation doesn't make him angry at this point, it just makes him want to collapse.

The doctor finally terminates the handshake and offers the detective coffee. "Come on. I could use one, too."

Coffee! At least, this damnable place doesn't ban that as well.

Mugs in hand, the two proceed to the doctor's office, which turns out to be by far the most conventional room the detective has seen yet. Save for a few ornamental details, this could almost be the office of any doctor or researcher back home.

Tuturo motions the detective to sit and hands him his report, which includes photographs.

Quickly leafing through the folder, Dovelander's eye catches a clue. "The flesh was tattooed?" And: "Were the previous body parts also tattooed? With similar markings?"

⌒ Back at the Mother House, a gargantuan Earth Sister is on night duty. She is by far the fattest person Dovelander has seen yet in Venera.

He had begun to suspect that fashionable slimness was mandatory in this demented, decadent city.

He's astonished at the elegance with which Sister Bettina, as she introduces herself, rises from her armchair. It's a mythic moment, like the Leviathan emerging from the depths. Venera tends to imbue the simplest of acts with gratuitous gravitas.

There's something straightforward about the Sister that immediately endears her to Pietro. That, plus the fact the she responds to his urgent request without any hesitation or obfuscation. "I'll be but a moment fetching Sister Agnes, detective."

While he waits, Pietro tries to understand the layout of the lobby, but, despite himself, his eye keeps being distracted by the sexual acts painted onto the floor. Couldn't they have chosen Moriano for this job? He's both an atheist and a degenerate. He's not too bad a detective, either. So what if the High Countess had asked for Dovelander? Both his captain and his commissioner know him well enough to understand that he's not the right man for this job. Or at least, for this place.

"What's the news, detective?" Sister Agnes's long hair is dishevelled, and her shirt is tucked crookedly into her pants. She's still wiping the sleep from her eyes.

"We should have held that man for questioning."

It takes a moment for Agnes to understand. "You mean Amore?"

"Is that his name? That crazy naked man with the tattoos?"

"Yes. Magus Amore. Once a brilliant writer, now one of our most renowned eccentrics."

Magus Amore. Even Dovelander, who reads at most two or three novels a year, knows the name. Twenty years ago, Amore had been the darling of the international literary world. Winner of the Booker, the Nobel, and numerous other awards. Dovelander had tried to read one of his books, *The League of Anarchy*. A thriller, the cover blurb had said. Impenetrable nonsense, filled with deranged sex and cruelty, pagan mumbo-jumbo, and subversive rants, was more what Dovelander thought of it, although he'd given up on it after a few dozen pages.

"Do you have any photos of him on file? Especially of his tattoos?"

6. THE GARDEN OF THE GODDESSES

In the lush garden of the Goddesses, naked, prepubescent sycophants tend to their every need. It is the night of Belinda's initiation, her ascension to godhood; for the occasion she once more wears the body of a sixteen-year-old. Her cunt grows moist as the Goddesses' gazes fall on her once-more ripe breasts.

An insistent ringing interrupts the proceedings. No-one else seems to notice the jarring sound. Belinda's concentration is shattered. Her body regains its true age. The Goddesses laugh. A loud thumping joins the ringing. Belinda grows even older, so old that all her hair falls out. Her shrivelled tits hang down to her waist.

As the skin begins peeling off her bones, she wakes up. The doorbell is ringing. Someone's beating hard on the door.

She forces herself out of bed. Picking up her nightgown, she sees her 45-year-old body in the bedroom mirror and yearns for firmer years. She wraps herself in the nightgown to find out what the commotion is about. She's certain it's about Magus. What's her crazy old darling done this time?

At the door, she finds a man in a worn, grey raincoat. He fidgets too much with his hands, and he's scowling. At his side, a tall, nervous Earth Sister avoids her gaze.

Without greeting or preamble, the man says: "We need to talk to Magus Amore."

"And you would be ...?"

"My name's Detective-Inspector Pietro Dovelander, and this is Sister Agnes from the Mother House." The detective reaches into his raincoat. "We're on official business, acting with full authority from the High Countess." He shows Belinda an official document, with the holographic seal of the Church, granting him full emergency powers. "Are you Belinda Gerda?"

"Yes. And I haven't seen Magus for days. It's not unusual for him to disappear for long stretches."

The detective seems somewhat less tense when he addresses her again: "I apologize for the intrusion at this inconvenient hour, but this is truly urgent. May we come in?"

7. THE AUTOMATA OF HEMERO VOLKANUS

No edifice better illustrates the fact that most buildings are machines than the home of Hemero Volkanus. The guts of the building are turned inside out, so that the plumbing and wiring are all visible, albeit protected by acrylic glass. In addition, the house moves. The many windows of various sizes are all built with photosensitive transistors that guide their frames to rotate so as to best capture the sunlight, or avoid it, depending on weather and temperature. It's also a noisy house, as the various gears and parts are constantly in subtle motion.

There is no doorbell and no doorknob, and Belinda knows better than to knock. Within a few seconds the door slides open to reveal one of the Kourai Khryseai, as Hemero calls his chillingly lifelike female automata, after the mechanical servants the god Hephaestus created to help him in his Olympian smithy.

The gynoid greets her in the nonsense language the machines have been programmed to speak. Nonsense, perhaps, but undeniably beautiful, ethereal in its musical beauty. Sometimes, Belinda is tempted to accept Hemero's claims that it is indeed the language of the gods, unintelligible to mere mortals. Magus, who grows ever more desperately credulous, takes everything Hemero says at face value. Magus believes Hemero's story that he did not invent these beautiful machines but found them buried deep in the bowels of Venera, among the ruins of the forgotten civilizations that once prospered on the archipelago's main island, that they are in fact the true Kourai Khryseai of myth. The inventor may be brilliant, but his penchant for tall tales doesn't fool Belinda.

The gynoid guides Belinda through the house. They reach the workshop of Venera's self-styled Hephaestus as he tinkers on a pair of mechanical legs.

"Trying to improve on the current model, Hemero?" Volkanus, who was born in Italy, lost both his legs in a childhood automobile accident.

"You know that for years I've been trying to reverse-engineer the Kourai Khryseai" — computer screens on his work table display schemata of a robot designed to look like a human female — "but I still haven't cracked Hephaestus's technology."

"Save it for Magus, Hemero. I'm not buying today." Despite herself, her voice breaks a bit.

Volkanus turns to look at Belinda. "Always the skeptic, eh?" Then he falls silent and scrutinizes her so intently that Belinda squirms.

Finally, she asks: "Is Magus here?"

"Magus? ... No. I haven't seen him for ... two weeks, I think. What's the matter, Belinda?"

It cascades out of her: "I haven't seen Magus either. For nearly three days. And I was just interrogated at the Mother House. They've called in a foreign detective, and he thinks that Magus is involved with those body parts that have been popping up in the waterways. They've taken my passport. They've confiscated my latest painting because of the tattoos, and —"

"Belinda. Slow down. Let's move to the parlour. One of the Kourai Khryseai can serve us tea, and you can tell me exactly what —"

The house interrupts Volkanus: "Magus Amore has arrived."

Volkanus raises his eyebrows, looking amused and curious, while Belinda gasps: "Magus ..."

The madman bursts naked into the room. "Belinda! I've come from your studio. Where's *The Thirteenth Goddess*? The time has come. Venera needs your sacred masterwork."

8. REVELATIONS

Every time Sister Agnes comes close to sleep, as she closes her eyes, she is visited by visions of the goddess from Belinda Gerda's painting and is almost instantly shocked awake. She can scarcely understand what happens in these phantasmagorias: they are populated by technobiological creatures whose morphology defies her understanding of animal life; these creatures all tend, in some manner beyond Agnes's ken, to the goddess.

What is the connection between Amore, Gerda's artwork, and the severed body parts?

Detective Dovelander had wanted to store Gerda's painting at his embassy, but Sister Agnes was under orders to monitor what he could or could not take out of Veneran jurisdiction. There was no doubt in Agnes's mind that the High Countess did not want that piece of evidence to leave Venera proper. Agnes requisitioned the use of a large storage closet at the Mother House, a 24-hour guard, and a padlock whose only two keys were in the hands of herself and the High Countess.

Agnes gives up on sleep. She dresses and heads to the ad hoc evidence room. The gargantuan Sister Bettina — on guard duty, sitting by the door — acknowledges Agnes with a bored nod.

Inside, instead of darkness, Agnes finds the small room bathing in vermilion-red glow, emanating from Belinda Gerda's painting.

Her painting of a goddess ...

... of the Goddess.

The Goddess, who now talks to her in a language she should not understand but does. The Goddess, who bestows upon her revelation. Agnes begins to see the outline of an iridescent whirlpool, enveloping her and the painting, when an insistent knock on the door breaks the spell, returning the storage closet to darkness and leaving only wisps of the Goddess's divine language in her conscious memory.

When Sister Agnes emerges from the storage closet, Sister Bettina introduces an attaché from Dovelander's embassy. Exuding pompousness and impatience, the too-handsome young man asks: "Where is the detective-inspector?"

"I haven't seen him since late afternoon, after we finished examining some new evidence. He told me he was heading back to the embassy."

"You let him wander Venera unescorted? I'm certain your superior instructed you otherwise. Should anything happen to the detective-inspector, my government shall hold you directly responsible."

The revelations of the Goddess recede ever farther from Agnes's consciousness. She's annoyed at this bureaucratic troll and concerned for Dovelander, with whom she has quickly developed an amiable and respectful camaraderie. Without a word, she hurries away while the attaché is still addressing her. She knows the city. She'll find Dovelander.

9. THE KOURAI KHRYSEAI

During the age of fable, when Hephaestus built the four Kourai Khryseai, he imbued them with attributes of his fellow Olympians. Hemero Volkanus knows this, and so does Magus Amore, who can speak the language of the gods.

After Gerda tells him of the painting's confiscation, Amore addresses the Kourai Khryseai in the divine tongue, overriding Volkanus's reprogramming.

In a flash, two of the gynoids zoom out of sight, with the speed and cunning of Hermes.

Belinda opens her mouth, as if on the verge of speaking, but stays agape.

Answering her unspoken query, Amore says: "They've gone to fetch the likeness of the Goddess. Your painting. *The Thirteenth Goddess*."

10. URBAN MYTH

Tales are told around the world of people getting lost within the labyrinthine streets of Venera, of the city transforming itself with malignant sentience, obliterating any recognizable points of reference, rearranging its complex grid of streets and waterways and transmogrifying its buildings, warping time and geography, so as to capture and consume those foolish enough to be tempted by its surreal decadence.

Dovelander had long dismissed these ridiculous tales as urban myths, or as an obvious metaphor for the spiritual dangers of this blasphemous metropolis.

But, on his walk from the Mother House to his embassy, the detective-inspector lost all sense of time and place. Now, he does not recognize any of the buildings, which look even more deranged than usual. The city appears entirely deserted. The sky has become otherworldly — no: infernal, of an oppressive rust-red tinge. He can smell the brine of the sea, but he never manages to escape the ever-tighter grip of the city streets and vegetation. Sometimes, the plants whisper to him, but he cannot decipher the language they speak.

II. VENERA RISING

Less than a minute elapses, and the Kourai Khryseai return to Hemero's parlour with *The Thirteenth Goddess* and hand it to Magus. The madman sets it on the floor and chants to it in the same language he used when speaking to the automata. The painting shimmers with otherworldly light and the image within acquires a barely tangible three-dimensionality.

Belinda gapes in wonder: *I painted that?*

On the extended palm of the ethereal thirteenth goddess, an iridescent whirlpool, vermilion in colour, takes shape, growing until it engulfs Magus, Hemero, the Kourai Khryseai, and Belinda.

Belinda is momentarily blinded. Before her vision returns, she feels the wind in her hair. When she can see again, she recognizes where she has been transported: the roof garden of the Venera Church of Mother Earth, lush with vermilion plant.

Magus is kneeling before the painting, chanting in that same strange language. But now Belinda can understand him. She is granted a revelation and finally understands who the thirteenth goddess is.

Venera. Venera herself is the thirteenth goddess. Venera herself gifts Belinda with yet more divine visions. Venera is returning to reclaim her city. And she and Magus have been the instruments of her plan.

The Goddess is furious at the Church of Mother Earth for trying to eradicate her existence from history, for usurping her mysteries in the name of their Earth worship. It is her menses that flow through her city at every full moon, and not that of the Earth. The body parts that have been washing onto the core island are those of her sycophants, transmogrified and sacrificed in preparation of her return. Soon, they will live again.

Soon, Venera herself will live again.

Beneath the feet of her new worshippers, the Mother House crumbles to the ground, amid the screams of the blasphemous Sisters inside. The vermilion garden remains intact.

Around Belinda and the others, one of the myriad bygone iterations of the city of Venera rises from its subterranean tomb, reconfiguring the metropolis into a new agglomeration. The Goddess herself rises from deeper still, from deeper even than the bowels of the Earth, to whisper her divine song to those Venerans who survived the divine transmogrification of the city-state.

12. LOVE SONG

The voice of Venera is a call to life and self-awareness for the Kourai Khryseai; they shed their mechanical bodies to reveal new flesh, blessed by the Goddess.

For Hemero Volkanus, the holy song is a source of power; he mines it to acquire the divine attributes of his patron god, Hephaestus.

The music of the Goddess inspires Belinda Gerda to new heights of creativity: as yet uncreated tableaux cascade through her mind's eye, nurturing her lust for art.

The melodies of Venera are too exquisite for Magus Amore to bear; swimming in the holy music, his body dissolves — and his organic particles waft toward the Goddess. She inhales the essence of her most devout and loving worshipper.

To Pietro Dovelander, lost in the ever-changing maze of the city-state, Venera's voice is a chaotic screech that further confuses whatever sanity remains within him.

Agnes, who has been unable to locate the foreign detective, is initially terrified at the scope of the unfurling bio-architectural transformations besetting the city of her birth; Venera's song is welcome serenity.

13. THE BLOOD OF VENERA

Come the gibbous moon, the waters of Venera start to flow red with the blood the Goddess. By the time of the full moon, the water coursing through the city's waterways is of a burnt-red hue. At that time, the goddess Venera's worshippers are invited to bathe in her menses.

Agnes takes off her shoes, her skirt, and her blouse. She walks down three steps on the stairs by the Via Olympia. The vermilion-red water caresses her toes, her feet, her freshly shaved calves. She delights in the briny smell of the salt water as it blends with the spicy tang of Venera's blood.

Still trapped within an urban geography he cannot grasp, Pietro Dovelander watches Venera's worshippers soak in her blood. He wants to call out to Agnes, whom he dimly recognizes, but the knowledge of language leaves him before he can utter even a word.

VERMILION WINE

⚮

That autumn afternoon, the acqua alta took Venice by surprise. Monica had been snapping pictures of the pigeons at the Piazza San Marco, her camera set to black-and-white, when she felt dampness seep into her socks. Before she could react, the water nipped at her ankles. She didn't so much run from the rising tide as she was swept by the rush of tourists scrambling to escape the calf-high flooding by scurrying to the north of the piazza.

As soon as she reached dry terrain and recovered her balance, all Monica could feel was her soggy footwear, emphasizing her growing irritation with Venice, which, despite its undeniable architectural beauty, she had so far experienced as scarcely more than a cynical tourist trap. She removed her designer sneakers and ankle socks and, in disgust, abandoned them there on the street, venturing barefoot further north, away from the encroaching acqua alta.

Walking up the bustling Calle dei Fabbri, she thrilled at the sensation of her bare feet treading the Venetian ground. Through this fleshly connection, Monica was astonished to suddenly uncover a profound connection to an essentially seductive Venice, as if, with every step, intimate parts of herself seeped down into the city's foundations and the ineffable secrets of the city welled up into her body through her naked soles. Every millimetre of her skin tingled, sensually charged. Other passersby strolled by her, and whether it was skin or fabric that brushed her bare arms every fleeting contact shot sparks of pleasure throughout her body. It was in that heightened state of sexual awareness that she stumbled onto the Museo d'Arte Erotica.

The entrance fee was merely a handful of euros; inside, the exhibit snaked over four storeys in a labyrinthine manner that was as sensually intriguing as the items on display. The various types of flooring — wood, marble, rug — caressed her bare feet, accentuating the sensuousness of the visit. Here was the key, she realized, to truly understanding Venice. Forget the dull history books; forget the official, so-called "masterpieces" of art; forget the sanitized, Disneyland-like version of the city presented to tourists; forget the greedy entrepreneurs eager to milk every cent from those same tourists. Venice — the real Venice — was unabashed pleasure: the sensuous, otherworldly architecture; the intoxicating aroma of the Adriatic Sea; that palpable aura of relaxed decadence that descended upon the city at night; the nooks along the streets and alleys, where trysts demanded to be initiated, inviting stolen moments during which hands and lips took whatever they could; mischievous, decadent, provocative artwork that celebrated the ribald joy of the senses. Yes, Monica had glimpsed all these things in the past three days, but the ubiquitous and opportunistic mercantilism that had evolved to take advantage of the abundant tourism that the compact city could scarcely manage to contain obscured their significance.

Here in the erotica museum she was able to ignore the crass veneer that hid the true Venice. The parade of sexually charged objects from throughout Venice's history — paintings, photographs, sculptures, curios, book pages, film clips — allowed her to find the primal wonderment she had initially hoped to discover in this legendary city. She scrutinized every item on display with hungry curiosity. On the third floor, she stopped in front of a glass case that contained an old book, bound in a reddish fibre that she could not identify. The tome was titled *La storia segreta dei vini sacri* (*The Secret History of Sacred Wines*), by an author with the unlikely name of Magus Amore.

Although Monica did not really want to think about work, her passion for wine went far beyond her weekly feature at the magazine. She could have used the connections she had amassed over her twelve years of writing the column to enhance her impulsive escape to Italy, but she had craved solitude and anonymity. She had just broken off an affair with her editor, Katherine, whose bullying bossiness she had at first mistaken for the masculine arrogance that she responded to, both viscerally and uncontrollably, in women. Honestly, she wasn't entirely certain she would still have a job when she returned; something told her Katherine was spiteful enough to find some justification to let her go. Monica had more than two months' worth of columns filed in advance, so she didn't have to worry about any of that yet.

Her Italian was a cut or two above serviceable; she deciphered what she could of the text on the two-page spread displayed under the glass. Most of it dealt with the rites of minor, forgotten Catholic sects whose subtle blasphemies of the flesh were lost on her irreligious mind, but on the last line of the second page she encountered the words "il vino vermiglio di Venera" ("the vermilion wine of Venera") and she was immediately consumed with the desire to turn the page and learn what that mysterious phrase could mean. She had never heard of a city or region, or even a vineyard, called Venera; and, despite all her years of investigating the wines of the world, she had no clue as to what "vermilion wine" could be. But the book was encased, out of reach. She tried to reassure herself that armed with the book's title she could at any time satisfy this sudden obsession.

Still, her impatient need to understand that phrase nagged at her to distraction. She hadn't yet seen the entire exhibit at the Museo d'Arte Erotica, but she could no longer focus. Nothing registered in her memory; every item was forgotten as soon as her eyes moved on to the next thing.

There were books in the boutique downstairs. Monica asked the clerk if they had for sale any reprint editions of Magus Amore's *La storia segreta dei vini sacri*. The young woman — despite her aura of hipster chic, which in Monica's experience signalled bad service, especially toward other women — was surprisingly solicitous. She took the time to carefully inspect the inventory, and even looked up the title on the store computer, but she came up blank and acted sincerely apologetic that she could not be of any help.

Monica inquired if it would be possible to consult the copy of the work on display. Irritation flashed on the young clerk's face, and she replied with a curt "No." The manner of the refusal irked Monica, sparking her to insist; she took out her press ID, which identified her as a "wine columnist," and presented the card to the clerk. "I'm writing a piece on the ritual uses of wine," she lied. "Perhaps if you passed my card on to the curator?"

The young woman glanced sneeringly at the business card on the counter. Defiantly, Monica left it there anyway and hurried outside without another word. A sense of defeat overwhelmed her as she neared her hotel. Up in the room, she collapsed instantly, fully clothed on the tiny single bed.

She woke up in darkness. She checked her watch; it was a few minutes past midnight, but soft, muted sounds wafted in through the open window: the murmur of conversations, the slow clickety-clack of heels on cobblestone, the subtle vibrations of live acoustic music. Without giving it any thought, without changing her clothes or putting on shoes, Monica followed the siren call of nighttime Venice. Out she went. Around her, people walked unhurriedly, talking in calm tones, leaning into each other with complicit intimacy; faint music echoed on the masonry of the city. At this hour, Italian reasserted itself as the language of the city: the tourists had gone to bed and the Venetians had come out to play. The sounds and smells of the Adriatic Sea filtered and tuned all of this tranquil festivity into a surreal urban lullaby. From the soles of her naked feet, Monica felt her entire body vibrate in harmony with her surroundings. As she wandered, humming, along the rios and calles, she, too, became part of this Venetian nocturne.

She located a table in a restaurant that overlooked the water. Groups of Venetians supped relaxedly, the evidence of several courses littering their tables. Monica hadn't eaten all day but had no desire for food. She ordered a litre of the house red, and quickly, perhaps too quickly, another litre. And yet another.

She woke in a luxurious bed, in a room at least three times larger than her hotel accommodations. She called out a drowsy, tentative "Hello?" Then, in Italian, "Salve?" But there was no answer. Despite the potentially alarming circumstance of waking up naked in an unknown bed, Monica had to struggle to keep from succumbing to sleep again. The bedsheets were soft as clouds. Her insides felt gooey, as if her bones had lost all solidity. And then the smell hit her: the musk of sex with a man.

Her skin reeked of it. The sheets reeked of it. The air of the room was permeated with it.

On the floor next to the bed were her clothes and her purse. A soupçon of anxiety nibbled at her as she rifled through her handbag, but nothing was missing. She had no memory of having had sex, nor of the man she'd presumably had sex with. She did remember downing at least three litres of wine by herself, though. Whatever. She did feel good inside, and her skin still tingled pleasantly. This trip was supposed to be all about escape and adventure. She got dressed and pulled open the thick, opulent curtains. She recoiled at the glare of the early afternoon sun and was also instantly hit with ravenous hunger: how long had it been since she'd last eaten anything? More than a day, for certain; perhaps as long as two days.

She wandered through the empty rooms of the three-floor dwelling, intending to find the kitchen. Whoever the man was, he was unconcerned enough to have left her alone in this fabulous, high-ceilinged house, outfitted with ornate, antique furniture and vintage objets d'art. Beyond those treasures, everywhere were cabinets of curiosities, all under lock and key, as if this were a museum.

Inside the cabinets: figurines, coins, books, portfolios, papers, notebooks, bottles, posters, cases, jewellery, toys, relics, and curios of all kinds. But nothing she had ever seen before. Nearly always there was a detail or an elusive aura that marked the items as strange. Some of the text was in Italian, but most of the language was merely close to Italian; even to her less-than-fluent eyes, it was clearly a dialect, tinged with French and Arabic. The crests, the logos, the designs ... they were almost familiar but not quite, as if they belonged in dreams. And then she saw it stamped on a gold coin; she saw the word: *Venera*.

She inspected the other items in her mystery man's collection. The word did not appear on every item, but it could still be found on many. The collection became a puzzle to Monica. If only she could figure out how to assemble all these objects, all this information, then she would understand. She wasn't exactly sure what she was trying to understand, but the compulsion was too strong, too fundamental, somehow, to her sense of self to be ignored.

A florid symbol on a spoon was also reproduced as a wax seal on a letter addressed to a Venera location. An unnamed building on architectural blueprints was also the centrepiece of paper currency issued by the Instituzione de Credit dia Venera (a name in that not-quite-Italian found on most of the currency on display). A bronze figurine of some weird bipedal beast looking vaguely like a cross between an iguana and a wolf was pictured along with two other bizarre animals on the cover of a book entitled, again in that not-quite-Italian, *Creaturas Fantastica dia Venera*.

Books. Books!

She searched frantically but thoroughly through the items inside the locked cabinets. She examined every book, everything that might be a book, until, having lost count of the number of cabinets, she found it: *La storia segreta dei vini sacri*, by Magus Amore. Unlike the edition in the Museo d'Arte Erotica, this was a paperback, from a press called — and she did not believe this to be coincidence — Vermiglio Editore. Then she noticed the item next to the book: the true object of her obsession; not the book, but a bottle of wine. Unusually for wine, the bottle was clear; the liquid within was of a sanguine shade of red, both dark and bright. Vino vermiglio di Venera. Vermilion wine of Venera.

She could have searched for keys, but considering what she had already surrendered, under questionable circumstances, to this stranger, she barely hesitated before shattering the glass of the cabinet with the foot of a table lamp. Even as she gave herself that excuse, she knew that the obsession had ensnarled itself so deeply into her mind that she would have perpetrated the same offense, regardless. Still, she paused. Which of the two objects should she take? Which of the two would most likely quench her thirst for knowledge? She touched one, then the other; as she pondered a deep growl issued from her stomach and hunger assailed her once again. Why was she trying to choose? She wanted both items, and she wanted them now. She grabbed the two objects of her obsession a little too hastily and cut her forearm on the broken glass.

The wound was closer to a nick than a gash, but it nevertheless bled profusely. Monica lost focus, her mind exploding chaotically with conflicting ideas, fears, and impulses. Paralysed into inaction, she collapsed onto one of the rococo divans, her blood staining the period upholstery.

Unsure whether or not she had lost consciousness for a brief time, Monica regained volition when panic at the thought of running the risk of meeting the stranger if she lingered here any longer spurred her to rise and leave. She carefully fingered her small wound; it had scabbed over, and she was no longer bleeding. She resisted the impulse to unscrew the as yet untampered twist cap and take a sip of the vermilion wine. Not yet. Not here.

Finding the correct door to exit the premises turned out to be tricky. She couldn't get a handle on the layout of the place. She stumbled upon more rooms filled with cabinets of curiosities, but she resisted the urge to inspect their contents. With increasing frustration, she opened doors to utility closets and wardrobes. She fell upon a closet filled with hundreds of women's shoes; they were of various sizes and had clearly never been worn. They, too, were a collection.

Monica, who was still shoeless in the wake of her debacle with the acqua alta, decided to purloin footwear as well. She settled on a pair of vermilion leather open-toe dress sandals with two-inch heels. They were probably worth hundreds of euros. Perhaps thousands, or even more. These were mint-condition vintage designer shoes, with an aura of the 1960s about them.

She finally located the exit door: the one that had a rack with umbrellas and tote bags next to it. She grabbed a bag to lug her loot, then: outside. She felt conspicuously and fraudulently glamorous as she clickety-clacked her way to a restaurant near her hotel and ordered a full five-course meal. No wine this time, though.

No, the only wine she wanted any knowledge of was now at her fingertips, in the tote bag she held tightly against her ribs: vino vermiglio, the vermilion wine of Venera.

⌁ The bottle rested unopened by Monica's bedside. The dawn sunlight caught on the vermilion glass and reminded her of its tempting, teasing, confounding presence. She had spent the entire night reading and rereading select passages from *La storia segreta dei vini sacri*, and she had finally come to the conclusion that it must be a work of fiction, a fantastical alternate history written in the form of nonfiction.

But then: the bottle. How to explain the bottle? And all those other Veneran objects in the cabinets of curiosities? Had an Italian film or TV series been made, based on this book, and these were the props that had been created for it? Perhaps her secret lover had been the director, a producer, a designer, or an actor associated with the project? Maybe even the original author, this so-called "Magus Amore."

La storia segreta dei vini sacri, as far as her imperfect Italian allowed her to comprehend, was written in the form a pop history book, but the world it described was not the one she knew. The focus of the book was ostensibly the ritualistic role of wine — any number of wines, not just vino vermiglio — among minor cults, secret societies, and arcane religions. The text lingered on the details of lurid rites and the hallucinatory experiences of those who performed these often brutal, obscene, and even pornographic rituals. Peppered throughout were passing allusions to wars, disasters, and other events that diverged from what she knew of history. Also, there was somewhere in the Mediterranean (the text seemed to provide contradictory information as to its exact location) an island city-state called Venera; this make-believe land appeared to be a nexus for the otherness of the world imagined by the author. If Venera was indeed the catalyst for the creation of this rich, bizarre world of atavistic debauchery, then it loomed large over the text by its absence more than by its presence. Outside of occasional oblique references to both the fictional city-state and its signature wine, there were only three brief sections that dealt directly with Veneran cults and vino vermiglio. Why write a book in which the world was transformed by the presence of an invented nation to then barely explore it directly?

It was as if this book expected its readers to take for granted and be familiar with the existence of Venera. As if this book had in fact been written in the world of Venera. There were no characters as such, beyond the names of some religious figures and brazen iconoclasts. There was no plot per se; it was little more than an embellished catalogue of the various uses of wine within (presumably entirely fictional) underground religious cultures. It was hard to conceive that such a peculiar work could be popular enough to be adapted for television or cinema, if that was indeed the source of all those Veneran artefacts she had perused.

Still wearing the shoes she had stolen from her mystery man's collection — she had never worn anything so chic and refined, and she luxuriated in the decadent feeling it gave her to be shod in such exclusive footwear — Monica picked up the bottle of vermilion wine and scrunched herself down on the floor of the hotel room's tiny balcony. The ambiguous descriptions on the hotel website had led her to believe that the balcony would be standing over the water of Venice; instead, her view was of a narrow winding inner calle, but she could still smell the brine of the lagoon wafting through the Venetian air.

Contemplating the bottle, Monica once more reflected on what she could decipher of the vino vermiglio rituals recorded in *La storia segreta dei vini sacri*. Venera was the name of both the city and of its matron goddess, but Venera was not the only goddess worshipped in her eponymous city-state. The book also described rites pertaining to the worship of Nayadaga, a fish goddess associated with amphibious mermaids purported to live in the underbelly of the island city, and of Santadonnamaria — a perversion of Christianity's Mary, Mother of God — whose mass involved the ritual sacrifice of a prepubescent boy, mixing the blood of his slaughter with vermilion wine for the communion of the congregation.

Nayadaga's cult was something out of a pulp magazine, with lesbian orgies, half-human secret societies, and goddess-fuelled shapeshifting. Monica hadn't clearly understood that section, as several words seemed neither Italian nor like anything she'd ever encountered and some details were too fantastical and grotesque for her imagination to fully grasp.

Amore's descriptions of the cult of Venera herself were somewhat tamer. He mentioned two competing denominations devoted to the matron goddess. One, the Venera Church of Mother Earth, was the official state religion and equated Venera with the Earth Goddess of so many world religions. Its mass was open only to the members of the Church's various orders — all of whom were women — and Amore claimed its practices were descended from Greek mystery cults: the wine offered communion with the Goddess while ritual enactments, sometimes erotic and always mystical in nature, served to cement Church hierarchy. The other, unnamed sect devoted to the goddess Venera was banned by state orthodoxy, and those found guilty of practicing that cult were punished by banishment from the city-state. This secret sect claimed that the goddess and the city were one — a divine duality — and that the Church of Mother Earth neither celebrated nor communed with Venera: instead, it caged and suppressed her. In this passage, finally, Amore revealed the nature of vermilion wine: despite its reddish hue, it was in fact a fruity white wine that derived its colour from an extract of a plant called vermilion, which grew only in Venera. Consuming the plant resulted in euphoric, hallucinogenic, and transcendent experiences that could be channelled by ritual. According to Amore, the vermilion in the wine, coupled with orgiastic rituals, allowed the male and female congregants of this underground sect to commune directly with the Goddess and lend her the strength of their spirit so that she could eventually break free of the shackles of the Church of Mother Earth.

The rest of the book was no less strange and lurid — violent lucha libre bacchanals from Mexico City; sake-imbibing lizard worshippers from Tokyo; Catholic cannibals in Paris who used the metaphorical blood of Christ to wash down the meat of their victims — but Monica had hurriedly skimmed the parts that mentioned neither Venera nor vino vermiglio.

Staring at the reflection of the morning sunlight on the glass bottle and on the liquid inside, Monica's sleep-deprived imagination could almost taste the vino vermiglio and accept as true Amore's outré and sensationalistic scribblings.

A passing cloud obscured the sun and broke the spell. Exhaustion overcame Monica; she stumbled back into bed fully dressed but, haunted by the weird, grotesque imagery from Amore's book, could not fall asleep. The bottle once again rested unopened by Monica's bedside, tempting her, teasing her, confounding her. Finally, she succumbed. She twisted open its screw cap, and the delicate fragrance hit her like an enchantment. Monica sipped directly from the mouth of the bottle, and, although the fluid was unmistakably wine, it was the smoothest she had ever savoured — a liquid orgasm. After only one taste she calmly drifted to sleep.

⟃ Monica dreamt of Venice, aware of simultaneously watching and experiencing the dream. She soon recognized it as a memory, but a doubt lingered: perhaps it was her mind filling in the blanks for a time that alcohol had wiped from her consciousness.

In the dream, she was pathetically drunk, harassing the other patrons of the restaurant by interrogating them in a slurred jumble of English and Italian about Venera, vino vermiglio, and Magus Amore. The Venetians ignored her, pointedly avoiding eye contact. Soon, a waiter ejected her from the premises. She stumbled through the otherwise calm, serene streets of nighttime Venice, continuing to shout her questions at passersby.

... Until a man grabbed her by the shoulders, pulled her away from the main thoroughfare, and slammed her against the wall of a shadowy calle. Fear and, to be honest with herself, excitement jolted her out of her drunken obsession; with soft fingers he touched her lips delicately and said in a kind voice: "Hush. I know the answers to your questions. No, I can see in your face that it is more than that: to your quest. But there is no need to shout and disturb the quietude of others. Come, and I will reveal all there is to know."

His voice was melodious and mesmerizing; it eased her way down into a haze of drunkenness and sexual readiness, where she could hide from the embarrassment at her uncouth behaviour, an emotion that had briefly surfaced along with the momentary fear.

He took her by the hand, and at a slow but deliberate pace led her deeper into Venice. He was tall, slim, and at least twenty years older, with long grey hair tightly pulled back. He was dressed with stagelike, antiquated formality, giving him the air of a performing illusionist. His grip was firm and commanding; she abandoned herself to it as they progressed in silence.

The man paused in front of a doorway, took out his keys, and unlocked the door. "Before we continue on inside, I should introduce myself, especially as I heard you shout my name through the streets. I am Magus Amore."

In her bare feet, obeying an impulse she did not want to control or question, Monica stood up on tiptoe, grabbed his hair, pulled his mouth down to hers, and kissed him. His mouth was spicy and moist — and responsive. Monica let herself sink deeper, closer to unconsciousness.

He picked her up in his strong, taut, wiry arms; they crossed the threshold.

Monica woke up in darkness. She glanced at the open bottle of vino vermiglio by her bedside and took another intoxicating sip. Soft, muted sounds wafted in through her open window: the murmur of conversations, the slow clickety-clack of heels on cobblestone, the subtle vibrations of live acoustic music, the almost imperceptible damp resonances of the sea. Still shod in the stolen vermilion shoes, still holding the bottle of vino vermiglio, Monica followed the siren call of the nightlife. Out she went. Around her, people walked unhurriedly, talking in calm tones, leaning into each other with complicit intimacy. Almost every voice spoke a language she could not quite identify. It had the musicality of Italian, but the words were subtly different and sometimes utterly alien.

The shoes seemed to guide her; she followed them to wherever they might lead her.

The city Monica wandered through she could not recognize as Venice. Already the architecture of Venice was otherworldly, unlike that of anywhere else on the planet, but what she now beheld was exponentially stranger. The buildings had a partly biological feel to them, the shapes obeying a geometry that defied her comprehension. The cityscape was so alive that it appeared to change and shift as she stared at it, a perpetually metamorphosing mosaic work of art. The clothing of the people around her, although modern, followed fashions unfamiliar to her and were often more risqué and revealing than any city she knew would normally allow. Sometimes, out of the corner of her eye, she thought she espied denizens who might not be quite human. The very air around her shimmered with the potentiality of the impossible.

The word drifted to her ears from the conversations that wisped by: *Venera.*

Monica weighed the heft of the bottle in her hands. Once more, she drank from the vino vermiglio, the vermilion potion that had somehow transported her here, to this imaginary city dreamt up — she knew now beyond a doubt as more of the potent beverage seeped into her — not by Magus Amore and not by any person. Venera was the city of Venice's dreams: unfettered by the constraints of mundane reality, petty mores, or dreary human concerns. A phantasmagorical city-state dreamt up by an overcommodified city yearning for weird intrigue and grotesque romance, yearning to seduce and fulfill the fantasies of those with enough imagination to perceive the dark, ineffable mysteries that inspire its innermost heart.

Monica drank again from the vermilion wine. She drank deeply, then continued to wander the impossible streets of Venera.

Acknowledgements

Appreciation

The Canada Council for the Arts, which provided funding during the early development of this project; my friend Roberto Quaglia for his help with the Italian. (However, I am entirely responsible for the eccentricities of the Veneran language.)

Inspiration

The Arabian Nights, J.G. Ballard, Edward Bryant, Salvador Dalí, Antoni Gaudí, Alexandra Camille Renwick, Roma, Venezia.

About the Author

∽

Claude Lalumière (claudepages.info) is the author of three previous books: *Objects of Worship* (CZP 2009), *The Door to Lost Pages* (CZP 2011), and *Nocturnes and Other Nocturnes* (Infinity Plus 2013). He has edited or co-edited fourteen anthologies in various genres, including *Island Dreams: Montreal Writers of the Fantastic* (Vehicule Press 2003), *Lust for Life: Tales of Sex & Love* (Vehicule Press 2006), *Masked Mosaic: Canadian Super Stories* (Tyche 2013), and *The Exile Book of New Canadian Noir* (Exile Editions 2015). Originally from Montreal, where he was a bookseller in the 1990s, he's also lived in Québec City, Portland, Austin, and Vancouver. He's currently headquartered in Ottawa.